John Holt Lord

A Memorial of Edward Brooke, of Fieldhouse, near Huddersfield

John Holt Lord

A Memorial of Edward Brooke, of Fieldhouse, near Huddersfield

ISBN/EAN: 9783337013806

Printed in Europe, USA, Canada, Australia, Japan

Cover: Foto ©Raphael Reischuk / pixelio.de

More available books at **www.hansebooks.com**

SQUIRE BROOKE.

A MEMORIAL

OF

EDWARD BROOKE,

OF FIELDHOUSE, NEAR HUDDERSFIELD.

WITH

EXTRACTS FROM HIS DIARY AND CORRESPONDENCE.

BY THE

REV. JOHN HOLT LORD.

THIRD THOUSAND.

LONDON:

HAMILTON, ADAMS, & Co., PATERNOSTER ROW;

SIMPKIN, MARSHALL, & Co., STATIONERS' HALL COURT;

SOLD ALSO AT 66, PATERNOSTER ROW.

LEEDS: H. W. WALKER, 37, BRIGGATE.

MDCCCLXXIII.

PREFACE.

MEN who have made self-gratification the great end of life, are justly forgotten when they die. To those who have done nothing for the world's benefit, the world owes no kind remembrance. No one cares to hear the story of their useless and wasted life. It could teach no pleasant lessons.

> "Their mould'ring clay
> Is but an emblem of their memories,
> The space quite closes up through which they
> Passed."

But men, who acknowledging the responsibilities of life, have lived to purpose, serving God and their own generation by the will of God,—lifting their fellow men out of the mire, and helping to make the world better and happier than they found it; we love to think upon, when they are gone. Their memory is fragrant. Like grateful perfume, it revives and invigorates. By reading the story of a good man's life, many a slumbering nature has been roused, and many a young man whose life was aimless, has been stirred to well directed activity, and encouraged to go and do likewise.

The object of the following pages is to embalm the memory of one, who spurning all selfish considerations, lived to bless his fellow men :—that others contemplating his consecrated life, and influenced by his beautiful example, may aspire to similar devotedness, and " not live unto themselves, but to Him who died for them and rose again."

The value of this book lies in the excellence of its subject. The Superintendent Wesleyan Minister, in charge of a large and important Circuit, has small leisure for literary work. When it was first proposed to me to collect materials and

prepare a Memórial of my late honoured friend, the pressure
of numerous duties seemed to render compliance impossible,
and I respectfully declined the responsibility. But in the
absence of any other biographer, and to meet the just wish
of many friends, who were unwilling that a career so remarkable as Squire Brooke's, should have no record, I at length,
with many misgivings, consented to attempt the service.
The work has been done at intervals, and no small portion of
it, in night hours withdrawn from needed rest. It is now
offered to the public, in the earnest hope that the imper-
fections of the Memorial, of which no one is more conscious
than the writer, may not entirely prevent its utility.

To numerous friends who have placed letters and reminiscences at my disposal, and more especially, to the members
of Mr. Brooke's family, the Revs. John McOwan, James Loutit,
Edward Walker, John E. Coulson, Martin Jubb, Henry Richardson, Henry Graham, Thornley Smith, John Gostick, John
Brown, Henry W. Holland, William Tindall, Mr. John Hudson,
(Mr. Brooke's early companion in Christian work,) Mr. S.
Taylor and others, I take this opportunity of expressing
grateful acknowledgments.

JOHN H. LORD.

BRUNSWICK CHAPEL HOUSE,

LEEDS, *November*, 1872.

THE first Edition of " Squire Brooke " having met with a
rapid sale, the volume is reprinted with a few corrections and
additions.

It is an encouragement to the writer to have received from
various quarters, testimony to the fidelity of the biography,
and also to its usefulness.

J. H. L.

LEEDS, *April*, 1873.

CHAPTER I.

> " When in the slippery paths of youth,
>   With heedless steps I ran,
> Thine arm, unseen, convey'd me safe
>   And led me up to man."

EDWARD BROOKE, Esquire, popularly known throughout a wide circle, as Squire Brooke, was born on the estate of his ancestors, at Honley near Huddersfield, March 29th, 1799.

His father was engaged in the staple trade of the locality as a manufacturer of woollen cloth, and was a man of large wealth and an extensive employer of labour.

Both father and mother 'belonged to the Established Church, and were highly esteemed by the population of Honley and its neighbourhood. They lived to old age, and towards the close of life were made partakers of saving Christianity, through the instrumentality of their son Edward.

A grandmother of Edward Brooke heard the venerable Wesley preach, when he came to Honley, and blessed by his ministrations, she bravely cast in her lot with the Methodists, who in those days were held in small favour. She became exemplary for piety, and for some time sustained the office of class-leader in the Methodist Society. It was Edward Brooke's privilege to have intercourse with this godly grandmother, and her Christian character and counsels are supposed to have influenced his ultimate career.

Trees give colour to the insects which lodge upon their leaves. The river's bed imparts its hue of sombre rock or lighter gravel to the fish disporting in its waters; and the physique and morale of men are largely determined by the surroundings of their early years. Children reared in the highlands of the north, familiar from infancy with bold mountains, rugged rocks and wild moorlands; with roaring torrents and dashing cataracts; with mist and storm and whirlwind, we expect to develop a hardier manhood and more vigorous character than the children of the lowlands, where the scenery is soft and beautiful and the climate mild and enervating; and, possibly, the birthplace of Edward Brooke and the associations of his youth may account for much that was characteristic of his after life.

The Honley of seventy years ago was widely different from the Honley of the present. It was an antiquated town. The old houses were low roofed and roughly built of stone, quarried from the neighbouring hills. The houses of later date were loftier and square looking, with large upper windows extending across the entire house front, that the weavers, who in " the good old times" plied their looms at home, assisted by wife and children, instead of crowding in mills as now, might be well lighted for their work. And there were old hostelries with quaint names and quainter signboards, where the slow going stage wagon stopped, and travellers refreshed themselves; but which, since railways have robbed the old roads of their traffic, have mostly degenerated into beerhouses.

The town stood upon a somewhat lofty hill. It was ventilated by the breeze and washed by driving rains, and wore the aspect of cleanliness and health. It looked down upon a valley of rare verdure. A trout stream meandered through rich pastures, its bright waters purling amongst

the rocks and discoursing sweet music as they flowed.
The hills on either side were covered with forest trees,
which, dressed in rich summer foliage, gave an air of
seclusion and beauty to the scene, that might have suggested the classic tale of "The Happy Valley."

The high lands beyond were mostly unenclosed. What
now are well fenced fields, tilled by the plough of the
husbandman and yielding rich harvests of golden grain,
were then wild moors covered with blushing heather and
flaming gorse. Those fragrant solitudes were well tenanted
by game. They were grand natural preserves where hale
generous sportsmen of the olden time, who had disdained
the modern battue with its sickening slaughter and sordid
traffic, loved well to range, regardless of fatigue, and
where a good shot might count on making a heavy bag,
and supplying an extra course for the dinner table of
his friends.

The population of Honley was in keeping with its
scenery. There were families which harmonised with the
valley scene of such rare beauty; families well born and
cultured, surrounded by all the refinements and elegancies
of polished life. Such was the family from which sprang
Edward Brooke; a family still represented, and which
has lost none of its social prestige in the neighbourhood.
And there were people as rough and uncultivated as the
unreclaimed and wild moors amid which they dwelt; and
it is said there were some who had strangely perverted
views of the rights of property, who chafed under the
restraints of law, and spurned its authority, especially
when gamekeepers were off their guard, and when, with
appetite sharpened by the fresh air of early morning, they
saw hare or partridge in tempting proximity.

These were the surroundings amid which Edward Brooke
first saw the light, and spent his earlier life.

His ancestors were stalwart and long-lived men, such as the neighbourhood of Honley might be expected to produce. From them he inherited a sound constitution and an impulsive nature; and breathing from infancy the bracing air which wafted over the hills and moors of Honley, he developed into a youth of fine proportions, of exuberant spirits and rare vigour.

The wealth and social status of the family placed all educational advantages within young Edward's reach. For some time he was under the care of Mr. Kemplay, of Vicar's Croft, Leeds, the principal of a classical academy of considerable note. Mr. Kemplay was a somewhat stern disciplinarian, and having a strong conviction that the most wayward natures may be subdued by physical suffering, he freely tested his theory upon the unfortunate person of Master Brooke, but alas! for his theory, with no very decided result.

On leaving the Leeds academy, Edward Brooke's parents had gladly sent him to Eton, Harrow, or Rugby, and amid the inspirations of one or other of those famous schools, and in company with embryo statesmen he might have laid broad and deep the foundations of classic learning, and at Oxford or Cambridge built up the structure and crowned it with honours; but according to the testimony of a surviving schoolfellow, the tastes of his boyhood were more in favour of muscular than mental activity. He preferred nature to art, and the mysteries of sport to classic lore. He was

> "A noble boy,
> A brave, true-hearted careless one,
> Full of uncheck'd, unbounded joy,
> Of dread of books and love of fun."

Well content with the scant scholarship that passed muster with country squires, he left classical studies and scientific researches to those who liked them, or the necessities of whose position compelled application.

Edward Brooke's school life terminated when he was about sixteen years of age. Soon afterwards, he took his place at the works, which were already located in the valley, and disturbed its peacefulness, and which have since developed into the great manufacturing establishment at Armitage Bridge, that has long found employment and bread for a large population.

Edward Brooke's career now appeared to be marked out. The ever enlarging mills with their great out-turn of production and revenue of wealth, seemed likely to find him his life-work. The early reminiscences, with which in after years he sometimes entertained his friends, gave the impression, however, that his devotion to business was by no means excessive, and that work was unduly relieved by recreation.

Young men born to wealth, rarely apply themselves to business with the resolute and self-denying energy which characterised the wealth-makers who preceded them, and by which they won success; and it often happens that wealth gathered by one generation is lessened or dispersed by the generation following. Most natures require the stimulus of necessity to develop their latent energies, and are in danger of wasting or perverting their powers when such stimulus is wanting. Many a noble spirit has been dwarfed in its growth by an inheritance of wealth, and he who bequeaths a large fortune to his child, exempting him from the necessity of industry, leaves him at best, a doubtful blessing.

The amusements of young Edward Brooke were not of the luxurious type, in favour with young exquisites who pride themselves upon their small white hand and jewelled fingers, and venture upon no more athletic sport, than a game of croquet with fair ladies on the smooth cut lawn. They were in keeping with the robustness of his nature and the wild moor scene about his home. Like Esau, the cunning hunter of old world renown, his delight was in the sports of the field. He loved the fragrance of the heather and the gorse, and the music of nature, heard only by those who penetrate her solitudes, and listen to her notes with unsophisticated ear.

He had a passion for horses, worthy of an Arab sheik ; a passion, the fire of which, still smouldered in old age, and burst into flame, whenever the old man looked upon a noble steed, or descanted upon the points and paces of his favourite mare.

A horse, not the long backed, narrow chested, spindle legged caricature, which modern racing has developed for base gambling purposes, but a veritable horse, with blood and bone well balanced, limbs rightly placed, and symmetry complete, answering, in some sort, to the magnificent description drawn by the patriarch Job, he regarded as the perfection of animal beauty. By close observation, he became so skilled in horse-flesh, that it required a clever sharper to deceive the squire's practised eye and introduce " a screw" into his stables.

In his own circle, his judgment became a last appeal, and whoever purchased hack, hunter, or carriage horse, deemed himself fortunate, if before striking the bargain he could have the advantage of the squire's inspection and curtly expressed opinion. The squire became so famous for the discovery of incipient blemishes, that friends who had purchased magnificent horses at fancy prices, were half fearful, and yet half wishful to submit their purchase to his notice; and many a gentleman looked upon his handsome horse with less favour, when informed by an authority he could not question, that perfection was not there, and that half the price given had been a full value.

A few old men still live who remember young master
Edward's feats of horsemanship, how he startled the quiet
townsfolk as he dashed like a mounted phantom through
the streets of Honley, his horse's hoofs leaving a bright
trail of fire as they rapidly struck the hard pavement; the
horseman scarce seen, ere he was out of sight, away over
hedge and ditch, and wherever his spirited steed and wild
fancy took him; and some still tell of the wondrous
journeys he performed of sixty and seventy miles a day,
when, in after years, he went on better errands and was
influenced by loftier motives; his horse, like its master,
seeming none the worse for a hard day's work.

A marvellous horsemanship was his. He has been
heard to say, when driving a friend, that horses have no
knowledge of their speed till taught by a master; that he
had astonished many a horse by putting him into a pace
he never dreamed of; and then giving a well known sign,
without touch of whip, his favourite mare dashed off and
flew along the road as though she had winged heels and
scorned all contact with the earth.

Like most country gentlemen, the young squire had a
liking for dogs. The kennels at the old homestead were
well stocked with various breeds, in training more or less
advanced. A sportsman's license was part of his annual
equipment. The habits and haunts of game he studied in
the grey dawn of morning, under the auspices of old
proficients who, repudiating legal restrictions, claimed a
divine right to capture and kill all undomesticated fowl or
beast. He gave himself to field sports with an enthusiasm,
which no fatigue abated, and which in mercantile or
professional pursuits must have gained him celebrity and
wealth. With gun in hand, and dogs cowering behind or
ranging far and near, the young sportsman might be seen
day after day, striding across the wild moors of Honley
blithe as the lark and ruddy as the morn.

In those early days, Edward Brooke was troubled by no sense of life's responsibilities. To him life was a jolly and not a serious thing. Born to a large fortune, his wants were all anticipated. Indulgent parents placed ample means of self-gratification at his disposal, and unfettered by restraints, he threw himself into the enjoyment of worldly pleasure with all the zest and eagerness of an impetuous nature, and as though self-gratification were the great end of man's existence.

Nor were the ministrations of the Established Church, which he attended in his youth, calculated to alarm his slumbering soul and to awaken a true estimate of life.

Like many rural parishes, Honley was less favoured in its clergy in those old times than of later years. Sin was less faithfully denounced. The way of salvation was less plainly taught, and the responsibilities of life were less urgently enforced. If tradition may be trusted, the parishioners of Honley were under small obligation to their spiritual guide. The shepherd slumbered, and sheep and lambs were left to stray unchecked, an easy prey to the devouring wolf.

Forgetful of God, forgetful of the claims of others and of the great reckoning day when all must give an account of their stewardship, and associating with boon companions as reckless as himself, young Edward Brooke, though a church-goer, was a gay worldling. Wild and wayward as an unbroken colt, he sought happiness in the delights of sense. Like Solomon, before he learned wisdom, he " commended mirth, because a man hath no better thing under the sun, than to eat and drink and to be merry," and he had yet to learn that " surely this also is vanity and vexation of spirit."

CHAPTER II.

CONVERSION.

"Mercy he doth for thousands keep ;
He goes and seeks the one lost sheep,
And brings the wanderer home."

THE wayward youth who, impatient of restraint breaks
loose from parental discipline, wanders into the far country,
and amid the excitements of sensual pleasures forgets the
home of his childhood, is not lost sight of and forgotten.
In that forsaken home the prodigal is remembered. Go
where he may, debase himself as he may, he is followed
by kind loving thoughts, warm wishes, and earnest prayers ;
and many an effort is put forth to reach his heart and win
back his love.

Edward Brooke, whilst forgetful of God, was not forgotten
by God. Were the inner life of his youth made known, it
would doubtless appear that there were seasons of thought-
fulness and conviction,—times when the solemnities of
death, judgment, and eternity looked him in the face, and
forced themselves on his attention ; and when the Divine
Spirit moved upon his mind and heart, and grappled with
his conscience, and lovingly and mightily endeavoured to
turn him from the error of his way.

He who gave His Son to die for all, gives His Spirit to
strive with all, and the man is not to be found whom, in
childhood and youth, that Good Spirit has not sought to
save. But though, in the case of Edward Brooke, all these
earlier ministries were ineffectual, at length came a time
in his early manhood, when his stout heart was bowed

and broken, and when coming to himself, he exclaimed
with the prodigal, "I will arise and go to my father, and
will say unto him, Father, I have sinned against heaven
and before thee, and am no more worthy to be called thy
son : make me as one of thy hired servants."

Who has not been struck by the diversity of instru-
mentalities and operations by which God brings men to
their senses and accomplishes their salvation. With infinite wisdom and love He adapts Himself to the endless
varieties of human temper and condition, and those who
are inaccessible in one way He reaches by another.

Men are often shut up to one line of action, and if
baffled in one course are effectually foiled ; but God's
resources are unlimited.   Silver trumpets and rams' horns,
polished shafts from the quiver of sanctified intellect, and
smooth stones from the brook, untouched by human art,
are all wielded by God, and in His hand are all effectual.
It is not "by might nor by power," not by "excellency of
speech and man's wisdom," that men are converted and
saved, "but by my Spirit saith the Lord of hosts."   Sometimes, God meets the sinner in the sanctuary and sometimes
in the way, in scenes of pleasure and in haunts of vice ;
sometimes conviction is carried by a sermon, and sometimes by a casual remark ; but the same Spirit worketh
all in all, and to God be all the glory.

Early in the year of 1821, Edward Brooke rose one morning, intent on pleasure. Equipped for his favourite sport, with
gun in hand and followed by his dogs, he was crossing the
Honley Moors, when a lone man met him with a message
from God.   The man was a Primitive Methodist preacher,
named Thomas Holladay, one of those strong-minded, earnest
evangelists, the validity of whose orders is disdainfully
denied by many, but who, judged by the results of their
ministry, hold a commission higher than bishops can

bestow—a commission signed and sealed by Him who is "head over all things to His church."

Intent upon His Master's work, "in season and out of season," Holladay was prompt to seize an opportunity of usefulness. Passing the young sportsman, he respectfully saluted him, and said, with pitying earnestness, "Master, you are seeking happiness where you will never find it." On went the man of God, perhaps little dreaming, that the arrow thus shot at a venture, had pierced the joints of the armour, encasing the young sportsman's heart. Yet so it was. Those few simple words, winged by the Spirit, entered and stuck like a barbed arrow in the young master's soul. However the moor game fared that day, the sportsman himself was shot. That was a grand day's work for Holladay. He had preached many a laboured sermon with less result. If that one stroke had been Holladay's life work he had not lived in vain, or been an uncrowned minister of Christ in the great day of recompense.

Home went the wounded sportsman, the words of Holladay still sounding in his ears, "Master, you are seeking happiness where you will never find it." The time was opportune. It was a day of visitation for that neighbourhood. The Spirit of God was moving upon the population. A great revival was in progress. It commenced at Thong, and spread from house to house, till nearly every family felt its power. On every hand sinners were strangely affected by a sense of their guilt and danger, as transgressors of the law of God, and exclaimed "Men and brethren, what must we do?" Many believed on the Lord Jesus Christ, and found peace through believing; their altered and happy life proclaiming them to be new creatures in Christ Jesus. Drunkards became sober, and abodes of misery were transformed into homes of peace.

Rains caught the blessed influence, and conversions were so marked and numerous in that locality, and awakened such wide interest, that the good work came to be known as the Rains' Revival. Then Honley was reached, and one and another were awakened. About fifty resolved to flee from the wrath to come, and joined the Methodist Society.

Prayer-meetings were held, where penitents sought mercy, and where those who had laboured under like sorrow and found rest in Christ, endeavoured to lead their fellow sinners to the Saviour and to help them by their intercessions. Some of these prayer-meetings were held in cottages convenient for the purpose; and one evening Edward Brooke, still followed by the words of Holladay and ill at ease, stood outside a cottage door, listening to the service held within, but not venturing to enter.

Nicodemus, a ruler of the Jews, went to Jesus by night, wishful to have intercourse with Him, whom wondrous miracles proclaimed to be "a teacher come from God." Though not sufficiently in earnest to go as an avowed disciple, and brave the reproach and scorn of his fellow rulers; Nicodemus still went to Jesus, and met with no harsh rebuke for his timidity. He was not roughly driven from the door, and told to come like a man, by daylight, regardless of the consequences. Nicodemus was a babe in grace and Jesus bore with his weakness and timidity, fulfilling the prediction, "a bruised reed shall he not break, the smoking flax shall he not quench, till he send forth judgment unto victory," and at length, when Nicodemus, thus nursed by the gentle Saviour, grew into a true and vigorous believer, he showed himself brave as the bravest; for at Christ's crucifixion, when older disciples were stricken with fear and crept out of sight, he came with "myrrh and aloes, about an hundred pound weight," and in company with the once timid but now emboldened Joseph of Arimathea, he embalmed the dead body of his Lord and fulfilled the last sad rites of sepulture, not caring who observed and reported his procedure.

He who is the Saviour of all men disdained not the half-awakened youth, who, troubled by a sense of sin, shrank from entering the lowly cottage where sinners were seeking mercy; and yet, by some strange fascination had found his way to the cottage door, and stood spell-bound and listening without, to the new strange sounds escaping from within. Christ saw and appreciated the spark of grace within the young man's soul, which surrounding temptations combined to quench; and He gently blew upon it till it burst into a fiame, which blazed for long years after, and kindled many a mighty blaze elsewhere.

The cottage service embraced both prayer and song; and whilst Edward Brooke still listened at the door, the verse was given out and sung,

> "A charge to keep I have,
>   A God to glorify;
> A never-dying soul to savo,
>   And fit it for the sky."

Sung with unwonted solemnity and feeling, these words not only fell upon the listener's ear but they reached his heart, deepening the conviction already made, and he retired more wretched than he came.

He was now thoroughly awakened to a sense of his lost condition. He saw with terrible clearness that his whole past life had been a life of transgression. He felt himself lying under the condemnation of the law of God; that against him was denounced the righteous penalty "the soul that sinneth it shall die," and that the wrath of God was upon him. Go where he might he found no rest. Horses and dogs and gun had all lost their charm. What interest has a doomed felon immured in his gloomy cell, and who hears the workmen hammering at his scaffold, in the frivolities of the world outside ? However he once prized them, they are all charmless now.

Just so, to Edward Brooke were the vain pleasures in which he once delighted. He felt himself a sinner on the eve of perishing,—hell opening to receive him and himself held back, only by the pure mercy of an insulted and angry God. To him there was but one question of importance, "What must I do to be saved ?" Day after day, and for three long weeks, he sought the Lord sorrowing, his sorrow amounting sometimes to agony.

A dark night was that in his soul's history; but, just when the darkness was deepest, the morning broke. It was the day of his sister's wedding. Ill prepared to join in the festivities of the occasion, because of the sorrow of his heart, Edward Brooke spent the previous night hours in reading his Bible and wrestling with God for salvation.

> "All night the lonely suppliant prayed,
> All night his earnest crying made."

About four o'clock in the morning, whilst kneeling by the old arm chair in his father's kitchen, still pleading for mercy through the mediation of Jesus, his soul grew desperate, and like Jacob wrestling with the angel till break of day, he resolved, "I will not let thee go except thou bless me."

That mighty importunity was the manifestation of true faith. He was enabled to receive Jesus as his Saviour, and believing with the heart unto righteousness, these words were applied to his heart, as distinctly and impressively as though spoken by a voice from heaven, "Thy sins which are many are all forgiven thee, go in peace and sin no more."

Just as the words of Jesus, "peace be still," quelled the storm upon the sea of Galilee, when the big waves broke into the ship, and the terrified disciples cried, "Lord save us, we perish," so did these words, divinely spoken, "Thy sins which are many are all forgiven thee, go in peace and sin no more," bring instant quietness to the storm-tossed heart of that struggling penitent, and there was "a great calm." He felt they were God's answer to his prayer, and was sweetly assured that he was now a sinner saved by grace; his sins all blotted out from the book of God's remembrance, and his soul accepted in the beloved. All fear and sorrow vanished, and still believing, he rejoiced with joy unspeakable and full of glory.

Exulting in his wonderful deliverance, his first impulse was to make it known. He hastened to his sister's chamber and told her the glad news that Christ had saved him,— a glorious announcement on her bridal morn : then, early though it was, he ran out into the village and roused a praying man called Ben Naylor, whose heart he knew would be in sympathy with his, and told him how he had found the Lord; and they two called up a third, named Joseph Donkersley, to share their joy; and from the rejoicing trio up went a song of praise, the jubilant and sweet notes of which were music in God's ear, and woke up the songs of angels, and gave new impulse to the happiness of heaven, "for there is joy in the presence of the angels of God over one sinner that repenteth."

What has been just described was the grand crisis in Edward Brooke's existence, to which, through all eternity, he will look back with grateful interest and adoring praise. It was the great change in which a true Christianity

commences ; the change, which Methodists denominate
conversion, and which, if not always wrought with such
marked definiteness, must nevertheless take place in all
who enter into life.

It would be difficult to find a clearer, grander illustration of the doctrine of conversion, than is here furnished
in the experience of Edward Brooke.   There was conviction of sin, deep and bitter, wrought by the Divine
Spirit through the instrumentality of the few simple
words spoken by the zealous evangelist who met the gay
young squire upon the moor, with gun and dogs, intent on
sport, and without one thought of God ; and which sent
him home like a wounded deer, to wander and mourn in
solitude. —There was godly sorrow, so all-absorbing, as to
leave no room and no desire for his old worldly pleasures
and besetting sins.   There was confession, and prayer, and
·mighty wrestling, extending into the small hours of night,
and the long night through ; and at length, with the re-
nouncement of all self dependence and all creature trust,
there was the desperate exercise of faith in Jesus as the
only foundation of the sinners' hope and the one way of
salvation ; and then came the sweet peace which follows
on believing, the superhuman peace created by the Divine
Comforter's assurance of acceptance and adoption into the
family of God.

That was a clear case of conversion, if ever one took
place ; hardly less clear than Saul's, when journeying
to Damascus, " breathing out threatenings and slaughter
against the disciples of the Lord," Christ met him in the
way, spoke to his heart, and transformed the raging per-
secutor into a meek follower of the crucified.   With his
heart Edward Brooke believed unto righteousness, and
with his mouth he made confession unto salvation.

The providential circumstances of a sinner's conversion,

—the mode of his awakening, the intensity and duration of his sorrow, and the manner in which the divine Spirit conveys the assurance of adoption, may vary as widely as human temperament and circumstances. All are not terrified by a startling revelation of their nearness to perdition; all ·are not comforted by the application of specific Scripture to their hearts, as though it were spoken by a voice from heaven : and to expect this sameness of operation is unwise and injurious ; but the essential elements enumerated, are never wanting where true conversion is experienced and salvation really enjoyed.

There is another gospel, too popular in the present day, which seems to exclude conviction of sin and repentance from the scheme of salvation ; which demands from the sinner a mere intellectual assent to the fact of his guilt and sinfulness, and a like intellectual assent to the fact and sufficiency of Christ's atonement; and such assent yielded, tells him to go in peace, and be happy in the assurance that the Lord Jesus has made all right between his soul and God; thus crying peace, peace, when there is no peace.

Flimsy and false conversions of this sort may be one reason, why so many who assume the Christian profession, dishonour God and bring reproach on the church by their inconsistent lives, and by their ultimate relapse into worldliness and sin. As in the olden time, it may still be said " They went out from us, but they were not of us; for if they had been of us, they would no doubt have continued with us; but they went out, that they might be made manifest that they were not all of us."

The doctrine of the cross is the grand central truth of the Christian system; the staple of the Christian ministry, —Christ, first, midst, last, throughout and evermore. But the preaching of Christ crucified must not supersede the

preaching of the law. The whole counsel of God must b⸠
declared. "By the law is the kuowledge of sin." Si⸠
must be felt, before it can be mourned. Sinners mus
sorrow, before they can be comforted.

True conversions are the great want of the times. Con
versions such as all Methodists believe in. Conversion
such as are witnessed now and then, such as were commo⸠
once, and shall be again, when the church shakes off he
lethargy, takes hold upon God's strength, and brings dow⸠
the ancient power. Then, as of old, sinners will qua⸠
before "the terror of the Lord," and have such percep
tions of the exceeding sinfulness of sin, as shall mak
sin permanently hateful; and believing in Jeṣus, sha⸠
have a sense of His preciousness, commensurate with th
intensity of their convictions and the bitterness of thei
distress, that will lead them, by His grace, to hold th
beginning of their confidence steadfast unto the end.

Conversion is the commencement of a new life. ⸠
change of nature invariably declares itself in altered an⸠
holy conduct. The sweetened fountain sends forth swee
waters. When Zaccheus believed in Jesus, his besettin⸠
sins were forthwith abandoned; he exclaimed, "Behold
Lord, the half of my goods I give to the poor : and if .
have taken any thing from any man by false accusation
I restore him fourfold." And where conduct before con
version has been outwardly correct, and no marked chang⸠
is possible, love gives a new charm and invests the lif⸠
with heightened beauty, which men cannot fail to see.

With bold decisiveness and sanctified manliness mos
beautiful to see, Edward Brooke, when converted, cam⸠
out from among the ungodly, and broke off his sins b⸠
righteousness, and stood forth a contrast to his former sel⸠

Some who profess Christianity, study to retain as man⸠
of· their worldly pleasures as possible, and to make th⸠

fewest possible sacrifices; and we can imagine a young man addicted to field sports, saying, what harm in taking the dogs, and carrying a gun, shooting over the moors, and supplying the table with game? Bodily exercise profiteth : man must have recreation, and game was made for man's use; and few would venture to unchristianise all who take out a licence to kill game.

In professional and mercantile life, men work at high pressure, and under a continuous strain. The nine hours' movement which empties the workshop of its toilers before they are weary, and sends them forth to recreate as they list, leaves the employer in his office poring over his plans and calculations till his brain whirls, and he is ready to envy his men, who, when they lay down their tools, have no further care till the morrow; and it takes no cognizance of the tens of thousands who work with their brain the long day through, and far on into the night, till their nerves quiver and refuse to be quieted, even when at length sleep overpowers.

Workers of this class, whose nervous energy is taxed to the uttermost, must occasionally have absolute relief, or nature will suddenly give way, brain fever or paralysis prematurely terminating their career; and some insist that no relief is more thorough, and no recreation more exhilarating and healthful to an overtaxed mind and shattered body, than shooting over the moors. The weary worker gets clear away from the scene of his toil, into the pure country, which God made, and which man has not defiled; where the sky is bright and the air fresh; and dressed in the free and easy garb of the field, which favours forgetfulness of himself, he strides over the rough land, bounding from ridge to ridge, his every muscle brought into activity, his eye following the ranging dogs, his senses all wide awake : when, sighting the game, quick as thought, bang goes the gun, and whether the game falls or escapes th shooter is conscious of quickened circulation, and ever tiny vessel of his body is flushed with vitalized blood and new energy is stored up to meet the stern demand of the future.

Undoubtedly there are Christian men, who seek relie from exhausting toil and the renewal of their strengtl after this fashion; who pray in the shooting-box with n less filial confidence and consciousness of access to thei heavenly Father, than at the family altar ; and alike ii labour and in recreation set the Lord always before them.

The late Sir Thomas Fowell Buxton, a Christian states man, prominent in anti-slavery legislation, thus writes ii relation to this subject.

" As for myself, I feel about shooting that it is not tim lost, if it contributes to my health and cheerfulness. . have many burdens, and it is well to cast them off les they should dispirit and 'oppress me, so that I become les capable of active exertion. But now my holiday is nearl over. Shooting may be my recreation, but it is not m business. It has pleased God to place some duties upor me with regard to the poor slaves, and those duties I mus not abandon. Grant, O Lord, that I may be enabled t discharge my solemn duties to them."

Then follow devout and earnest prayers for grace, wisdom and strength, to meet the responsibilities of his position.

Exhausted by hard work, this Christian statesman tool a month's shooting as a restorative, on which he could ask the divine benediction as confidently as on the steel mixture or port-wine and quinine prescribed by his phy. sician ; a restorative which he discontinued as soon as the benefit was realized.

But all things that are lawful may not be expedient. What to some might be harmless and healthful recreation to others, might be a temptation and snare, and by them, must be avoided at whatever cost of self-denial. It is better to make sacrifices than to risk spiritual loss. It is better to give up lawful indulgences, and to content ourselves with recreations less pleasurable, and even less healthful, than to make a weak brother to offend. It is an absolute duty to avoid what under some circumstances might be an innocent enjoyment, if the possible result, be the lowering of the tone of the spiritual life and the soul's partial estrangement from God. It is an absolute duty to avoid every pleasure of the lawfulness and Christian expediency of which we are not fully persuaded in our own mind, for whatsoever is not of faith is sin, and he who indulges in doubtful pleasure is condemned. The Saviour's mandate applies to all times and to all conditions of human life, " If any man will be My disciple, let him deny himself and take up his cross and follow Me :" and if Christians, and especially young Christians, would but deny themselves in things lawful for Christ's sake, it would be vastly better for themselves, for the church, and for the world.

By a true instinct of the new nature, Edward Brooke knew how to act in relation to his old and loved recreations. He knew that if he allowed himself in field pleasures, they might lead him astray; that if he kept to his dogs and gun, he would most likely keep to his associates also, and rather than run the risk of denying his Lord, he would give up his pleasures as well as his sins. With heroic spirit, he resolved to deny himself for Christ's sake; to cut off the right hand, to pluck out the right eye, to forsake all that he had rather than renounce his discipleship; and from the day of his conversion, as he often said in the pulpit, suiting the action to the word, "this finger never pulled trigger more." His sports were abandoned, his altered life declaring him to be "a new creature in Christ Jesus."

Mrs. Brooke remarked her son's altered conduct, and how he had lost all interest in field sports; and fearing that his dogs might be neglected, she requested the cook to see that they were fed. The cook replied, "O ma'am, Mr. Edward sent his dogs and gun away before five o'clock this morning." When his mother next saw him, she said, "Edward, why have you sent the dogs away?" He answered, "Mother, I awoke in the morning with this passage of Scripture on my mind, 'My son, give Me thy heart.' I replied, I will, Lord, and I immediately got up and sent the dogs away." And that act of self-denial, so prompt, so beautiful, was but an indication of the spirit of self-sacrifice, which ruled in the heart of the young disciple, and shaped his course through life. "Lord, what wilt thou have me to do?" was the constant inquiry of his heart, and no sooner was the will of God made known, than, conferring not with flesh and blood, he promptly and cheerfully obeyed.

CHAPTER III.

CHRISTIAN FELLOWSHIP.

> " The riches of His grace
>   In fellowship are given
> To Sion's chosen race,
>   The citizens of heaven :
> He fills them with the choicest store,
> He gives them life for evermore."

THERE is small hope of the stability of Christian converts, who, from whatever motive, hold aloof from their fellow Christians, and attempt to travel the heavenly road alone. " Two are better than one, because they have a good reward for their labour, for if they fall, the one will lift up his fellow ; but woe to him that is alone when he falleth ; for he hath not another to help him up."

Christian fellowship is a necessity of the new nature, and one of the best helps and safeguards of the spiritual life. Breaking through conventional restraints, all Christians should seek the companionship of saints, who are the excellent of the earth. Christianity is not designed to obliterate social distinctions. It gives no sanction to communistic theories. But faith in Christ is a bond of union between all true believers. Christians are a loving brotherhood, and are all members of the one Family of God. Nay, Christians sustain to each other a still more intimate relationship ; they are members of one body, and are all one in Christ, who is their living head. None can say to the other, I have no need of thee. Each is essential to the other. Poor and illiterate Christians may derive instruction and refinement from their cultured brethren, and Christians of cultivated intellect and polished manners, may learn precious lessons and derive rich spiritual profit from communion with brethren "of low degree."

The godly in all ages, have recognised the value and necessity of fellowship. David, though a king, said, " I am a companion of all them that fear Thee, and of them that keep Thy precepts." In the days of Malachi, when God's people had largely apostatized, "they that feared the Lord spake often one to another," and their fellowship was favoured with divine approbation. The early Christians lived as one family. As churches were organized in apostolic times, their members were commanded "to consider one another to provoke unto love and to good works," "not forsaking the assembling of themselves together,"—but exhorting one another, and so much the more, as they saw the day approaching.

When God honoured John Wesley's ministry by numerous converts, he was prompt to recognize the importance and necessity of Christian fellowship, and by the good providence of God, was led to organise the institution of the class-meeting, which is simply a systematic provision for the enjoyment of Christian fellowship. In this respect, the Methodist people have an advantage over every other branch of the Christian church. Week by week, at a given place, and at an appointed hour, few or more, animated by the same desire "to flee from the wrath to come" and to strengthen their spiritual life, assemble under the guidance of "the leader," whose matured experience, and cultivated gifts, have marked him out as fitted, by the grace of God, to address to each member such counsels as the experience related may demand. By instruction, exhortation and prayer, the ignorant are taught, the timid are encouraged, the tempted and sorrowful are comforted and strengthened, and the lukewarm and unfaithful are admonished.

Tens of thousands, scattered the world over, bear glad testimony to the value of this means of grace. Multitudes, who otherwise would find it difficult to secure the fellowship which their soul needs and craves, and who, possibly, for want of it, would grow disheartened, yield to temptation and fall away; find spiritual stimulus and nurture in the weekly class-meeting, and "grow in grace and in the knowledge of our Lord and Saviour Jesus Christ."

It may be questioned whether any human institution has yielded richer results of spiritual profit than the class-meeting; and how, at a time when other churches, impelled by necessity, are feeling their way to the establishment of something similar, any bearing the name of Methodist can speak lightly of this ordinance, or seek to lower it in the estimation of the Methodist people, is passing strange, and almost compels the assertion. "an enemy hath done this."

Improve the class-meeting by all means; let the leaders appointed, be intelligent and earnest Christians, who have experimental acquaintance with the deep things of God; and who, forgetting the things that are behind, reach forth to those that are before. Let leaders inform their minds and warm their hearts by the diligent and devout study of the word of God, and by the free use of religious literature, and out of a well-furnished treasury bring forth things new and old. Let leaders be Christians who have power with God, and whose prayers are prevalent, who take personal and deep interest in the spiritul welfare of their class, and study through the week to make the class-meeting a means of instruction and grace and salvation. Let the members of the class be in earnest about the salvation of their souls, not attending now and then, just to secure recognition of their membership; but regularly meeting, with warm desire for spiritual good. Let members prepare for the class-meeting by self-examination and secret prayer; and instead of a few common place utterances, which mean anything or nothing, tell with childlike simplicity the actual experience and condition of their souls, all sympathising with each other, and all interceding for each other; then the class-meeting will be baptized with its ancient power, and will everywhere become what it was in the olden time, and what even now, in many a place it is; a means of grace and salvation, a season of Christian fellowship, longed for and delighted in.

Soon as Edward Brooke had experienced a change of heart and consecrated his life to God, he felt irresistibly drawn towards those who were like minded with himself; and at once exchanged his old companionships and follies for the advantages of Christian fellowship. The Methodist Society at Honley was composed of persons in humble life. Many of them were weavers and "mill hands," so called, in the employ of the manufacturing firm at Armitage Bridge. Worldly pride no doubt suggested to the young convert, the possibility of going to heaven in better company, and with associates in the same social position as himself. But conversion is an humbling process. Whoever gets through the strait gate accomplishes the passage on his knees, and by the prostration of unfeigned self-abasement; and whatever airs of superiority the young squire might have before assumed, all vanished. He humbled himself as a little child. Poor working people though they chiefly were, who met in the Methodist chapel, and in each other's cottages for fellowship; he at once recognised them as Christian brethren, and to the lowliest said, " Is thine heart right, as my heart is with thy heart? If it be, give me thine hand." Without hesitation, he identified himself with the Methodist Society, in whose simple and earnest services were the unmistakable manifestations of spiritual life; and joining the class of Joseph Donkersley, one of the two men whom he called out of bed, to help his new-born soul to praise God, at four o'clock in the morning; he said, once for all, "This people shall be my people, and their God shall be my God."

It is to be regretted, that through the mutilation of the diary, relating to this period of Edward Brooke's spiritual life, no record is found, referring to those early class-meetings, in which, with all the ardour of a new-born soul and impulsive nature, he told the story of his wonderful deliverance, his temptations, conflicts and triumphs; and was encouraged and strengthened, by the sympathy and love, the counsels, experience and prayers of his leader and class-mates. Those, however, who are familiar with the class-meeting, and especially those who knew the squire in the heyday of his youth, or the vigour of his manhood, will readily believe, that in the class-meeting where he and other young converts were present, telling of their joy and sorrow, singing the spirit-stirring songs of Zion to lively meters, and with music of the heart; and pleading for present blessings on each other, for the conversion of their friends and kindred, and the salvation of the world; there would be no want of life, and no complaint of the tameness of the meeting.

Even in these days of decorum, when fastidious Methodists demur to the propriety of the inspired direction for public worship, "and let all the people say amen," and lay the cruel hand of oppression upon impulsive brethren, who, when the fire burns, speak with their tongue, a Honley class-meeting is not the best place to sleep in; especially in a time of revival. There are warm hearts at Honley still, and lusty voices, and leaders, who bear the

honoured name of Donkersley, and others, good and true ;
and there are glorious class-meetings, where babes in
Christ and strong men meet for spiritual help, where life's
troubles are all forgotten in the great present joy of
fellowship ; where, as one and another tell of God's
dealings, and praise the Lord for his goodness, the fire
burns, and vents itself in vigorous response, somewhat
trying to the nerves of weaklings, and the class-room
seems filled with heavenly influence ; and the souls of the
people rising above all earthly things, gain the suburbs of
the New Jerusalem, and catch glimpses of its glory, and
hear the faint echoes of its music, till in their ecstasy of
holy joy, whether in the body or out of the body they can
hardly tell, and their pent up emotion seeks relief in song,

> " And if our fellowship below,
>   In Jesus be so sweet,
> What heights of rapture shall we know,
> When round His throne we meet ?"

In the great revival, when Edward Brooke and scores
beside, were awakened and brought into the liberty of the
sons of God, the class-meeting was a scene of spiritual
life and power, where he found his right element. Amongst
the simple, warm-hearted people, who gathered week by
week in Joseph Donkersley's cottage, to edify and help one
another ; and who, not in set phrases and stereotyped
forms of speech, but in the simple utterance of the heart,
told of God's goodness, and breathed forth their soul in
prayer and praise, his heart was entirely at home ; and
many a time has he borne grateful testimony to the
advantage which he derived from these means of grace
peculiar to the people of his choice.

Methodism not only enjoys its class-meeting, but its
lovefeast ; an ordinance observed by the Moravians, among
whom John Wesley learned the way of salvation ; and

which he regarded as closely resembling the Agapæ of the early Christian church. In all ecclesiastical regulations, the Founder of Methodism endeavoured to conform as closely as possible, to the model presented in the New Testament Scriptures, and in the records of the first Christian age; and he was quick to perceive the adaptation of the love-feast to the spiritual wants of his people, and to adopt it as a recognised means of grace. The lovefeast has at once, more and less of formality than the class-meeting. After preliminary worship, followed by breaking of bread and a collection for the poor, as an expression of brotherly union and love, the minister presiding relates his Christian experience, accompanied by such exhortations as he may deem expedient; after which, any and all of the assembly are at liberty to rise and declare what God hath done for their soul. The minister, at his discretion, relieves the attention or enlivens the interest of the meeting, by announcing a verse or two of a hymn, bearing upon Christian fellowship, which is sung to a lively tune and in hearty style; and after repeated testimonies to the power of grace, the service is concluded by singing and prayer.

As may be readily supposed, by those who have know-ledge of Methodism, these lovefeast services were appreciated by the early Methodists. They were held at various hours, sometimes at night, but generally on the Lord's day afternoon or evening; when the preaching places were thronged by eager worshippers, and congregations were thrilled and overcome by the artless story of conversion and Christian experience told by old and young. And if through the increase of these services in the rapidly multiplying chapels of the body, the lovefeast may appear to have lost somewhat of its old popularity; it still holds its place in the heart of the Methodist people, and is an element of power in the Methodist economy not to be dispensed with. Tens of thousands of Methodists look eagerly at the circuit plans, to see where and when the lovefeasts are appointed, and attend them as church festivals, hallowed by precious memories, and with expectations of good not often disappointed. Many a trembling penitent whilst listening to the story of his brother's sorrow, and how at length he found the Lord, and believing, rejoiced in the clear sense of sin forgiven, has been made a partaker of like precious faith and joy; and many a weak believer, whilst listening to the experience of Christians strong in faith and filled with the Spirit, has been encouraged to the exercise of that all-appropriating faith which brings into the believer's heart the fulness of the blessings of the Gospel of peace.

The relation of Christian experience is an ordinance of God, which didactic teaching cannot supersede. It comes from the heart and reaches the heart, and wields a power which mere orators may envy but cannot gain. No lines of Cowper have stirred deeper emotion in the hearts of readers, than those sweetly simple lines, in which his heart tells the story of its wound and healing.

> "I was a stricken deer that left the herd
> Long since; with many an arrow deep infixt
> My panting side was charg'd, when I withdrew
> To seek a tranquil death in distant shades.
> There was I found by one, who had himself
> Been hurt by the archers. In his side he bore,
> And in his hands and feet, the cruel scars.
> With gentle force soliciting the darts,
> He drew them forth, and heal'd and bade me live.
> Since then, with few associates, in remote
> And silent woods, I wander, far from those
> My former partners of the peopled scene;
> With few associates and not wishing more."

Many a strong man has brushed away the tear as he has read these lines, which are simply a poetic version of the story told in varying phrase, and with endless variety of detail in the lovefeast, and which is never told from a warm full heart without impression.

Soon after Edward Brooke's conversion, there was a lovefeast in the old Greencliffe chapel. It was a wonderful lovefeast, as lovefeasts in great revivals mostly are. It was thronged by new converts attending a lovefeast for the first time; their hearts aglow in the warmth of their first love, and swelling with large expectations of spiritual good. As one and another rose and told the simple story of their soul's conversion, how, though awakened by various means and in different ways, they all found peace through believing on the Lord Jesus Christ; the fire burned, the whole assembly was ablaze, and old and young rejoiced together. A proud day was that for old Ben Naylor, the good man whom Edward Brooke selected, as the first sharer of his joy, on the morning of his new birth; for there was he, his young master by his side, their hearts brimfull and overflowing with holy joy. Impatient to hear his young master speak, Ben intimated by an intelligible sign, that his time was come; when, up rose Edward Brooke, the converted squire, all eyes upon him,—and in his own quaint style, he said, "a camel has got through the needle's eye!"—and many a heart sang hallelujah! and not many eyes were dry.

The salvation of a rich young man is a miracle of grace, which Christians contemplate with special joy. Not that a rich man's soul is of greater intrinsic worth than a poor man's soul. The same ransom price was paid for both Prince and peasant, rich man and pauper, it cost the blood of Jesus to redeem; and all are alike precious in God's sight; but, the difficulties in the way of a rich man's salvation are so numerous and great; the conversion of a rich man is an event so rare, and the influence of a rich man when faithful to his Christian calling and stewardship, is so immense, that we wonder not at the thrill of feeling which passed through the village lovefeast, when the young squire rose in the midst of his poor neighbours, and avowed himself to be their brother in Christ, their companion in tribulation, and in the kingdom and patience of Jesus. It was an emotion shared by angels, and shared by Christ. The camel had got through the needle's eye, and, by the omnipotence of grace, was the human impossibility accomplished.

The appearance of Edward Brooke amongst his new associates was not occasional or casual. Public worship on Sabbath days and on week day evenings, the class-meeting, the band-meeting, the prayer-meeting, the cottage services, all offering their opportunity for Christian fellowship, Divine communion and Christian work, were all frequented. In them he found his recreation and his joy. In singing the lines of Wesley, it was not mere sentiment he uttered, but the deep feeling of his heart,

> "O happy souls that pray
> Where God delights to hear!
> O happy men that pay
> Their constant service there,
> They praise Thee still ; and happy they
> Who love the way to Zion's hill !"

The assemblies of the saints were his loved resort. With David he could say, "A day in Thy courts is better than a thousand, I had rather be a door-keeper in the house of my God than to dwell in the tents of wickedness."

CHAPTER IV.

"Thee Son of man, by faith we see,
And glory in our Guide ;
Surrounded and upheld by Thee,
The fiery test abide."

UNASSAYED gold is open to continual suspicion. Precious metals must be tested and stamped with the royal arms, ere they pass current in the world and fulfil high uses. For his own sake, and for the sake of others, the Christian's graces must be subjected to trial, that their reality may be apparent and indisputable. "Now for a season, if need be, ye are in heaviness through manifold temptations; that the trial of your faith, being much more precious than of gold that perisheth, though it be tried with fire, might be found unto praise and honour, and glory at the appearing of Jesus Christ."

The graces of new converts are often tried by the scornful strictures and opposition of the unconverted. Worldly men are their observers, and perplexed by conduct which their carnal mind cannot appreciate, they pronounce it to be folly. "Paul thou art beside thyself, much learning doth make thee mad," said Festus to the fettered Apostle, when making his defence before Cæsar's judgment seat. What, thought Festus, but some strange hallucination could induce so gifted a man as the prisoner at the bar to profess faith in a Crucified Saviour, and to commit himself to so wild and hopeless an enterprise as the conversion of

D

the world to this faith; sacrificing ease, comfort, reputation, friends, worldly prospects, and all that men hold dear, whilst persecuted from city to city, he had nothing but imprisonment and martyrdom in prospect. On mere worldly principles, Festus was justified in his conclusion; and, when Edward Brooke abandoned his old pastimes and companions, and so entirely gave himself up to Christian worship and work; there were those who pronounced all this to be wildfire, which would soon burn out, whilst others pitied the young man as a lunatic.

In his zeal to get rid of everything that could remind him of his old habits, or be a temptation to resume them, Edward Brooke not only sent his dogs and gun away, but gave orders to have the dog kennels pulled down; on hearing which, his father interposed, and countermanded his instructions, saying, " I know Edward will want the kennels again." His old companions could hardly believe they had lost their jovial friend, and declared they would soon have him back, some said within a fortnight; but the fortnight passed, and the young squire was still praying with the Methodists. At length, a day was fixed, when, he would certainly rejoin them. It was arranged to form a grand shooting party, and to have a long day's sport upon the moors, with all the attractions incident to such occasion. Edward Brooke was to be invited and pressed to join the party, and no persuasions or inducements spared, that seemed likely to bring their old friend back to them once more. So assured was their hope of success, that it was currently rumoured that on a given day, the young Methodist would break with his new friends and join the gay company upon the moor, with gun and dogs, as in days past; and this point gained, all else was sure to follow.

All this might have been, had the young convert been

half decided or self-confident, trusting in the arm of flesh. But he was neither. He had counted the cost, ere he assumed the Christian profession, and was resolved to abide by his choice. He had felt how bitter and evil a thing it is to sin against the Lord, and was determined to renounce sin for ever. He had drunk at the fountain of the water of life, and he felt no hankering after the foul cup of sensual pleasures. His soul's thirst was slaked, and his heart was satisfied.

Alive to the greatness of the crisis, and assured that if faithful, he must be strengthened from above, he asked for grace to help him in time of need. He sought the sympathy and prayers of Christian friends, and, as when Peter's life was in peril, "prayer was made without ceasing, of the church unto God for him;" so now, at this critical period of the young convert's history, the church came to his help, and he realised the wonderful advantage of Christian fellowship. All the members who resided in the neighbourhood of the mills, assembled at a fixed hour for special prayer, the great object of their intercession, that their young master might be strengthened to resist the threatened attack upon his piety, and "be steadfast and unmoveable." The prayer of the sympathising church was prevalent; the abundant answer appearing not only in Edward Brooke's victory over the immediate temptation, but in his whole after life.

Was ever a soul converted, whom, sooner or later, Satan failed to assail with temptation? To see the prey escaping from his toils, awakens the devil's utmost rage, and with all his energy and craft, he endeavours its recapture. No captive of the devil may calculate upon escaping without conflict. Moreover, temptation is God's ordinance, and is a necessity of the spiritual life. Temptation is not an evil, mysteriously permitted for the gratification of Satan's

malignity. It is a test ordained for the trial and establishment of the believer's faith ; and if withstood yields
unfailing and permanent advantage.   When the storm
blows, and the quivering tree, caught by the blast, is
strained to the uttermost, and spectators predict its down-
fall ; it strikes its roots more deeply in the soil, and
grapples the firm rock beneath, and laughs defiance at all
storms to come.   And in the case of the steadfast
Christan, the devil, by his most malicious temptations,
but frustrates his own designs, promoting the future
stability and welfare of the tempted one.

Satan had never asked God's permission to tempt Job,
had he foreseen that the result of the cruel process to
which he subjected that righteous man, would be the
development of perfect patience, the · maturing of Job's
spiritual life, his ultimate aggrandisement in this world, his
glorification in the world to come, the strengthening of
multitudes by the contemplation of his wonderful example ;
and the emblazonment of Job's triumph on the page of
inspiration, so that to millions of readers of the blessed
book, throughout all time, it should be said, "Ye have heard
of the patience of Job."   The devil had never put it into the
heart of Judas, to betray his Lord into the hands of the
murderers who killed him, had he forseen that Christ's
crucifixion would be the consummation of God's grand
mediatorial scheme for the redemption of the world ; and
that by his malicious temptation, he was helping to
accomplish what God had before determined to be done,
and the result of which should be the bruising of Satan's
head, the destruction of his power and his ultimate
consignment to the everlasting infamy and torment of the
bottomless abyss, . "the lake which burneth with fire and
brimstone."   Malignity in man or devil frequently outwits
itself ; and still, with shortsighted policy, and to the

sure enhancement of his condemnation, Satan goes to and fro in the earth, laying snares to catch the unwary and to accomplish the ruin of men.

Like other new converts Edward Brooke was not long unassailed by temptation. Whilst exulting in the sweet sense of pardon, and the assurance of the favour of God, there came the suggestion that he was deceiving himself; that his conversion was not a reality, that he was still unsaved, his joy in God but the offspring of excitement. Instead of simply looking to Jesus and driving back the temptation by instant faith in his Saviour, he listened to the tempter, his faith faltered, his joy vanished, and Satan got the advantage of him.

It is an old temptation this, with which Satan seldom fails to try the faith of the babe in Christ; and ofttimes he dresses it up into such near resemblance to the godly jealousy, which we are enjoined to entertain; and whilst plying the temptation, he so transforms himself into an angel of light, that he overcomes his unsuspecting victim and plunges him into despondency, if not deep down into despair. Many a young Christian knows by bitter experience, the horror of great darkness which such temptation, artfully timed and persistently applied, brings over a new-born soul, even when repelled, much more when it overpowers.

Sorely harassed by this temptation, Edward Brooke in the agony of his mind, betook himself for counsel and aid to the man of God whom he had met on the moor, and whose words had been the means of his awakening. Who more likely to advise a child than his father? So to Holladay, who had begotten him in the gospel, he told his sad story of doubt. A skilled casuist this earnest evangelist might not be. Some cases of conscience, if presented, had most likely perplexed and baffled him; but with cases

of this sort he was familiar.   Holladay at once divined the
young convert's position.   He looked him in the face, and
like a true son of thunder, he said with terrible emphasis,
" He that doubteth is damned," and abruptly left him.

The mistakes of good men, and even their misinterpreta-
tions of Holy Scripture are not always fatal to their
usefulness.   The Divine Spirit condescends to honour the
good intention and sincere endeavour, notwithstanding the
faultiness that mars them ; and by the Great Master's
mercy, the unskilled workman turns out sound work.
However doubtful the use of that particular Scripture in
this instance, it was a word in season.   The doubter
realised his danger, and at once grasped his Saviour as
with a death grip.   The snare was broken.   The love of
God was shed abroad in his heart.   The inward witness
obscured, or lost under the power of that terrible temptation, shone forth again clear and distinct, " and he went on
his way rejoicing."

From this time Edward Brooke seems to have been
" established with grace," " not laying again the foundation
of repentance from dead works and of faith toward God."
He henceforth observed the apostolic injunction, " Let us
go on unto perfection."

CHAPTER V.

CHRISTIAN WORK.

" Not many lives, but only one have we—
Frail, fleeting man !
How sacred should that one life ever be—
That narrow span !
Day after day filled up with blessed toil,
Hour after hour still bringing in new spoil,"

WHOEVER receives divine grace, is under obligation to communicate. Each convert to the Christian faith should aim
at converting others, who in their turn shall act on others,
and through them on others still ; the circle of Christian
influence ever extending, till it embraces the whole world.

Those vast primeval forests whose mighty depths no
man has penetrated, were not always in possession of the
ground they occupy. In all likelihood, they all sprang
from a single tree, which grew from a tiny seed, dropped
by a bird, that winged its weary flight across the wilderness. That solitary tree, having seed in itself, cast its
seed into the virgin soil; and up rose young saplings,
which flourished, and in due course, shed seed around
them, and trees arose in all directions, till the forest, ever
extending, took undisputed possession of a continent.

So is a living Christianity to be propagated and extended in the earth; each one whom the Spirit quickeneth,
imparting by the grace of God, his new life to others, and
spreading Christianity around. " Go home to thy friends,"
said Jesus to the healed demoniac, who longed to make
one of the Saviour's revenue, "tell them how great things

the Lord hath done for thee, and hath had compassion
upon thee." And what Christ said to him, He says to all
whom He delivers from the devil's tyranny. The impulse
to declare what God hath done for our soul, and by
personal testimony to win others for Christ, is felt by
every new-born soul; and nothing more powerfully affects
the spiritual life of the new convert, for good or evil, than
obedience, or disobedience to this impulse.

Edward Brooke not only felt but obeyed the impulse to
do good. He conversed with his beloved parents, who
at that time, were strangers to experimental godliness,
and with affectionate concern, endeavoured to lead them
to the Saviour. With their concurrence, he conducted
family worship and sought to bless the household. An
old domestic testifies that after his conversion, he came
once and again, into the kitchen, and told the servants
how Christ had saved him, and besought them to seek
mercy. He talked with the workpeople at the mill, and
when impression was made, knelt down and prayed with
them. He went out into the highways, and with loving
and earnest words urged strangers and friends to flee from
the wrath to come.

And whilst thus diligently embracing incidental opportunities of usefulness, and often marking out his own
course, he placed himself at the disposal of the church,
and worked in harmony with others like minded with
himself, and was never more thoroughly at home, than in
helping to conduct religious services in the cottages of his
native village.

Cottage prayer-meetings are institutions which were
marvellously owned of God in the early history of Methodism, and which in these days when the church is
yearning after a revival of the work of God ought to be
multiplied by thousands. Many a poor besotted sinner,

whom no influence can induce to enter church or chapel, where he must face the great congregation, may be persuaded to slip into a neighbour's cottage, where he sees none but familiar faces; and when found there, he may, without fear of offence, be addressed, in terms more homely and direct, than would be at all prudent in a larger or more promiscuous gathering. Prayer in the cottage service, is often more free and fervent, and more minute in detail and individual in its allusions, than prayer offered in great assemblies. The poor man in the cottage prayer-meeting, feels more completely in sympathy with those about him and exercises less self-repression. A thorough reorganization and effectual working of the old cottage prayer-meeting system, where it has unhappily fallen into neglect, would soon be followed by marked results in the conversion of the careless and the outcast, and the quickening and enlargement of the church.

The cottage prayer-meeting is certainly one of the best training schools for the development of Christian gifts. In some of our town circuits, where chapels are few and large, and the pulpits invariably supplied by ordained ministers, and where Sunday afternoon services have been discontinued, and no rooms or cottages are open for mission work; what opportunity have those whom the Spirit moves to preach His word, to test their call by actual experiment, and to develop their preaching power by frequent practice?

The present tendency in Methodism is to create a class of circuits, from which the ministry has small hope of replenishment; in which the local preachers from whose ranks the future ministry must come, find such inadequate employment, that they have but little stimulus to study, and seek no accessions to their number, and as a body are in danger of dying out for want of work. This evil

would be largely obviated by a well organized system of
cottage prayer-meetings and home mission services, where,
new converts whose hearts are full of zeal, and divinely
prompted to work for God, may under suitable leadership
and supervision, attempt the evangelization of neglected
neighbourhoods.

In such meetings, Edward Brooke first ventured to
deliver the message of salvation, which was as a burning
fire shut up in his bones, till he was weary with forbearing
and could not stay; and there he found encouragement
and strength for further service.

About two years after his conversion, Edward Brooke
was appointed to raise a class. Good Joseph Donkersley,
not fearing to be overdone with means of grace, and
believing, that wherever the ark of God found shelter,
a blessing rested, opened his house to receive it. Within
twelve months of the establishment of the new class the
house was filled to overflowing, backsliders and others
joined, till the class numbered from forty to fifty members.

Some in whose character the element of prudence
largely predominates, may possibly question the wisdom
of so early promoting a young convert to important office
in the church, and entrusting to a comparative youth,
responsibilities so grave as those involved in leading a
class and moulding the spiritual character of others.
Undoubtedly the utmost care and discretion should be
exercised in the creation of leaders; the same direction
should influence the appointment to this, as to the higher
office of the Christian ministry : " not a novice, lest being
lifted up with pride he fall into the condemnation of the
devil." All candidates for the office should give unmistakable evidence of earnest piety and sanctified intelligence, and sound judgment and aptitude to teach; but
that comparative youth should be a disqualification where
these qualities exist is not to be admitted.

Timothy was a youth when set apart to the highest of all church offices. Most whom God calls to the Christian ministry are called in early life. And when the ministrations of a youthful preacher are in harmony with the oracles of God, and his conduct characterised by Christian consistency and gravity, none gives less heed to the sermon because of the preacher's youth.

The mere circumstance of youth never prevented John Wesley's appointment to the office of leader of those whom he judged qualified, and many of the most successful leaders in former and later times, have been those upon whom the responsibility was laid in early life. If any church officer needs energy for the successful fulfilment of his duties, it is the leader whose duty it is to watch for souls as one that must give account, to reprove, rebuke, exhort with all long-suffering and doctrine; who has not only to meet his class once a week, but to visit the absentees, from whatever cause their absence may arise; and to look after those, who impressed under the ministry of the word, may by timely invitation and encouragement, be induced to give themselves unto the Lord and join the church.

Whilst fully admitting that " age should speak and multitude of years teach wisdom," the infusion of youthful energy and zeal into this department of church work is supremely desirable, and is commonly followed by the best results. An increased supply of young, energetic, intelligent, and holy leaders of both sexes, is one of the most pressing necessities of Methodism in the present day.

As a class-leader, Edward Brooke worked with characteristic energy. The diary which he kept at this period, and which has escaped destruction, affords ample evidence that the responsibilities of this important office were duly appreciated. Not satisfied with meeting his members at the appointed hour of fellowship, he called upon them at their homes, familiarised himself with their various conditions, and in cases in which he had cause to suspect a want of sincerity, or candour, instituted minute inquiry, and administered more direct rebuke than had tended to edification if given before others. He anxiously sought to conduct his members into the clear enjoyment of God's favour, and soon as they rejoiced in conscious acceptance with God, he encouraged them to " go on unto perfection." The diary supplies such records as the following.

March 8th, 1827. Rose about half-past five. This has been a day of good. The Lord upholds me by His power, and saves me by His grace. This evening at our class-meeting we had a gracious season. Two souls crying for mercy, one received whilst I was there, the other continued to wrestle, and I hope obtained before she left. Gaining souls, as Bramwell says, " is best of all." Lord make me successful.

March 22nd. I feel that the Lord has possession of my heart. This evening at the class-meeting He poured out His Spirit. A young woman began to wrestle for full redemption, and the blood was applied. Her soul was released from the burden of corruption, and she rose and praised God. Others are seeking. My God let this work of holiness go on.

April 8th. At the class-meeting, we had an outpouring of the Spirit. Two or three found redemption in the blood of Jesus and rejoiced in His salvation. God is reviving His work. Penitents are getting justified, and believers sanctified. Glory be to God.

May 17th. Went to the class-meeting, felt encouraged. The members were lively and the Spirit descended. Two young boys came to the meeting, and I have every reason to believe the Lord is at work in their souls. My God, save them and make them Thine.

And yet, with all the life that characterised the class-meeting which Edward Brooke conducted, like other leaders, he had difficulties and discouragements. One instance he records, of a member, who, whilst retaining the garb of her Christian profession, shocked and distressed him by gross misconduct, and to whom, in the warmth of his holy indignation, he privately administered a most terrible rebuke. "All are not Israel that are of Israel, neither because they are the seed of Abraham are they all children." Few though Christ's immediate disciples were, a traitor found admission to their fellowship, and partook with them and their blessed Lord, of the last Passover; and since then, wherever the wheat has grown, the devil has seldom failed to sow his tares.

But there were cases besides those of flagrant inconsistency and outward sin, which caused perplexity and harassment.

April 18th. This evening, I went to my class, and there again, the Lord blessed me. I feel rather tried with one woman. What to make of her I know not. She does not, I think, give up all for salvation. She keeps complaining about her unfaithfulness, her hard heart, etc., etc., and has done so for weeks and weeks. I think all is not right. Lord help me to sift her, to try her, to find out the idol, if there be one.

It involves no small strain upon a leader's sensibilities, to sympathize with his members in their trials, and to encourage sincere but desponding seekers of salvation to persist in their endeavours to find Jesus : but the most depressing of all work, to a leader, is the fruitless endeavour to lead those who will not be led ; who week after week, come to their class with the old story of unfaithfulness, and the reiterated complaint of their shortcomings, and whom it is simply impossible to help on, through sheer

want of earnestness on their part. One member of this
sort is often a greater burden to a faithful leader than a
whole class beside; and what can he do in such case, but
seek help from God.

In addition to the systematic visitation of his members,
Edward Brooke sought access to the general population.
In his own neighbourhood he did the work of a Home
Missionary with a thoroughness which but few had ventured to attempt. He called upon rich and poor without
distinction, and instead of timidly watching an opportunity to edge in some inoffensive allusion to religion,
that might quiet his own conscience, but could never
disturb the consciences of others; he bravely addressed
himself to the object of his visit, and with the earnestness of a man who had the terrible realities of eternity
in view, he told his neighbours of their danger, exhorted
them to flee from the wrath to come, and when permitted,
kneeled down and prayed for their immediate salvation.

His convictions in relation to this work, and his efforts
in this department of Christian service, are frequently
recorded in his diary.

1826, July 21st. A good day till afternoon. I then saw
I had erred in not being obedient to the Spirit. I believe
the Lord intends me to go more amongst the people,
visiting from house to house. The Lord direct me.

1827, January 12th. This day has been a day of encouragement. Whilst visiting various families at their
different homes I saw the power of God manifested. Tears
rolled from the cheeks of many. Here I see the goodness
of God, in the way He takes to encourage me to go forward in His work. This morning I felt a little of the fear
of man, but I acknowledged it before the Lord, and He
graciously delivered my poor unworthy and unfaithful
soul. O for a heart to praise Him. May all my thoughts,
words, and actions be one continued sacrifice through life.

February 3rd. Rose about five and twenty minutes past four. This has been a day of trial, but I have found great encouragement whilst preaching Christ from house to house. God help me to do Thy will with all my heart.

March 31st. (Saturday.) Rose a little after five. A day of good to my soul. Went this afternoon amongst the butchers in the village to talk with them about their souls, and the awful consequences of selling meat on the Sabbath, which I thought some of them practised. One of them appeared much wrought upon : tears flowed from his eyes, and I hope, ere long, a mighty cry for mercy may break from his heart. God grant it.

September 21st. This has been a day of good to my soul. In the morning I felt rather discouraged, but found it would not do to reason : I earnestly begged to know the Lord's will concerning me, and felt impressed to visit every house in the village. I began, and went to many. In time I shall go through all, God willing : Lord help me. By so doing, I find some who are afflicted of whom I had no knowledge, and I shall find out any who may be desirous of salvation. But what can I do of myself. I shall fail in the attempt without much prayer. Lord help me. Honley is low. I long to see her rise. Lord lift us up.

September 25th. This has been a strange day. Set off to go to Mr. S——'s, to talk with the family; found the young people at home; talked and prayed with them, but one or two of them seemed backward. From thence I went to John W——n's, at Huddersfield. I told him I was impressed to go to Mr. J. H——'s, and to other great people. I wished his opinion. He advised me to make it a matter of prayer, and expressed a fear that I should set myself more work than I could do. However, I want to do the will of God and to serve Him better.

October 26th. This has been a day of peace. I felt rather tried at a gentleman's house. I asked permission to pray, but the lady said she was a " Churchwoman," and her father wished her never to be a Methodist. Strange Churchwoman, I thought, when she did not like to bow her knee. Returned home praising God.

The foregoing extracts from the diary abundantly show that Edward Brooke's religion was not a sentiment, but a divine principle of wonderful intensity and power, impelling him to seek the salvation of his fellow men with a strength of purpose and endeavour which no difficulty or discouragement could daunt; and because he was thus willing and obedient God led him, step by step, into a wide sphere of Christian work and usefulness.

CHAPTER VI.

"The love of Christ doth me constrain
To seek the wandering souls of men;
With cries, entreaties, tears, to save,
To snatch them from the gaping grave."

VISITING one day, an old member of Society, who lay upon his death-bed awaiting the Master's call, and rejoicing in hope of the inheritance above; Edward Brooke and the sick man conversed, till the youthful visitor felt lifted up, and, as if he already trode the confines of the better land, and breathed its exhilarating air. Envious of the aged saint, whom the angels were beckoning across the border, he said to the old man going, "I wish I could change places with you." "No," replied the dying man, "you have to preach the gospel for many years to come, and to be the means of bringing hundreds of sinners to God."

When a sanctified soul is breaking away from mortality, it would seem as if, sometimes, all its faculties were intensified. It appears to see what is invisible to others, to hear what others cannot hear, to penetrate into the far future, and to read the Almighty's purposes. A good man departing, appears sometimes, as if transformed into a seer, and gifted with prophetic foresight; and certainly it might have been so in this case, for no truer word ever fell from the lips of hoary prophet, in the olden time, than the words which fell from the lips of that dying saint, as he addressed the young man standing by his bed, "You

E

have to preach the gospel for many years to come, and to be the means of turning hundreds of souls to God."

Whether that remarkable prediction, uttered under circumstances of such deep solemnity, developed the impression which Edward Brooke had previously received into a conviction of duty, is unknown ; it is certain, however, that he now felt that he must preach the gospel, not only as heretofore, from house to house, and in cottage meetings, but in the great congregation. His membership with the Methodist church, which recognises an order of lay-preachers, and admits to her pulpits not only those who are set apart to the office and work of the Christian ministry, but men who, whilst following their worldly avocations, still believe themselves moved by the Holy Ghost to call sinners to repentance, offered him facilities for obeying this conviction.

Lay-preaching, like other institutions of Methodism, was not part of a preconceived scheme of church organisation, but was the offspring of a providential necessity, which the founder of Methodism, with his high churchism, was unwilling and slow to acknowledge.

With holy indignation, and feelings akin to horror, John Wesley, when at Bristol, learned that Thomas Maxfield, whom he had left in charge of the Foundry Society, with instructions to pray and expound the Scriptures, but in nowise to preach, had ventured to ascend the pulpit and deliver a sermon. Had Maxfield been slain with fire from the Lord, like Nadab and Abihu, who " offered strange fire before the Lord, which He commanded them not ;" John Wesley had felt no surprise and but small pity. With the least possible delay he hastened back to London to lay his strong hand upon the presumptuous youth, and forthwith arrest the sacreligious innovation. On entering his home, at the Foundry, his venerable mother at once saw, from his beclouded countenance, that his usually calm spirit was perturbed ; and inquiring the cause, was met with the sharp reply, "Thomas Maxfield has turned preacher I find." But Mrs. Wesley, who was no less strong in her regard for church order than her son, had heard the young man preach ; and, notwithstanding her prejudice, had felt, whilst listening, that though wanting the Bishop's ordination, the hand of the Lord was on the preacher and the heavenly unction with his word ; and, with characteristic judgment, she cautioned her excited son, saying, "take care what you do respecting that young man, for he is as surely called of God. to preach as you are," and further advised that he should hear the young man preach and make inquiry as to the fruit resulting.

Methodism owes much to the mother of the Wesleys, and perhaps, for nothing is more indebted, than for this sage Christian advice, given at this critical juncture ; for, obeying his mother's counsel, John Wesley stayed proceedings till he had heard young Maxfield preach, and was himself so impressed, that though shocked and staggered by the unauthorized proceeding, he could but submit to what he felt to be a mysterious and divine ordination, saying, "It is the Lord, let Him do what seemeth Him good."

The principle of lay-preaching once admitted, John Wesley was speedily surrounded by lay-"helpers," called of God, and wonderfully qualified for the difficult work they had to do. Some he entirely withdrew from their secular pursuits, appointing them to circuits, where, under his supervision, they watched over the Societies which he had raised, and did "the work of an evangelist," contentedly subsisting upon slender pittances but little larger than the out-door relief which careful guardians grant in these days to paupers. Others still followed their worldly callings, maintaining themselves and families by industry, and preaching on Sabbaths and week evenings when opportunity presented.

From those days till now, Methodism has never lacked a supply of converted, intelligent, and spiritual men, whose hearts God has touched, and who, while devoting six days to worldly business, give their strength upon the seventh to evangelical labours, which severely test their physical and intellectual powers, and, involve no small sacrifice of domestic comfort.

There are wide circuits in Methodism where, on Sabbath days, local preachers travel long miles, ofttimes on foot, regardless of the storm, and preach twice and three times a day, reaching their homes late at night, weary and worn with the labours of the day. There are rural districts in which four-fifths of the preaching on Sabbath days is done by local preachers, and where the suppression of lay-preaching would involve the closing of numerous chapels, the scattering of Societies, the ruin of circuits, the withdrawal from many a village of all gospel ministrations, and a positive famine of the word of life.

Methodism has just cause to think well of her lay-preachers, and to thank God who, in this agency, has given her so vast an advantage over numerous branches of the Christian church ; an advantage which less favoured communities are beginning to recognise, and in some cases are cautiously endeavouring to secure.

As to gifts and usefulness, the local preachers of Methodism need no apology. The congregations and Societies which, in hundreds of cases, are mainly gathered and held together by their ministrations, afford ample evidence that He who calls abundantly qualifies them for their work.

Samuel Drew, the metaphysician ; William Dawson, a pulpit orator of marvellous dramatic power and holy unction; the learned Dr. George Smith; the cultured and polished Thomas Garland; Samuel Hick, from whose untutored mind flew sparks, bright and burning as those of his own anvil; Charles Richardson, whose words were pure, wholesome, and nutritious as the fine wheat from his master's threshing floor; Edward Brooke, who dashed over the devil's lines with the impetuous daring of an Uhlan, and rescued many a captive from the mighty; and others, too numerous to mention,—some fallen asleep, and many remaining unto this present,—represent no insignificant amount of intellectual gifts and culture, and spiritual power and usefulness. Such men shed lustre on their order, and indicate an average ability and fitness that not only speaks well of the past, but gives fair promise for the future.

To her lay-preachers Methodism has done scant justice in the past; whilst of generosity she has been strangely and culpably neglectful. In but few circuits is anything like systematic training attempted; but young men, however slender their advantages, are left to grope their way to the attainment of necessary knowledge, with only the casual assistance which some kindly minister or brother local preacher may afford; and when prematurely worn out, as not seldom happens, from the continuous strain of seven days' labour, no adequate provision has existed for the relief of the necessitous. There seems, however, in these respects, to be the dawning of a better day.

Impressions relating to Christian work are not always from above. What is supposed to be a call to preach, may be a temptation from beneath. The devil has many devices by which he seeks to get the advantage of young converts and inexperienced Christians. Failing to seduce them into their old sins, he ofttimes endeavours to beguile them into spheres of Christian work, to which they have

no divine call and no adaptation; that discouraged and
weakened by the unanticipated difficulties of their false
position, or lifted up by pride, they may fall into condemnation.

It is a melancholy thing for a young Christian, under a
mistaken sense of duty, to abandon a sphere of usefulness
where God owns and blesses his labours, and in which he
finds joy and recompense, for one of higher distinction,
where, for want of a divine call and qualifications, failure,
mortification, and sorrow are inevitable. Young men who
feel impressed that they should preach the gospel; before
accepting the impression as divine, should search their
hearts and scrutinize their motives, and take counsel with
judicious Christian friends; and above all, should earnestly
seek the guidance of Him who, if they be sincere, engages
to direct their steps. In relation to worldly occupations
and pursuits let men adventure if they will, but before
entering the pulpit and claiming to be heard as an ambas-
sador of heaven, let every man be fully persuaded in
his own mind."

After prayerful consideration and consultation with
Christian friends, it was arranged that Edward Brooke
should submit his convictions of duty to the judgment
of others, by preaching in James Donkersley's chamber;
a large room which answered the threefold purpose of a
workshop, a bedroom, and a place where the neighbours
might gather to worship God. The service was duly
announced, and great interest awakened in the young
squire's first appearance as a preacher. The chamber was
thronged, and many a heart uplifted in earnest prayer that
God would encourage and help His young servant in this
first trial of his pulpit gifts. After singing and prayer, the
preacher took for his text a passage in harmony with
his intense convictions; "The wicked shall be turned into

hell." Acting upon a sense of duty and humbly relying
on God, the preacher was divinely assisted, and the effort
was considered a success.

An old schoolmaster now living, who in his youth
possessed a retentive memory and ready pen, heard the
squire's first sermon on two occasions; and writing it out
at length, showed it to the preacher, who endorsed it as a
correct report. As a first effort the sermon is highly
creditable, both to the preacher's intellect and heart. It
contains a clear exposition of the text, and a tender, faithful and powerful application of its awful teaching to the
sinner's conscience. The sermon bears evidence of careful
preparation, and whilst free from all eccentricity, is characterised by a bold and forceful putting of the truth that
could hardly fail to arrest the attention of his hearers,
and by God's blessing to affect their hearts.

The delivery of that first sermon settled the question of
Edward Brooke's call to preach. However assailed in
relation to other duties, his conviction that he must call
sinners to repentance seemed strengthened beyond assault,
and shaped his whole subsequent career. They who heard
him preach in that upper room and witnessed the impression, also felt that the young man who addressed them
was "a chosen vessel."

The news that the young squire had begun to preach
soon spread through the neighbourhood and district, and
created no small sensation. Opportunity to exercise his
gifts offered on every hand, which he accepted as a call
from God. Those who had known the squire in his wild
days, and those who had heard of his remarkable conversion, all flocked to hear him. The announcement that
Squire Brooke would preach, not only drew young squires
but emptied the public houses far and near; and was the
signal for many an old poacher, dog fighter, pigeon flyer,

drunkard, and habitual Sabbath-breaker, to find his way
to the house of God. The squire attracted congregations
such as no other man could get, comprising the fast men,
the publicans and harlots, the roughs and outcasts of
society, the sight of whom, in the house of God, must
have made the heart of the preacher leap for joy, and
carried him out of himself.

Influenced by the strange character of the congregations
which thronged to hear him, and by the fact that many
heard him, to whose untaught, sensual minds, theological
terms and doctrinal definitions, conveyed no meaning, and
ordinary preaching was unintelligible; he, of set purpose,
renounced the style of his first sermon in favour of another,
which but for the preacher's motive and exceptional position, might be open to criticism; and which, in a copyist,
would be most reprehensible.

The carefully prepared discourse, with its elaborate
argument and rounded periods and memoriter deliverance,
he found to be utterly unsuitable to the rough work he
undertook. The excitability of the motley congregations
he addressed constantly endangered the preacher's con-
tinuity of thought, and exercise of memory; and he felt
shackled and embarassed in the attempt to remember and
deliver the paragraphs which he had written, learned, and
rehearsed in his study; and which, at the time of utterance
in the pulpit, he felt were not always what the occasion
called for. In the name of the Lord he resolved to sacrifice taste for effect, and to adopt a free and easy style of
address that should leave him at liberty to adapt himself
to his strange congregations, and to the varying requirements of each separate occasion, to catch the inspirations
of the time, and to avail himself of suggestions from
above.

Two circumstances contributed to determine this change

of pulpit style. When the squire preached on one occasion at Scarborough his valued friend, the Rev. David Stoner, was amongst his hearers. The preacher laboured under embarrassment, painful to himself and congregation; embarrassment which Mr. Stoner rightly attributed to the preacher's attempting an exact recitation of his written discourse; an effort to which his memory, which was not a verbal one, was clearly unequal. At a subsequent interview, Mr Stoner advised his young friend to throw off his chains, and whilst preparing his discourses with care to clothe his thoughts with such language as might present itself at the time.

About the same period Mr. Brooke attended a service conducted by Mr. Joseph Mortimer, who was at that time "a hired local preacher," and known on the Yorkshire wolds as a successful "revivalist." Mr. Mortimer, who delighted in curt, homely phrases, which captivated rustic ears, delivered a brief, characteristic sermon of the exhortatory class, and wound up with a lively prayer-meeting, when about thirty penitents were brought into liberty. Mr. Brooke at once perceived the adaptation of this style of preaching to his mental conformation and to the evangelistic work on which his heart was set. The next morning he sent for Mr. Mortimer to his lodgings, conversed with him at length on the subject of preaching, and before separating said, " I have given up my dogs and gun, and last night I got baptised into the work of soul saving, and from this time I mean to save souls in your way, by preaching short, holding a prayer-meeting, and expecting God to work with me, and to give " signs following."

The Rev. Edward Walker, in a communication with which he has kindly favoured the writer, says, " In the early period of Mr. Brooke's work he took great pains in preparing for the pulpit, and I have heard him preach sermons, which as to ability, accuracy, pathos and power, at that time, at 'least, appeared to me to be worthy of any pulpit in the land; and the success of his labours, the revelations of the last day only will fully disclose.

"He knew and greatly admired that distinguished servant of God, the Rev. David Stoner, who was a remarkable instance of careful and conscientious preparation for the pulpit, and I know that for some time, he tried to follow that excellent man's example in this respect.

"In subsequent years, however, he became less elaborate in his pulpit preparations, believing that a more extemporaneous method of preaching, by gathering facts illustrative of divine truth, from extended observation as well as reading, and, from his own experience and that of others, would be more congenial to his habits, and more likely to be useful to his fellow men, which object, was certainly the great aim and endeavour of his life,"

In his diary, Mr. Brooke refers to his first attempt to preach without committing his written preparation to memory: and tells how, like many an one beside, he was surprised and delighted to find that his thoughts found natural and happy expression.

Released from the fetters imposed by a memoriter deliverance, the preacher rejoiced in his liberty, though ofttimes with trembling. But now, a new danger assailed him from an opposite direction. Excitable himself, and commonly addressing excitable assemblies; pulpit and pew acted and reacted on each other, until sometimes, the preacher broke away from the line of thought suggested by the text, mapped out in his preparations, and which, on entering the pulpit, he purposed to pursue, and like a wild steed that has thrown its rider, he roamed here and there, and far and wide. But, when he thus wandered, he always kept the goal in view, and commonly wandered to his hearers' hearts, who not only forgave but welcomed the digression.

Sometimes, he told, in his own quaint way, the story of his wild days and wonderful conversion. How, when he sought mercy, horses and dogs and gun and all the idols of his heart were at once and entirely given up for Christ. How he had found ten thousand times more joy in the service of his Heavenly Master than ever he found in the devil's drudgery ; a story which carried the conviction of its truthfulness to every heart, and which though told for the twentieth time, rarely failed to move the most stolid hearer and melt the congregation into tears.

The leader of a large class in a London circuit tells, how, when a young man, listening to this story of the dogs and gun, in City Road Chapel, (where the squire was conducting a series of special services,) he was led to see the absolute necessity of parting with his idols, which for nine long months of sorrow, had held him back from Christ, and how, forthwith following the example of the preacher, he that night lost his burden, and found peace through believing.

At times, when the heat was oppressive, or the attention of his hearers flagged, or his strength was failing, or his mind moved slowly and thoughts flowed less freely than he liked ; the squire, who had a good voice and a command of lively metres, would strike up a familiar and stirring tune to a well-known verse, which the congregation at once caught up ; and in a trice, preacher and people were all alive. Sometimes the sermon was largely interspersed with song, for dulness was about the last fault that the squire would tolerate.

Occasionally, at the risk of offending fastidious ears, the squire used expressions which he knew would unlock the hearts of rough men before him, and give him access to the inmost sanctuary of their soul, where he might lodge the incorruptible seed of the kingdom : which, if not then, yet some day, should bring forth fruit to the praise of God's name. And what wonder that he felt himself justified in thus overstepping the bounds of severe decorum, when he saw the big tears course down the cheeks of stalwart men who gloried in the ring, and could bear any amount of pummelling and punishment without showing "the white feather," when he heard poachers, dog-fighters and drunkards roaring in the agony of their soul, and crying "God be merciful to me a sinner."

He has been heard to say, that with the consciousness of his power to wield a more cultivated style, he on principle, adopted the eccentric that he might lay hold of those whom others could not reach, "pulling them out of the fire." In the spirit of one greater than himself, to the weak he became as weak that he might gain the weak, and was willing to be made all things to all men, that he might by all means save some; and whatever judgment fastidious hearers might pronounce, the great Master honoured his motive and gave unmistakable signs of approval.

It was no uncommon circumstance for the whole congregation to be moved under the squire's discourse, whilst here and there, sinners overpowered by conviction, cried out until the preacher, unable to proceed, was glad to resolve the service into a prayer-meeting, to make intercession for the mourners, till one and another obtained mercy and stepped into the liberty of the sons of God; and prayer gave place to praise and exultation.

The squire's personal appearance and bearing in the pulpit favoured impression. Tall and erect in figure, of handsome features, dark hair and fresh complexion; with a keen penetrating eye of singular expressiveness, and manners which indicated supreme contempt for the finical; he was a fine specimen of the country gentleman, whom none could look upon without prepossession.

His colloquial address and allusions to common life soon captivated the attention of the most illiterate and dull. All felt, at once, that the preacher meant what he said, and was resolved that his hearers should understand and feel it. His earnestness often rose into passion and became overwhelming. It occasionally betrayed him into extravagances which none deprecated more than himself. After an unusually exciting service, he wrote in his diary, "Too wild myself," and doubtless, there were some who endorsed the preacher's own animadversion. But men of phlegmatic nature should deal gently with those whose nature is the opposite of theirs; and surely, we have enough tame men in the world, and we need not lay the rough hand of repression upon the few here and there, who overcome by strong feeling, and with pure zeal for the Master's glory, sometimes break over the line of severe propriety.

It was a fine critique upon Edward Brooke's preaching given by a poor woman, who once heard him preach and felt what he said. "I think," said the woman, "he is like one who has just escaped from falling into a great fire, and he wishes to save every one from falling into it."

What wonder that the preaching which called forth such a just and grand critique, produced remarkable results. An earnest man is a power in the world; and an earnest minister of Christ, whose ministrations are sustained by the Holy Ghost, can hardly fail to have converts.

Awakenings were so numerous under the squire's preaching, that he soon came to regard the prayer-meeting as a necessary appendage to every service he conducted. Preach when he might, on Sunday or on week-day, morning, afternoon, or night, he generally wound up his service with public intercession. He had faith in the

preached word. He believed that under every sermon he
delivered, the good Spirit fulfilled His office, convincing of
sin and of righteousness and of judgment ; and he looked
upon the prayer-meeting as a means of pressing divine
convictions and good desires to an immediate issue, when,
otherwise they might be " as a morning cloud, and as the
early dew."

In the prayer-meeting, the preacher scanned the congregation with keen eye and with acute perception, which
seldom failed to detect even incipient penitence, and no
matter where the penitent might be, however inaccessible
to others, the squire found means to reach him. Hedges
and walls, and ditches broad and deep, were no obstruction
when following the game, in his wild sporting days; nor
should pews, or high-backed forms, or stately and stiff
notions of propriety baffle him in his eager pursuit of a
nobler object, when he had reason to believe that personal
intercourse with a stricken soul might deepen its convictions, or help that soul to lay hold of Jesus and secure
salvation. So with agility which surprised, shocked, or
amused, as the case might be, the squire made his way
over every obstruction, till he reached the object of his
solicitude, ascertained his condition, and advised and
encouraged him, as his state required. "Glory be to God !"
he would often say to the penitent, struggling to give up
his idols, and to receive Jesus, "if God could save Brooke
from dogs and gun He can save you; come let us go to
work."

Whilst clambering over the pew tops on one occasion,
a young woman who had a keen sense of the ridiculous
laughed immoderately at his unusual and grotesque procedure : his eye observed her merriment, and passing her
shortly after, he said, with deep seriousness, " Young
woman, five minutes in hell will cure you of laughing to

all eternity." It was a terrible reproof : some might pronounce it unduly harsh and severe, considering how the offence had arisen ; but the reproof penetrated, and driven home by the Spirit, was fastened as a "a nail in a sure place." . Shortly after, the offender truly awakened, sought and found salvation.

Rare were the instances in which the squire had no immediate and visible fruit of his labour. Such occasions invariably led to close self-examination and deep humiliation before God. Assured of God's willingness to save, he feared lest pride, or unbelief, still lurking in his heart, should have limited the Holy One of Israel. He chastised himself with pitiless severity, and took no comfort till he again witnessed the manifestation of God's mercy in the salvation of souls. His mourning was commonly of short duration. Delighting himself in the Lord, God granted him the desire of his heart.

In numerous places sinners were saved ; notorious sinners, whose conversion was the wonder of the neighbourhood. Many of these, after giving full evidence of the reality of God's work of grace in their souls, adorning the doctrine of God their saviour in all things, finished their course with joy, and preceded the preacher to the heavenly city ; and when at length he followed, were they not found waiting at the gates to give him welcome, to escort him through the hosts of shining ones up to the throne of God and of the Lamb, and to present him to the Saviour, saying, this is the man who condescended to our low estate, and to whom we owe, through Thy mercy, our salvation ?

A few extracts from the diary, may serve to illustrate the spirit in which Mr. Brooke gave himself to God's work at this early stage of his Christian course.

1826, April 2nd. Preached in Hepworth chapel, in the

afternoon, from Proverbs xi. 30, "He that winneth souls
is wise." Very much tried before I began preaching, and
for a few minutes after I had commenced, but still kept
my eye of faith fixed on the Master of assemblies,—Jesus
the Great Head of the Church,—and He soon burst in upon
my soul, and filled me with life, light, and power. The cloud
was dispersed. The word was accompanied by His blessed
Spirit to the hearts of many. Some were in tears, others
were praising God with all their hearts, and there appeared
to be a good feeling throughout the whole congregation.
After preaching held a prayer-meeting, and as near as I
could learn from my brethren, there were about ten souls
in distress, all seeking for pardon, peace, and holiness. Six
or seven found peace with God. Praised be His holy name,
the work is His. Went to Thurstiland in the evening.
Felt very weak in body but strong in faith, and well I
might, after such wonders wrought in the afternoon.
Preached from Zechariah viii. 23, "We will go with you
for we have heard that God is with you," and blessed
be His name I found Him to be with me. Though weak
in body, I was strengthened and wonderfully assisted.
Stopped in preaching for a little rest and gave out a verse,
which the congregation sang with melody in their heart to
the Lord. Then went on, and through God's assistance
finished the discourse. After preaching, held a prayer-
meeting. Five souls in distress. Two found salvation
and rejoiced in God. Praise the Lord.

April 3rd. Happy in God whilst evening, and then did
not find that sweet communion I had done in the morning.
Self-examination immediately took place. The cause was
soon discovered. I had given way to spiritual pride, by telling others what God had done on the Sabbath, and wanting, as it were, the praise of men. God save me from it in
the future. "Let another man praise thee," says Solomon,

"and not thine own mouth ; a stranger, and not thine own lips."

April 4th. Suffered in consequence of this cursed thing. ·

April 5th. Went to Huddersfield to hear Mr. Watson. A prayer-meeting was held in the afternoon, and there, according to the promise of God, I again found His comfortable presence, but am not fully satisfied. Went after the prayer-meeting, to visit a sick person, and whilst pouring out my soul in prayer to God, on her behalf, I found full deliverance from spiritual pride. May God ever save me.

April 9th. Preached at Kirkburton in the morning, from these words, "Finally my brethren, rejoice in the Lord." Found God to be with me in a particular manner. Wonderfully assisted. In the afternoon preached from " He that hateth reproof shall die." I think I never spoke with more authority and power. Held a prayer-meeting, and as near as I could tell, nine or ten souls were seeking salvation. Five found and rejoiced. Praise the Lord ! The work is His. "Not by might, nor by power, but by My Spirit saith the Lord." O for more faith. May God increase my faith. Before the prayer-meeting was concluded, I lost in a great measure the presence of God. The cause was this. Many hardened sinners were crowding around those who wanted salvation. I tried to keep them at a distance. One young man was very stupid and obstinate ; and I felt something within me which was contrary to purity, a bone of the old man. I was led to mourn, and did not find myself comfortable in the meeting after. Visiting a sick person, to my sorrow, I felt neither liberty nor power, I continued to moan and groan, but whilst taking tea at another friend's house, I found deliverance, the blood was applied, and I could again rejoice.

F

Praise God! He is gracious and merciful. O for full redemption : may God sanctify me.

April 19th. Lost by some means or other, the confidence I had enjoyed. Preached in the evening at Cowms, and felt distressed, held a prayer-meeting as usual, but had no faith, though there were two or three souls seeking salvation.

April 20th, 21st, 22nd. Powerfully distressed in my mind, which arose from a sight of my unfaithfulness and little love to God.

April 23rd. Unsatisfied till the evening, when the Lord revealed Himself more fully to my soul, whilst preaching in Honley chapel. After preaching, we held a prayer-meeting and the spirit of prayer was wonderfully poured out upon the people. Souls were crying out on every hand. I think at least nineteen or twenty were seeking salvation, and to the praise and glory of God, twelve or thirteen, I think, some said more, received pardon. Glory! Glory! Glory! The Lord ride on.

April 30th. Went to Holmfirth. Preached in the afternoon, and found it hard work. Examined myself, but could not find out the cause to my own satisfaction, so left it all to God. In the evening I preached again, when to my astonishment, I found great liberty, I felt my heart warmed. "The fire burned," and my tongue was loosed. Such was my ecstasy of joy that several times, during the sermon, I cried Hallelujah! After the services of the day, we held a prayer-meeting. The Spirit from on high was imparted. Souls were awakened. Sixteen or more were crying for mercy, and as near as we could tell, twelve or thirteen found salvation. Glory be to God! Saving souls is the best work after all. The Lord make me wise to win souls.

May 1st. Preached at Golcar in the evening. Much

weakness of body, but found the Lord present to heal my body in a great measure, and had liberty in preaching. One soul seeking salvation, but did not find.

May 2nd. Happy.

May 3rd. Happy. Preached at Houses in the evening. Found the Lord precious. Held a prayer-meeting. Four souls seeking salvation and three found. "Bless the Lord, O my soul, and all that is within me bless His holy name."

May 4th. Preached at Whitfield, in the Dewsbury circuit, for the benefit of the new chapel. Found the Lord precious. Held a prayer-meeting. Two souls were seeking. They did not get clear in their acceptance, but found good. The Lord be praised.

May 7th. Went to preach at Crosland Moor in the evening. The Lord condescended to grant me light, liberty and influence. Many were affected. At the prayer-meeting there was a mighty cry for salvation. Fifteen or more were seeking, and seven or eight found the forgiving love of God. My soul praise the Lord.

May 10th and 11th. Passed through the fire of temptation.

May 12th. Went to Greetland and preached in the evening. Never felt so much in God. The people under my feet. Held a prayer-meeting. Six or more seeking salvation. Three found.

May 14th. Happy in God at Greetland. Preached morning and afternoon, and held two prayer-meetings, after both services. Fifteen or sixteen, or more, in distress. Some were backsliders. Nine or ten, as near as I could learn found liberty. Glory! Glory! Glory! The Lord God Omnipotent reigneth.

CHAPTER VII.

"That I thy mercy may proclaim,
  That all mankind Thy truth may see,
Hallow Thy great and glorious name,
  And perfect holiness in me."

WHERE there is life there is development. In vegetation we see "first the blade, then the ear, then the full corn in the ear." The acorn when put into the earth, sprouts into a seedling, which shoots up into a sapling, and ultimately develops into the full-grown oak, beneath whose wide spread branches and luxuriant foliage, the flocks find shade and shelter. In animal life the same law of development obtains. The babe whose only signs of sentient life are the plaintive cry and instinctive search for nourishment; develops, as months pass over, into the laughing, sportive child, which enlivens and gladdens the whole household, and in due course, into the buoyant youth, and eventually, into the vigorous man, who, it may be, moves a nation, and makes his influence felt the wide world over.

So is it with the spiritual life. The babe in Christ, remains not a babe in perpetuity, but grows "in grace and in the knowledge of our Lord and Saviour Jesus Christ," till he comes "unto a perfect man, unto the measure of the stature of the fulness of Christ." "Leaving the principles of the doctrine of Christ, let us go on unto perfection," is authoritative counsel, addressed to all believers in Jesus. The maturity of holy love which

St. Paul presents under the term " perfection," John Wesley urged upon his converts as a blessing not only to be sought, but claimed and realized by faith in our Lord Jesus Christ, that being delivered out of the hand of their enemies, they might serve God without fear, in holiness and righteousness before him, all the days of their life; and just in proportion, as the Societies were stirred up to the attainment of their Christian privilege, were they influential on the world without.

Perfected in love, the early Methodists had power with God and with men and prevailed. Edward Brooke believed that He whose first and great commandment is, " Thou shalt love the Lord thy God with all thy heart and with all thy soul and with all thy mind," had not given His creatures an austere and impossible command, but one which divine grace would enable their regenerated nature to obey. Edward Brooke regarded perfect love as his blessed Christian privilege, and his necessary qualification for extensive Christian usefulness; and he sought it with an eagerness which his diary abundantly illustrates.

May 5th. When at family prayer, felt happy, but very soon after, felt a conviction that my soul was not so lively as it ought to be. I instituted self-examination, and the Lord awakened me in a powerful manner, to seek for full redemption with all my heart and soul and mind and strength, *through grace.* Previous to this, I had been seeking it by fervent prayer, performing my duties and so on, but now, the Lord applied to my heart the words, " Not by works of righteousness which we have done, but according to His mercy He saved us." I then began to cry for grace to help me, and it was granted. I felt heavily burdened. In this state I continued some time, weeping, groaning, mourning, praying, till at last the Lord gave me power to wrestle for it. I wrestled for some time, then gave up and

then began again. I was in my bedroom, next to the
room where I and my brothers dine, and whilst on my
knees it was suggested to my mind, that my brother John
who was dining would hear me. I gave way to the
temptation, desisted, and brought myself into misery.

May 8th and 9th. Felt happy in some measure, but
this great work of sanctification is still before me. For
this I weep, and mourn, and groan, and wrestle and strive
in mighty prayer. The Lord grant me the blessing.

May 15th and 16th. Happy, but low in body.

May 17th. Happy. Engaged to preach at Golcar.
Found myself very unwell and sent a friend to supply my
place. It is absolutely necessary to take more care of
myself, or else I shall very soon be fit for nothing. A
thought struck my mind that a few weeks at Scarborough
would be of service to me. I laid my case before the Lord
and found much encouragement.

May 18th. Happy. Set off for Scarborough. Arrived
at Leeds in the evening.

May 19th. Happy. Set off in the morning. Arrived
at York.

May 20th. Happy. Heard Mr. Stoner preach morning,
afternoon, and evening. Found it good and profitable. The
word came in the Holy Ghost and with power to my heart.

May 21st. Happy. Went to breakfast with friend
Stoner, and opened my mind to him upon many things.
One was the sanctification of the soul. I told him I had
mourned and groaned, wept, fasted, prayed, and laboured
to obtain the blessing. He appeared to listen with much
attention to my experience, and from what he said, I
almost believed I was in possession of the great blessing.
He expressed the opinion, that though some Christians
may have as clear an evidence of their entire sanctification
as of their justification, it was not generally so, and we

should not expect it, sanctification being a progressive work. I felt much encouraged.

May 22nd. Happy in God. Thought much on sanctification whilst on my journey to Malton.

May 23rd. Happy in God. Meditated on sanctification whilst journeying to Scarborough, and felt encouraged to believe the work accomplished in my soul. The Lord save me from self-deception.

May 24th. I still think the Lord has sanctified me. Temptations I have, but grace resists, and cries "it is written." Heard a sermon in the evening and found it good. Hallelujah!

May 25th. Happy in God. I now enjoy more of His light and life. The word of God is sweeter and sweeter. But dare I say I am sanctified? Lord save me from error.

May 28th. Heard three sermons, found them all profitable. Glory! Glory! Glory! to God and the Lamb. The desire of my heart is accomplished. The blood is applied, and my soul is sanctified. "The life which I now live in the flesh, I live by the faith of the Son of God, who loved me and gave Himself for me." The word of God says the blood of Christ cleanseth from all sin. Faith cries the blood has cleansed from all sin. Hallelujah! the Lord God Omnipotent reigneth. Satan tempts, accuses, etc. Grace resists, repels, stands and conquers. My faith is strong, my peace flows, my hope is bright. "I live, yet not I, but Christ liveth in me." Glory! Glory! God has my heart, and Satan is bruised under my feet. What shall I render unto the Lord for all His benefits? Grace cries,

> "My life my blood I here present,
> If for Thy truth they may be spent;
> Fulfil Thy Sovereign counsel Lord,
> Thy will be done, Thy name adored."

Glory! Glory! Glory! My soul burns with desire to be useful.

For some days after this remarkable manifestation of God's grace, Edward Brooke maintained an unwavering faith, and went on his way rejoicing. He seemed to live upon the verge of heaven, and to have closer affinity and fellowship with the church triumphant across the border, than with the militant host still warring the good warfare upon earth; but, though he had gained a higher region of the spiritual life, he was not beyond assault. His warfare was not ended, and his journey to the skies thenceforth a march of triumph.

In the Queen's army are household troops composed of picked men, dressed in bright uniform, who may possibly fulfil their whole term of service and never face a foe; soldiers whose military life is passed in snug barracks, and on the gay parade. But Christ's soldiers are not for show but service. They are all fighting men; and Edward Brooke now so exultant, was but just entering on a long campaign, and had many a hard fought battle between him and final victory. The great adversary watched his opportunity, and with characteristic subtlety plied various temptations so artfully disguised, that "ignorant of his devices," the youthful Christian was beguiled. Instead of promptly "looking unto Jesus," he listened to the tempter, reasoned and doubted. His ecstatic joy in God gave place to deep depression, and he was brought into "heaviness through manifold temptations."

Body and soul are closely united. Physical exhaustion may often account for mental depression; and undoubtedly, much of the mental suffering which Edward Brooke's diary records at this time, arose from physical causes, which he had not yet learned to take into account, when estimating his religious condition. Preaching night after night, and conducting prayer-meetings in crowded rooms, and in a stifling atmosphere; visiting the poor and sick, denying himself necessary sleep, fasting, praying, wrestling for long hours; and all this, to some extent, even when professing to take rest, nature at length resented the ill-usage. Body and mind were prostrated. The adversary took advantage of the sick man's weakness. Almost every thing he did became the occasion of temptation and distress, and he chastened himself with a pitiless severity, the artless record of which is painful.

June 8th. Did not find my mind in a good frame. First one thing struck me and then another. Horses that I had seen, kept passing before me, as it were. The Lord have mercy upon me for my worldly-mindedness, luke-warmness, unprofitableness, and instability. I feel in deep trouble whilst writing; the Lord have mercy upon me. Have been this evening to hear a sermon, but alas! I felt completely shorn of my strength. No light, life, or power did I feel. What must I do to regain my wonted health and strength in the divine life? O this world! or rather my worldly mind. The Lord save my poor soul and deliver me. What must I do?

" My God, if I may call Thee mine,"

What must I do to obtain Thy favour? My Lord hear my groans, my prayers, and for the sake of Jesus heal me again, love me freely, and bless me with Thy great salvation. Now, I see from what an immense height I have fallen. O my heart! my heart! Lord save me, save me, save me. Take not Thy Holy Spirit from me, remove not the candlestick out of its place, spare me to recover strength. Good Lord, now deliver and help me again.

June 11th. Miserable. Lord save me. Going to Malton after dinner, God willing. What must I do?

"O that I could the blessing prove
My heart's extreme desire,"

the salvation of my soul, the burning love of God. Lord
help me. On my journey this afternoon, never so much
tried by the devil. Now said he, thou didst profess and
declare to others that thou wast sanctified, and thou hast
lost the blessing and fallen to justification, and now thou
hast lost that blessing, and become a wandering star. Thou
art twice dead, and plucked up by the roots. This was
fighting with a witness. When I arrived at Malton and had
got up into my lodging-room, the devil attacked me with
all his hellish fury. . . . After this, I went to Mr.
Rawson's, the travelling preacher at Malton, and told him,
his good wife, and Mr. Mortimer my case, and for my
encouragement found that others had passed through
similar temptation. We afterwards went to prayer. The
glory of God was revealed, power was imparted to my soul,
and I felt a great deliverance. Here we see the value of
Christian fellowship.

June 12th. Happy in the Lord. Solicited to preach in
Malton chapel in the evening, and complied with the
request. Found the presence of the Lord. Held a prayer-
meeting. Many souls were in distress. Four or five
experienced salvation, and to my great surprise, two of
them were Mr. Rawson's sons. Hallelujah! praise the
Lord. The devil's kingdom is falling, and it will fall.
Lord pull it down.

June 14th. Happy. Went to meet Mortimer at Sheriff
Hutton, in the Easingwold circuit. There I found the
presence of the Lord. Mortimer preached, and I related
the conversion of Mr. Rawson's sons. The people during
the whole time appeared to be affected. We then held a
prayer-meeting, and such a mighty cry for salvation arose,
as I never witnessed. How many were seeking, the Lord
only knows; but it was supposed that upwards of forty
souls received pardon. Wonderful!

June 15th. Happy. Went with friend Mortimer to the houses of the people to converse with them and encourage them. Went to chapel in the evening. Mortimer exhorted, and I said a few words. Held a prayer-meeting, and souls were crying for mercy on every hand. About thirty experienced salvation, so that nearly seventy souls, if not more, were brought to God, in two evenings. From this we ask, is anything too hard for the Lord?

June 19th. Happy. Set off from Hovingham for Malton. Felt the Lord present and good. Went with Mr. Rawson into the pulpit and prayed for him. After he had preached, held a prayer-meeting. Several souls were in distress and six or seven received salvation.

June 20th. Happy. Set off from Malton for Scarborough. Had a pleasant journey, having the Lord with me. Heard a sermon at Scarborough in the evening and felt determined not to rest, till I again experience full redemption. For this I now groan and weep and pray and labour. The Lord grant me the desire of my heart. It can be done. The blood can cleanse and save from all sin. I know it can, and should I never obtain the blessing again, I would declare it to the world.

After spending a few days at Scarborough for his health's sake, still preaching and striving to do good; on Saturday, June 24th, Mr. Brooke set off towards home. He spent the Sunday in the Malton circuit, and preached at Ferrington for Mr. Mortimer, between whom and himself, acquaintance had ripened into friendship, such as can only subsist between kindred natures, " baptized into one Spirit," and consecrated to the Great Master's work. It would be difficult to imagine yoke-fellows more equally mated, than Edward Brooke and Joseph Mortimer; or a congregation which these two men of amazing natural energy, clothed with the spirit of holiness and might, when working in concert, would not move. Exhortation and prayer were their element. Pulling souls out of the fire was the work and joy of their life.

It was a hot summer's afternoon when the squire preached at Terrington. The little chapel was crowded with farmers and farm labourers. The preacher was mightily in earnest. Oppressed by the stifling atmosphere, he threw off his coat, saying, "You people strip to gather in the earthly harvest, and why should not I strip to gather in the heavenly harvest?" In his shirt sleeves, on he went as impetuously as before, enjoying wonderful physical relief, whilst the congregation was too impressed by his awful earnestness, to be at all shocked by the unusual spectacle.

His friend Mortimer preached in the evening, and in the midst of his discourse came to a dead lock. The silence which followed was happily broken by a loud shriek of distress. A poor woman saw herself to be a perishing sinner, and unable to repress her emotion, cried aloud for mercy. Down went the embarrassed preacher from the pulpit, and making the best of his way to the penitent, exclaimed, "This woman's praying is better than my preaching." The effect was wonderful. The little chapel became a Bochim. The whole congregation seemed broken down, and numbers were converted.

Riding through York, on his way to Huddersfield, Mr. Brooke called on Messrs. Stoner and Slack, by communion with whom, he felt greatly encouraged.

July 4th. Happy in the Lord, but powerfully tried till the afternoon, when the Lord delivered me and brought me safe through the fire. Felt particular liberty in thinking on a passage that was applied to my mind, "Be ye holy for I am holy," and at night experienced His power in a wonderful manner at the class-meeting, and especially, whilst conducting family prayer.

July 5th. Happy in the Lord. In the morning felt rather a backwardness to pray with Mr. R——, not knowing whether it would be acceptable or not. Still, I prayed with him and found liberty : since then, my mind has been tried. The Lord deliver me in His own time, and save me with His great salvation.

At this time, Squire Brooke's journeys, of whatever distance, were commonly performed on horseback : and we can easily imagine that his energy of will, which often put his own physical powers to the severest strain, would occasionally test the strength of his horse to the uttermost. The sort of horse which he required—a road-ster safe, swift, and with almost unlimited endurance, was not often to be met with. Talking over their horses one day, Edward Brooke and his friend Mortimer, then visiting at Honley, and who, through an infirmity of lameness, was literally a " riding preacher," both resolved to horse them-selves after a better fashion.

As the squire had a man on whose judgment in horse-flesh he relied, it was agreed to despatch him to Lee fair ; each entrusting him with money for the purchase of a serviceable steed. The man started with instructions and cautions, and the money securely placed in his safest pocket. He looked through the fair, and whilst making his observations fell in with fascinating men, who seemed to divine his wants, and kindly tendered him their friendly help. The pleasant and opportune acquaintanceship must be cemented by refreshment at the public-house, before pro-ceeding with the business of the day. Ale was ordered and generously paid for by the friendly strangers. Com-pany dropped in and joined them. The conversation became excited, rose at length to high words, and ulti-mately issued in a general scuffle, in course of which the simple horse-buyer was hustled. When the fray ended, the result may be readily surmised; the sharpers had vanished from the scene, having first cleared out the pockets of their victim, who had to return to his master without horse or cash, a sadder and wiser man.

The squire's manner of accounting for this mishap was characteristic, and must have been very consolatory to the swindled man. Mr. Brooke said to his friend Mortimer, what might have been further from the truth, "The devil has done this, having a grudge against us because of what we have done against him, I shall therefore refund you the money." Mr. Mortimer, in relating the story, added, "Thinking we could do better at soul saving than horse buying I accompanied him to Birstall, where he was announced to preach. Leaving me to fulfil his appointment he went on to Armley, where, through some oversight, he had engaged to preach at the same hour. The power of the Lord was present in both places, to kill and to make alive, and Mr. Brooke taking me up, on his return, we drove to his home rejoicing."

Shortly after this visit Mr. Mortimer was favoured with the following letter:

July 6th, 1826.

Dear Friend,

I write this afternoon, in order to inform you that I have sent by coach, the cloth I mentioned when at Malton. The £20 which is enclosed I beg you to accept, for the mare. As it respects my experience since I saw you, it has been various; sometimes rejoicing with joy unspeakable and full of glory, and sometimes dejected. The latter is my present state, yet I still hang by faith on the Son of God; and praised be His Holy Name, though He has declared He will bring the third part through the fire, He has promised that as our day is our strength shall be; therefore I feel determined to trust where I cannot trace. As

Mrs. Rogers says, I believe our faith is often made manifest by following God blindfold. Oh for an increase of faith. I still have faith to believe that God has cleansed my heart in a great measure, though at present my soul is passing through the fire; fightings without and fears within, and horrid suggestions from the devil. My life, as good Bramwell said, is more than ever a conflict. The devil hates me, and I want more courage and faith to pull his kingdom down. I often think and speak about the blessed seasons I enjoyed whilst with you and Mr. and Mrs. Rawson. When I think of the piety of that woman I stand amazed. The fruit of the Spirit, which is love, joy, peace, etc., appears to abound in her soul. Her kindness to me was great. My kind respects to Mr. and Mrs. R.

When you write acknowledge the receipt of the money, and tell me how Mr. Stoner went on at Sheriff Hutton, and how you have been since I was with you, and if souls are still saved. Pray for me. Pray for me. Pray for me. All hell is at my heels; and without much prayer I shall sink. Lord help me is the cry of my heart.

> Your affectionate friend,
> EDWARD BROOKE.

Again he writes in his diary:

July 10th. I still feel a need of full redemption. My soul cries out, how long, O Lord, how long? I have wept bitterly to-day and mourned in consequence of the little grace I enjoy. O Lord bless me with a full salvation.

July 14th. Felt condemned and cast down till evening, and then the Lord manifested His comforting presence to my soul. I clearly see I want wisdom to distinguish temptation from sin. It appears that I have given way to reasoning and unbelief, in the time of trial, and have not pursued my duty as before. The Lord help me for the future.

July 15th. Felt comfortable in the morning. At noon, I felt wrought upon to pray and to ask my brothers to stay. This was impressed upon my mind on the previous evening. I thought it would be inconvenient to have family prayer at noon, and neglected to fulfil the duty. I soon felt the impression I had resisted was from God, and was chastised, reproved, and punished. In the evening self-examination took place, and in the strength of grace I resolved and promised the Lord, that for the future I would perform the duty, and other duties which I clearly saw to devolve upon me; and that I would love Him with all my heart, and serve Him with all my powers. The Lord help me to pay my vows.

The Lord did help His young servant. Family prayer at noon became thenceforth his established custom, a custom which he bore with him when leaving his father's house, he formed a home circle of his own, and which he observed in perpetuity, as numbers who have enjoyed his hospitality can witness. Whilst many of the squire's friends glided into the fashionable habit of late dining, he steadfastly kept to the habit of his early life, and dined at noon, as being in his judgment, more favourable to health and more in harmony with the "simplicity of Christ." Soon as the repast was over, with a promptitude which often took the uninitiated by surprise, he dropped down upon his knees, and offered thanks and made intercession for his family, his guests, the church, the world. Great blessings were asked in few words, and with rapid utterance, but still with unmistakable fervour and devotion; and all present felt that the priest of that household had the true consecration and offered a spiritual sacrifice.

July 24th. A day of weeping and mourning. I long to

be saved with a full salvation. Lord help me. My body is very much out of order, arising from derangement of the liver. Without I alter my plan of procedure in the work of God, I shall not be long here.

To his friend Mortimer, he addressed the following letter.

August 12th, 1826.

Dear Friend,

I received your letter and was glad to hear of your glorious success. Take care and ever " cast the net on the right side of the ship," and you are sure to succeed. I frequently think of you, and the encouragement I received from you. Of late I have passed through severe trials, on account of being so very unfaithful and unprofitable. But amidst it all, the Lord is gracious and merciful. When I had read your letter I poured out my soul to God, and He baptized my soul again. Souls are being saved. In this I rejoice, and will rejoice. But still, I want stronger faith that with God I may prevail. . . .

You seem anxious that I should visit you, but at present I must decline, having so many engagements to fulfil. However, let us pray for each other, and that God who answers by fire, will answer our prayers and bless us.

" Praise God from whom all blessings flow."

This week the devil has tempted me horribly, but that God who delivered Daniel from the mouth of the lions, has delivered me from the lion of hell. Hallelujah ! the Lord God Omnipotent reigneth. May He reign as King on the throne of our hearts. Go on, our Captain is gone before, and has left us an example that we should follow His steps. Go on, our Captain is gone before, and has conquered death, hell, and the grave, and promised that His grace shall be sufficient for us, and His strength be made

G

perfect in our weakness. "Strengthened with might by His Spirit in the inner man," we shall conquer in spite of earth and hell. Hallelujah! God is here. I feel He blesses me in writing to you; may He apply the letter with power to your heart. Religion is good. God is love. What will be the happiness of heaven if a foretaste be so good and satisfying? May God fill us with His love. Pray, pray, pray for me. Pray that God may humble me. Self wants to get the dominion over me. Unbelief reigns. Pray that God may increase my faith. Pray that I may be faithful in the discharge of all my duties. Now pray. Just now, lift up your heart to heaven on my behalf, and cry, "Lord help him," and I am sure He will hear and answer. "The effectual fervent prayer of a righteous man availeth much;" therefore, pray for me and God will bless. Sometimes I have been wrought on to pray for you. It has struck me suddenly; and whilst praying for you, God has blessed me.

Remember me to Mr. and Mrs. Rawson. Were I to go out to travel—O how I should like to be with that blessed man. May God bless him at Tadcaster and make him useful.

Your affectionate friend,
Edward Brooke.

Feeble in body, depressed in spirit, and yearning after the fulness of joy which he had lost, Edward Brooke entered into correspondence with Thomas Holladay, his venerated spiritual father, and also with David Stoner, whom he honoured and loved as an elder brother in Christ. The letters which he addressed to these men of God are not forthcoming, but the replies which he received and carefully preserved amongst his best treasures, indicate how minutely he had described his case; how bitter had been his self-accusation of unfaithfulness; how deeply he lamented his spiritual loss, and how intensely he desired to recover the full joy of God's salvation. Both letters present spiritual counsel admirably adapted to the case which they were meant to serve; and are characterised by godly wisdom, which stamps them with permanent interest and value, and justifies their insertion in this memorial.

Manchester, August 18th, 1826.

To my much beloved and honoured Friend Brooke,

Grace and peace be multiplied. Amen. Yours came duly to hand this morning. I was pleased to hear from you, but sorry on account of the great loss you have sustained; and believe me, my prayers have ascended and shall continue to ascend, until you are filled again with all the fulness of God. I am pained at my heart to think that you did not *take up your cross,*—if a cross it were, to do your duty! and I am exceedingly sorrowful that you should afterwards enter into reasoning on the subject with the enemy, and unadvisedly give up your confidence.

To reason was not wise, and entirely to give up your confidence was neither needful nor prudent. You grieved the Spirit by an omission, and as a just punishment His most powerful consolations were withdrawn. But was the body of holiness destroyed? was the body of sin reinstated? Did inward corruptions exist as they did before you enjoyed sanctification? I answer, No. But you ask, "was there no guilt?" If it were the will of the Spirit that you should have done that which you name, there was guilt, and guilt which needed washing away by a fresh application of "the blood of the Lamb." But there is certainly a difference between that guilt and the rooted corruptions that exists prior to sanctification.

Although many cannot see this difference, yet think of
it in the spirit of prayer and Divine light will show you
a wide difference. Why then give up your confidence
entirely ?

You say you felt ashamed and confounded before the
Lord. All the better, seeing that you had not done right ;
and impressed with a sense of disobedience, and covered
with holy shame on account thereof, you should have
gone to the throne of grace, and through an ever adorable
Advocate pleaded the clemency of the Father, in full
confidence of your interest in the blood of the everlasting
covenant ; and peace would again "have flowed as a river."

You ask for direction. God help me to direct you
aright, for you are dear to me as my own soul, and I shall
feel a sacred pleasure in doing all I can to promote your
happiness and usefulness. Sometimes you think "you
should not preach till you receive the full glory again."
That would be adding disobedience to disobedience, and
consequently sin to sin. Sometimes it strikes you "that
you ought to do this or that, before you can receive it
again." This would be equally bad with the other, for it
would be seeking it by works. I do not recommend you
" to fast much," nor yet to "pray nearly all night through."
Why destroy "the temple of the Holy Ghost ?" If your
body were healthy, strong, and vigorous, and your natural
spirits high, I would say fast ; and if need be, fast much,
but your complaint, etc., will not admit of it. Nor must
you "pray nearly all night," except you intend to kill
your body to save your soul, which God does not require.

I would recommend the following line of proceeding.
If you have not told the people, do not tell them. It will
render you no more acceptable to God, and the devil may
make a handle of it among them. Pray, visit, and preach,
or in other words, attend to all your duties as before, and

attend to them in the same way, as much as possible. Hold forth and recommend full redemption as before, when necessary; or in other words preach the same Gospel, being careful not to say anything of your own experience. You have no need to do it, and it might do harm rather than good. By preaching full redemption to others, and fervently praying for its realization by the people, you will be assisted in getting it yourself.

Be constant, frequent, and fervent in private. Be careful not to reason about your own unworthiness. You have nothing whatever to do with that, only as it shows you your helplessness and need of a Saviour. Such reasoning is an eternal barrier against sanctification. You must not look so much inward as *upward! upward! upward!* What you have to do with, is the blood of Christ! the blood of Christ! the blood of Christ! Oh the precious blood of Christ, and the free mercy of God through his blood. Neither the length nor language of your prayers are any thing; but faith in the blood of Christ. Be *humble*, be *simple*, be *fervent*, be *confident*, and God will fill you with unutterable glory, which is the prayer of your

Affectionate and humble servant,

Thomas Holladay.

The same post brought Edward Brooke the following letter from the Rev. David Stoner, then stationed at York, where, as elsewhere, his pulpit ministrations were characterised by amazing power and followed by wonderful results, the memory of which still makes his name fragrant.

York, August 18th, 1826.

Dear Brother,

I thank you for your letter, but scarcely know how to answer it; partly on account of the situation of myself and family, and partly because you ask such a multiplicity of questions, and some of them hard to answer.

I am unexpectedly removed to Liverpool, as you will have heard, most probably. This appointment of Conference has taken us by surprise, so that we have all to prepare in a short time. In the midst of the bustle of packing and cleaning, etc., my wife has been taken very ill, which has increased our perplexity. However, thanks to the Giver of every blessing, she is rather better to-day.

As to the first of your questions, you ask, " What must I do ? I have lost the blessing of sanctification." I answer, " Believe in the Lord Jesus Christ and thou shalt be saved." It appears to me,

1. That you have a conscience not only *tender*, but *scrupulous*, excessively *sore*, even *red raw*, and,

2. You rob yourself by *reasoning*, instead of living by *faith*. As to the instance you mention, by which you lost the blessing, I question, first, whether you did not condemn yourself, where God did not condemn ; and second, if it should be true that it was unfaithfulness, you should immediately have humbled yourself, applied by faith to the blood of sprinkling, and prayed for grace to be more faithful in future.

You ask, " Did you ever feel in this manner ?" I answer yes, many a time.

You ask, " How must I proceed ? Must I fast much ?" I answer, No ! Your body is the temple of the Holy Ghost, and it is at your peril, if you undermine the foundation or injure the walls of that temple. *Fast* and *abstain* you may and ought, but not in any degree so as to *injure* your body but to *govern* it. " For no man ever yet hated his own flesh, but *nourisheth* and *cherisheth* it, even as the Lord the church."

In order to obtain the blessing again, the command is

not, pray much, fast' much, weep much, but *believe, only believe*: "all things are possible to him that believeth." Now, in this instant, while this paper is in your hand, hear His voice, " I will, be thou clean." Believe it, venture, dare, try to believe, and the work is done. Remember, the Saviour is *infinitely desirous* to save you to the uttermost *just now!* Then what shall hinder? Lord, here I am; I give up all. I am fully Thine. Thou art my Saviour: I will, I do believe. Hallelujah! Bless the Lord!

You certainly have erred, in seeking the blessing by *works* instead of coming by *faith.*

It is the devil who tells you, you ought not to preach till you have received the blessing again. He would be glad enough to shut your mouth. Preach on, and preach that blessing till you get it, and then you will preach it because you have it.

You say, " this is the second time I have lost it," and what then? If it were the thousandth time, still the command is believe.

You ask, " Must I tell others that I have lost it?" I would say, generally, this would be very improper. This would weaken the feeble minded and stagger those who are seeking. You know we are to preach not our own experience, but " the whole counsel of God." If you have an intimate friend or two, you might tell *them;* they would help you by their prayers, etc.

Do not write bitter things against yourself. Begin from this hour to spend all that time in *praising* that you have spent in *complaining,* and I am sure your soul will rise. In your prayers remember

D. STONER.

Happy the souls who, when perplexed and troubled, have access to such wise counsellors as the writers of the foregoing admirable letters, and have also the wisdom and grace to avail themselves of the advantage. Many a snare of Satan would be broken, and much suffering obviated, if youthful and inexperienced Christians would confide their temptations, perplexities, and sorrows to judicious Christian friends, and to those who are over them in the Lord.

August 19th. Mr. Brooke writes in his diary : Felt quickened by a letter I received from David Stoner, and am determined not to rest till I receive the blessing. In the evening, I felt encouraged to think that God would revive his work in Huddersfield on the coming Sabbath. A passage which I opened upon in the Bible struck me very forcibly, 1 Chron. xxviii. 10, " Take heed now for the Lord hath chosen thee to build an house for the sanctuary, be strong and do it."

August 20th (Sunday). Went to Huddersfield, and preached in the afternoon, but did not find much liberty. However, thank God, souls were saved in the prayer-meeting. Seven at least got good, and professed to be pardoned. In the evening the Lord broke into my soul in a wonderful manner. Praise the Lord !

October 1st (Sunday). Went to Lindley. Preached in the morning and held a lovefeast in the afternoon. Two or three, I think, found mercy.

October 2nd. Went to Cleckheaton and preached in the evening. Held a prayer-meeting, and three or four found mercy, it was said.

October 3rd. Remained at Cleckheaton, and conversed a good deal upon preaching with Messrs. Womersley and Woodcock. Held a prayer-meeting at Roberttown with Brother Woodcock in the afternoon, and in the evening at Cleckheaton. Some appeared to be labouring under conviction.

October 4th. Went to see a few of the Cleckheaton friends.

Found liberty whilst praying with them, and returned home in the afternoon. I find much company and long absence from my studies not profitable. The mind wanders. I feel I need a greater work of grace. The blessing of sanctification I long to enjoy in all its plenitude and fulness. With this, all is calm and serene. Lord help me. When I consider the unbounded goodness of my Lord in rewarding my poor labours, crowning me with success in the salvation of my fellow mortals, I fear I do not feel that gratitude which I ought to feel. Lord help me, and may all my powers praise Thee.

October 11th. Went to Bradford Moor and preached in the evening. Felt liberty to speak, but little energy. After preaching, the power of God fell upon the people, and there was a blessed feeling amongst them. Some received sanctification, and one, if not more, pardon. I never was so astonished as when in the vestry, I heard first one and then another declare that they had full redemption in Jesus' blood. I felt ashamed before God and man, but thank God I experienced a deliverance, and retired to rest in the favour of God. Hallelujah! praise the Lord!

October 18th. Went to Brighouse and preached in the evening. As I went, my faith kept increasing. I was greatly blessed at Mr. Brooke's. I continued to look up, and went to the chapel expecting a mighty work, and to my joy and satisfaction, my expectation was realised. The Lord appeared with His glory, and my soul was happy. After preaching we held a prayer-meeting, and there was a mighty cry for salvation. As near as I can tell, above twenty were seeking redemption, and fifteen or more received good and acknowledged Christ as their Saviour. I think, if ever I received an increase of faith it was in the chapel. A young woman who was in deep distress had been wrestling for some time. One of the members asked me to pray with her. I kneeled by her side, and spoke a few words. In a moment, I felt a strong assurance that the woman would presently be saved, and told the people. It was so. Jesus came and made her happy. Glory be to God! for one of the happiest nights I ever spent in all my life. Many, if not all these souls had no doubt been seeking salvation before : or at least, had been under conviction ; but this was the time of their deliverance, when they gave up all.

October 19th. At peace with God. I staid with Mr. Brooke in order to hold a prayer-meeting in the evening. We held it in the chapel, expecting the Lord to come and save many more; but for wise ends we were disappointed. The work is the Lord's, and when He withholds the blessing, man is nothing.

October 22nd. Went to Almondbury and preached in the morning, but with little influence. In the afternoon, in consequence of temptation and bodily infirmity, I gave up before I had finished my sermon, and told the people I could not preach.

November 5th (Sunday.) Went to Birstal and preached in the afternoon and evening. After sermon in the afternoon there was a mighty cry for mercy, and several, it was said, found peace, and some in the evening. The work is the Lord's : praise His holy name !

November 6th. Went to Hightown, and there I found the presence of Jehovah. The Lord revealed His power in the conversion of many souls. Twelve or more were seeking. Six or seven, I think, found pardon.

November 8th. I did not feel happy. I examined myself, and found I had not improved my time as I ought to have done, whilst from home. Long absence from the closet brings barrenness to the soul. If spared, I feel resolved in the strength of grace to improve my time better. I also see, by the light of Jesus' Spirit, that I often offend with my tongue. Lord help me to keep the door of my lips for the future, so that nothing may proceed out of my mouth but "that which is good to the use of edifying."

November 16th. Rose a little before four. Praise the Lord! less sleep is better for me. God blessed me in this act of self-denial.

November 17th. Felt the risings of an evil heart whilst distributing God's bounty to the poor. I shall never do the will of God, as angels do in heaven, until I receive a new heart.

November 22nd. Rose about four o'clock. This morning has been a time of strict self-examination. I find, when I fairly weigh myself, that I am an unprofitable, lukewarm, unstable, half-hearted, cowardly soul. I might have brought ten times more glory to God. I clearly see the will of God. I must be singular. I must be faithful in whatever sacrifices I have to make, or whatever opposition I have to meet with. If I vow and declare in my own strength to be more faithful, I shall again break my vows. Lord help me to vow in the strength of grace. In the afternoon I went to Halifax, and in the evening preached at Ovenden. There I felt the Lord present and precious, and rejoiced to hear sinners crying for mercy. I should suppose ten or more were seeking redemption in the blood of Christ, and four or five obtained the blessing. Hallelujah! Praise the Lord! Jesus is bringing lost sinners to God. May He bring more and more.

November 25th. Rose about three o'clock. A day of severe trial. I long for the blessing, but still I do not lay hold. I have vowed this day, and I hope in the strength of grace, to do the whole will of God. Lord help me.

CHAPTER VIII.

"Saviour, to Thee my soul looks up
  My present Saviour Thou !
In all the confidence of hope,
  I claim the blessing now.
'Tis done ; Thou dost this moment save,
  With full salvation bless ;
Redemption through Thy blood I have,
  And spotless love and peace."

THE Methodist chapel at Honley was a small, square built, unpretentious structure, standing in the outskirts of the village, capable of accommodating about two hundred and fifty people. Judged by his work, the leading idea of the architect who supplied the plans for this honoured sanctuary, was the stowing away the greatest number of human bodies in the smallest space, without regard to the philosophy of life, and in utter forgetfulness that an adequate supply of vital air is essential to mental activity and apprehension, and to the profitable hearing of the word of God.

After the great revival in which Squire Brooke was brought to the knowledge of the truth, and especially after the young convert became the occasional occupant of the chapel pulpit, and spent many hours between Sabbaths in visiting from house to house, endeavouring to awaken religious interest among the people; the little chapel was filled to overflowing. Some of the old folks were well content to put up with the pressure of the crowd, perhaps thinking, that when the excitement of the revival had passed away, the congregation would dwindle down to a more convenient size ; or possibly, they enjoyed the warmth, and never suspected that the drowsiness which stole over them in public worship, however demonstrative the preacher, was attributable to the close vitiated atmosphere they breathed ; and was in fact, incipient apoplexy, only requiring the prolongation of the service to result in a catastrophe like that which befel Eutychus when, as Paul was long preaching in the upper chamber with closed doors and many lights, the youthful hearer, overcome by sleep, fell down from the third loft and was taken up dead. Moreover, the old people were somewhat proud of their chapel, and not without cause, considering the times in which it was erected, and that God had so often blessed them there ; and possibly, they thought that what had met their case might well suffice for posterity.

The squire, however, read the signs of the times, and boldly mooted the question of a new chapel, in a central and public situation ; a chapel which should not only accommodate the existing congregation, but the hundreds more, whom his faith assured him would be attracted to the house of God ; and no doubt he was greatly surprised that a necessity so pressing, and a call to extension so marked, were not equally apparent to others and to all. Some cautious people protested, and others held aloof ; but the squire urged his views with the utmost force of his strong will, winding up his argument with the encouraging assurance that his broad shoulders were strong enough to bear the financial burden, and that no man's heart need fail through fear.

Sustained as he was, by the enthusiastic approval of the younger members of the church, who had unlimited confidence in their generous and devoted leader ; objections were all overruled, and it was decided to erect a new and

commodious chapel, to seat from six to seven hundred
people, with school-rooms and vestries ; a complete establishment, where the Methodist organization should have
full scope, and be worked under advantageous conditions,
that should facilitate success.   A site was accordingly
secured, and the work hurried on with all possible
despatch.

Nothing is remembered of the foundation stone cere-
monial, but a few old people, still surviving, tell how,
when the new building was roofed in and the shell com-
pleted and the frame-w rk of the gallery erected ; and
full six months before the formal opening by Mr. William
Dawson, the impetuous squire, impatient of delay, consecrated the unpewed structure by preaching to an enthusiastic crowd, who placed themselves as best they could,
on floor or gallery, and made the bare walls echo to
their song of praise.   The diary supplies the following
allusion.

November 26th.   Preached at Honley for the opening
of the new chapel, from these words, " Let us alone."
Found great liberty, but still feel a want of heavenly
power.   O for the further work of grace, the full baptism
of the Spirit.   Till I receive this again, I cannot be
so useful.

> " Jesus the hind'rance show
>   Which I have fear'd to see ;
> Yea let me now consent to know
>   What keeps me out of Thee."

At the prayer-meeting, a backslider cried out for mercy.

December 1st.   Rose a little before five.   After I had
taken breakfast, I felt an increase of faith, and maintained
it throughout the day, by the help of God.   I have thought
I should not stay long in the present world.   How this
may be I cannot tell, but the thought of leaving does not

distress me, for I firmly believe my reward will be in heaven. After all my conflicts, I shall end well, and get safe to heaven,

> "This all my hope and all my plea,
> For me the Saviour died."

God is faithful, my soul praise Him. I shall be sanctified. The glory will come. Lord send it quickly, and prepare me for Thy will.

December 2nd. Rose a little before five. A day of prayer and breathing after God, to behold His face to the full salvation of my soul.

> "Weaker than a bruised reed,
> Help I every moment need."

Lord help me. Jesus help me. May I continue to feel my helplessness, till Thou Thy strengthening, sanctifying power impart. When I look back on the past week, I feel thankful that it has been a better week than some before. Doing God's will is the way of peace.

December 3rd (Sunday). Rose about four. Went to Marsden, and preached in the afternoon. Felt happy in mind, but weak, very weak in body. I must give up a great deal of labour. Self-murder is not pleasing to God. Just before I began to preach, I wept like a child and thought I should not have been able to preach. However, I grew better after singing awhile. Redemption, full and complete, I must enjoy. My soul thirsts for it. Satan roars and yells. Christ speaks, believe, believe. My faith increases. Jesus is willing, more willing to give than I am to receive. Lord, help me now, just now, to lay hold. Come in, my Lord, come in.

December 5th. Rose about six o'clock. A day of much prayer. I think my soul rises. My desires grow stronger, and my soul feels restless for the blessing. The cry of my

inmost soul is, come in, my Lord, come in. Delay not to
take possession of my heart.

> "My life, my blood, I here present,
>   If for Thy truth they may be spent."

Accept the offering,

> "Small as it is, 'tis all my store,
>   More should'st Thou have, if I had more."

December 6th. Rose a little before five. I think I
never had such a sight of God's goodness towards me, as
within the last few days. I see myself to be laden with
blessings. Woe! woe! woe! to me, if I do not give God
my heart, my whole heart, my soul, my all. Lord, help
me. I have found these last few days, that visiting the
people under my care, at their own homes, has been a
blessing to my soul; and when I consider that Jesus, my
Saviour (would to God I could just now say, my all and in
all), "went about doing good," went about, not stayed at
home in His study, as I have frequently done all day long,
but "went about doing good" to the bodies and souls of
men, I long to copy His example. Thanks be to heaven!
I yet feel a hope that God will reclaim me to perfect love.
Till then, I cannot do and suffer all His will as I ought.

December 8th. Rose between five and six. Did not
feel my mind so well this morning, and, upon strict examination, I found that I had grieved the Lord, in some
measure; at least, I think so, by speaking to a friend of
the faults of absent brethren. The Lord appeared to
reprove me for it. I resolved, however, to be more careful
for the future. I still remain faithless and unbelieving,
respecting the great salvation; but, amid all, I feel
encouraged to wrestle, like Israel, till I with God prevail.

December 10th. Rose a little before five. A day of
prayer, trial, and peace. My desires increase, my faith
grows stronger and stronger.

December 11th. Rose a few minutes before four. This has been a day of light, peace, and holy wrestling with God. I feel determined in the strength of grace, to conquer or die. Jesus has died to purchase for me redemption from sin, from all sin ; and this He will accomplish in me, ere long, if I be faithful ; Lord help me to be more in earnest. O for an act of living faith. One simple act of faith would bring the Deity into my soul. Lord help my unbelief.

December 12th. Rose before four. A day of prayer. A day of conflict with visible and invisible enemies. But Jehovah sitteth upon the waterflood, and the waters have not overflowed me. My head is out of water, and with the eye of faith I can still see the promised land. Glory! glory! glory! Through God I shall yet do valiantly, for He it is that shall tread down my enemies. I shall conquer. God is almighty. My soul exalt His name, and live to Him, and Him alone.

December 13th. Rose this morning about a quarter after four. I do not feel satisfied with this. I would rather it had been a quarter before. When on my knees, scripture after scripture was applied to my soul, and one passage in particular, which had never, to my recollection, been applied before. "The Lord shall be unto thee an everlasting light, and thy God thy glory." O the weight of this passage, the fulness of the glory here promised. My God, what am I? A worm, nay less, and yet Thou deignest to visit me. O for a heart to praise my God.

December 14th. Rose a little before four. This has been a day of much prayer. This afternoon my faith increases. Jesus applied the following words to my soul, which have greatly encouraged me. "I have prayed for thee, that thy faith fail not." O for a heart to praise the Lamb, for His interest on my behalf. I shall through

H

grace prevail, and find full redemption in His blood. This
evening, I took up the first volume of *Josephus*, but could
not get on at all. My mind was so dark, I could not
understand what I read. This might arise from various
causes; weakness of body; depression of soul, through
earnest but unsuccessful seeking for purity; and, above
all, the Lord showing me my utter inability to do anything
without Him. This has humbled me, and I trust that ere
long the dark cloud that hangs over my poor soul will be
dispersed by the bright sun of righteousness, diffusing his
sacred light throughout my whole nature. Lord increase
my faith. Save me, save me now, just now, this moment.

> " Lord, I believe Thy precious blood
> Which, at the mercy-seat of God,
> For ever doth for sinners plead,
> For me, even for my soul was shed."

Then now, even just now, apply it. Wash me throughout.
Visiting the sick and poor is made a blessing to my soul.

December 15th. Rose a little after five. Later than
usual, through taking supper, which caused me to feel
heavy. I think I shall give up taking much supper, if
any. I have done little this day, but visit the poor and
sick. O for a heart to feel for them, as well as to help
them. Lord give it me. My souls thirsts for all Thy
fulness. Why do Thy chariot wheels so long delay?
Come Lord Jesus, come quickly, and reign in my heart
without a rival. This day my body is weak, and if an
alteration does not take place, I must sink and die. Lord
prepare me for all. My soul longs to be filled. O God
remove the hindrance and send the Holy Ghost. Help
me to believe, the faith impart, the blood apply, and seal
me for Thine own. Come Jesus, come. I will not let
Thee go, till I the great salvation prove, and know Thy
sanctifying power.

December 16th. Rose between seven and eight, in consequence of affliction. I find that I cannot labour as I have done. After I had retired to rest last evening, I was led to serious reflection on the past day. I mused on what I had witnessed while visiting the poor, and I never had such a feeling of boundless charity diffused through my soul; I thought that should God spare me, I could almost lay my life down for the poor.

Mr. William Dawson, of Barnbow, near Leeds, and Mr. Roberts, of Holmfirth, called to see me this evening. Mr. Dawson prayed with me very soon after he entered the room, and prayed a second time after we had had some conversation about God and heavenly things. He appears to be a man of much information, simple, humble, honest, pious, cheerful, and in earnest for his own soul and the souls of others. My soul to-night longs to be dissolved in love, and to dwell in God. Lord increase my faith.

December 19th. Rose this morning between three and four. A day of good to my soul, but much of my time has been taken up with thoughts about leaving the house I dwell in. It certainly is not a healthy one. I have mentioned it to my mother, who thinks I shall do well to change for a healthier situation. Went on to Honley Moor, and looked at different houses, but I saw none so suitable as Abraham Chapel's. But, in changing my residence, am I doing the will of God? If not, I had better never think of it. I had better live in a dungeon, than grieve God. I have made it matter of earnest prayer, pleading the promise, " in all thy ways acknowledge Him, and He shall direct thy path." As far as I can judge, the Lord approves of my removal. At my class-meeting, at Thomas Oldham's, I felt the Lord wonderfully precious, "near to save, strong to deliver," but did not fully realise salvation from all sin. However, He is faithful, the blood

is efficacious, and, through faith, I shall realise all the life
of God. My soul is hungry, thirsty, restless, and the
promise is, " Blessed are they that hunger and thirst after
righteousness, for they shall be filled." Whilst crossing
Netherton Moor, O how powerfully did the Lord apply to
my mind this passage, "sanctify them through Thy truth,"
and ere long I expect its fulfilment. Lord help me.

The foregoing extracts reveal a depth of religious conviction, an intensity of feeling, a persistency of effort, a
continuous agony of strife, that must perfectly astonish
religious formalists, and easy going Christian professors,
who having once found peace through believing, are trusting in their conversion, instead of "forgetting those things
which are behind and reaching forth unto those things
which are before ;" and who know nothing of the strife so
frequently referred to by Christ and His Apostles. A
simpler faith in Jesus, "who of God is made unto us,
wisdom and righteousness and sanctification, and redemption," resulting in pardon and purity and perfect peace,
was Edward Brooke's undoubted privilege ; and yet who
shall say, that this long and terrible struggle which broke
down his health and threatened his very life, was not
the discipline best fitted to bring his ardent nature into
captivity to the obedience of Christ, and to fit him for
the work of an evangelist ?

Who so prepared to sympathise with spiritual mourners
as they who have drunk deeply of the wormwood and the
gall ? Who so qualified to guide the feet of lost sinners
straight to the cross of Christ, and into the way of peace
and purity and life, as they who found it after long and
weary and all but despairing search, and then were
astonished to see how simple and straightforward was
the way, had they but followed the teachings of God's
word and Spirit, instead of listening to the suggestions
of their own "evil heart of unbelief ?"

Men who are called to special service, have commonly special training, and by the sore conflict which the diary describes, God was graciously preparing his servant for Christian work and usefulness. But the conflict was drawing to a termination. Christmas day, which breaks so joyously on most, found Edward Brooke still mourning; but it brought him a letter from a Christian friend, which was sanctified to his encouragement and ultimate deliverance.

December 25th. Christmas day, so called; may it be a day of salvation to my soul; a day of rejoicing, that ever Jesus came to "seek and to save that which was lost." Rose this morning a little before five. I groan, and mourn, and sigh, and weep from a deep conviction of inward depravity. Lord help me to-day. Heard a sermon this afternoon. Felt low in my mind, in consequence of not having the great, the mighty, glorious, heavenly salvation from all sin. I long for it, more than for my wine or my oil to increase, I pray for it, as far as I know with all my heart. I plead the blood, the promises and the faithfulness of Jehovah. Here I rest. Here I will rest, till the spirit of burning comes and consumes the whole mass of corruption. The foundations of the great deep have been broken up, this day, in my soul, and my tongue cannot describe my feelings. Truly I may say with Hezekiah, "O Lord I am oppressed, undertake for me."

This afternoon I received a letter from William Dawson, and my soul was humbled whilst reading and meditating on it. Tears flowed from my eyes, and I felt thankful for the encouragement I received from the letter. He wrote, "you are hungering and thirsting after righteousness, and therefore you may expect the accomplishment of that rich, deep, and unfathomable promise, '*They shall be filled.*'" This promise has rested upon my mind some time. But what must I do? I believe the Lord will ere long fulfil it

to the joy and satisfaction of my mind ; and, therefore, I
must rest in the Lord and wait patiently for him.   I have
lost the blessing by my own unfaithfulness, and the Lord
cannot err, He knows when and How to deliver me.   O for
grace, grace, grace to wait.   Lord help me.

The following is a copy of the characteristic letter
addressed by Mr. Dawson to his friend, and to which
allusion has just been made.

Barnbow, December 22nd, 1826.

Dear Sir,

Grace, mercy, and peace be multiplied upon you, from
God our Father and the Lord Jesus Christ, was the inspired
prayer of an Apostle for his brethren, and is the humble
and heartfelt petition of W. Dawson for his friend and
brother Brooke.   But Paul could not only *pray* for the
churches which he had been a means of planting, but also
give thanks on their account.   When writing to the
Romans, he says, "I thank my God through Jesus Christ
that your faith is spoken of through the whole world;" so
also your ministers and brethren can thank God that your
faith is spoken of through the neighbourhood.   When we
look at you, we cannot but exclaim, Hail miracle of mercy!
of double mercy,   Not only born of God, but also born in
circumstances, especially of a temporal nature, which, when
sanctified by the word of God and prayer, are a talent
committed to your care, by which you may most eminently
promote the highest end of creation, that is, the glory of
God.   In the day of judgment the poor believer is noticed
and honoured by the Judge as a brother, but not so noticed
as the rich members of Christ's mystical body, who attended
to Paul's counsel to the rich : who "were not high minded,
nor trusted in uncertain riches, but in the living God ; who
did good, who were rich in good works, ready to distribute,

willing to communicate." I say it will be seen in that day, that such exercises of faith and love will be especially owned and honoured by Him, by whose grace they were performed, to whose people they were applied, and for whose glory and honour they were directed. Long may you live to enjoy with increasing pleasure these vital and active principles, which always present every act of the soul and body to God through the meritorious hand of Jesus Christ. Long may you live to exercise these principles which produce " the fruits of righteousness, which are by Jesus Christ unto the glory and praise of God."

The richest enjoyments of faith and love are most deeply felt through the soul, when, by their exercises, self is annihilated and God is glorified; thus the soul that is most freed from sin and most filled with love, most actively serves the Lord Jesus Christ, and most delightfully exclaims, " not I, but the grace of God that is in me." O my dear brother, when I look at you, I cannot but cry out, What has the Lord done for you! and what is it that He will not do for you? He has brought the camel through the needle's eye, nay more, He has transformed the camel into a sheep; and now puts you into His pasture by day, and into His fold by night; continue there, and He will one day place you at His right hand for ever. O, that grace which conquered your will, when, at the first it opposed, what conquests can it not now make, what salvation can it not now effect when it yields? That blood which pardoned your numerous and aggravated sins, which stained and stung a guilty conscience, what can it not now do upon your enlightened and sprinkled conscience? That love which sprung up in your heart, when you first believed, what a well of water can it not rise to, by repeated exercises of faith? Who can fathom the depths, who can measure the breadth, who can explore the height of the

love of Christ to which a Christian believer may now
attain ?   May he not experience the answer of that somewhat parodoxical prayer of the Apostle, for the Ephesians,
and know the love of Christ which passeth knowledge ?
surely he may, and blessed be God, that you do, in a small
degree, know it, and the knowledge at the same time
increases and satisfies the desire of the heart, and you are
panting to be filled with the fulness of God.

My dear brother, the fourth blessing in the fifth of
Matthew, sixth verse, is yours.   You are hungering and
thirsting after righteousness, and, therefore, you may expect
the accomplishment of that rich, unfathomable promise,
" *they shall be filled.*"   They shall be filled.   Who says so ?
You know who says so.   It is He who possesses infinite
fulness of everything, which a soul hungering and thirsting
after righteousness can ask for, or think of; and He
possesses this fulness, the same as the sun possesses a
fulness of light and heat, on purpose to bestow upon those
who stand in need of it, without money and without price.
They shall be filled, but with what shall they be filled ?
With the two grand attributes in the nature and essence
of God, viz., light and love.   They shall be " children of
light."   They shall walk in the light, nay, more, they shall
be light in the Lord.   Light shall shine upon their soul,
and give them the clearest evidence of their interest in the
blood of Christ.   Light shall shine upon their path, and
their steps shall be ordered by the Lord.   In this light
may you always stand.   In this light may you grow.   In
this light may you always march toward the grave, and
when you come to the sides of the pit, may your setting
sun be marked by beams of mild unclouded glory ; and
then may you rise in heaven to shine with the glory you
see to all eternity ; and we know that this will be the life
and death of a child of light ; because this light may be

known from all other lights in this characteristic peculiarity; it always begets and supports love, pure, fervent, humble, self-abasing, Christ-exalting love. That love which the Apostle so vividly describes, 1 Cor. xii., is the twin brother of this light. They almost breathe at the same moment. They grow together, or they decline together. They live together and they die together. In hell both are absent, and in heaven both are gloriously present to all eternity. O may we both experimentally know in time and eternity the full meaning of those texts, 1 John iv. 16, 17. Amen and Amen.

When I began, I intended only writing a few remarks upon your being careful of your health, and a wish that you would favour us with a copy of Mr. Stoner's letter, and now pardon me that I have detained you from this important, very important subject of your health. I would say, attend to the word of God in its letter, and to the Spirit which speaks in that word, and speaks in your soul through that work, and speaks in the minds of God's people, and that you will fix upon the golden mean, and bring your charge to land. You will not shipwreck your health upon the rock of imprudence, nor be becalmed in the dead sea of lukewarmness. A holy breeze will fill your sails. Your Bible will be your compass. The Holy Spirit will be your sunshine, by which you will see all its varyings and all its bearings. Jesus will be your Pilot and Captain. The excellent of the earth will be your comrades. Your closet will be your private cabin, where you will hold communion with your pilot. Your class-meeting will be the large cabin where you will converse with the Captain and your fellow passengers, who are bound for the same port as yourself; and you will sometimes mount the deck and blow the trumpet, and sound a few sweet notes upon the unsearchable riches of Christ,

and point the sinner to the Saviour, and when you have
got his eyes fixed upon Him, preach to him from Luke
iv. 18, 19, until his broken heart dances for joy, his
captive soul is delivered, his blind eyes are opened and
illuminated, and his spirit, once bruised with his chains,
finds at the same time soundness, health, and liberty, and
he springs forth and shouts his deliverer's praise. But
health is required for this. Without this you will be an
invalid in the cabin, and we shall have to visit you, to
cheer your drooping spirit, or share your overflowing
joys, and instead of profiting hundreds at once, only an
individual or two can participate in the profit and the
pleasure of your company. I would therefore conclude
with a sentence borrowed from Paul's letter to Timothy,
and repeat his words, " consider what I say, and the Lord
give you understanding in all things." But time, pen, and
paper say conclude, with assuring Mr. Brooke that you are
his well wisher in the Lord. So, indeed, is

W. DAWSON.

The encouragement which Edward Brooke derived from
the perusal of this Christian letter was decided and
abiding. The entries in his diary forthwith assume a
brighter character. The lost blessing which he sought
with such painful eagerness was soon recovered, and
mourning gave place to joy and exultation.

December 26th. Rose about four. This has been a day
of peace. Praise my God ! Notwithstanding I have been
much in the world, He has been my strength ; His grace,
saving, comforting, directing, encouraging. Grace has
been with me. O may I ever live to him. My soul
praise the Lord. He will have my heart. He wants to
sanctify me. He assures me it is His will that I should
be sanctified. May I soon rejoice in the possession of the
blessing. Amen, Lord Jesus.

December 27th. Rose this morning too early. When I got down stairs I found it was between twelve and one. Before I rose from my bed O what light I received from the Lord upon a passage on which I was musing. As it was so early I retired to rest again. Just before I fell asleep, these words seemed to sound in my ears. Prepare for further trials. I feel, however, this morning strong in the Lord, and in the power of His might, and I do believe the great salvation is coming. Hallelujah ! Lord send it. Rode a few miles on business. As I was going, these words were applied to my mind. "Now is the prince of this world cast out." Still I could not fully lay hold. One hindrance no doubt was, giving my mind too much to the horse I was trying. O this worldly spirit, if once given way to, how it grows : how it blinds and stupifies the soul. Lord save me from it.

> "Take my poor heart and let it be
> For ever closed to all but Thee."

December 28th. Rose a little before five. Glory ! glory ! glory ! be to God. This day I believe my soul is fully sanctified. Christ reigns without a rival on the throne of my heart. Glory be to God ! everlasting life is won, if I thus continue to hold fast. My soul praise the Lord. The Lord has shown me that the work was wrought, at least, as far as I am enabled to understand, when I awoke so early on Wednesday morning. Since then I have felt victory, victory, victory through grace, over myself. Praise the Lord ! May I ever be faithful, ever love Him with all my heart. Lord help me and save me.

December 29th. Rose about five. This has been a day of peace and holy joy. My life I find is warfare. Pray I must without ceasing, or else I shall fall. I stand in jeopardy every hour ; every moment. I dread being found unfaithful. Lord help me. He does, thanks be to His name; and He graciously assures me through the medium of His word and Spirit, "As thy day is so shall thy strength be."

December 30th. Rose about four. This has been a day of joy. The Lord has enraptured my soul with foretastes of bliss. Glory! glory! glory be to His name. "I live; yet not I, but Christ liveth in me; and the life which I now live in the flesh I live by the faith of the Son of God, who loved me and gave Himself for me." Every moment I feel him near. In Him I live and move, and have my being. Through Him I receive wisdom to direct me, grace to support and keep me in every trial, and He assures me that I am His. Glory be to His name!. Lord help me to do Thy will.

December 31st (Sunday). Rose about five this morning. God has told me that I am an heir of *all* He has. Tears flowed from mine eyes, and my soul rejoiced in His salvation. I went to Huddersfield in the morning, and heard Mr. Bowers preach from "Examine yourselves." It was certainly a word of reproof. Went to Mr. Shaw's to dinner. Before we sat down, two of us engaged in prayer, and I felt let into God. The glory of God filled my soul, and my heart rejoiced in His salvation. In the afternoon we went to the lovefeast, and there I told of God's unbounded love to my soul. My body this evening is very weak, I do not yet take sufficient care of it. Lord give me more wisdom and prudence, for my body is become Thy temple, in it Thou dwellest; in it Thou reignest without a rival. Lord save me.

January 1st, 1827. Hallelujah! praise the Lord! He reigns, the Lord God Omnipotent in my heart. Rose a little before four. Got on to my knees in bed, and as soon as I began to pray, I remembered that this is the first day in the new year. Presently the passage struck my mind, "This year thou shalt die." Whether from the Lord or the devil I leave, but from my present weak state it is very probable I shall finish my warfare in the course of this year. Lord prepare me for all Thy will, and make me meet for heaven. Went to Huddersfield, it being our quarter day. At the quarterly meeting, I found the fire of love to burn in my soul and came home rejoicing, and also mourning on account of my little love to God and His cause. Lord set me all on fire. Engaged Timothy Oldham's boy to-day to assist me. Hope he will suit. If it be Thy will, O Lord, grant that he may remain with me, and in answer to his father's prayer save him in his younger days.

January 2nd. Rose about ten minutes after four. This I don't like : Lord help me to be more punctual for the future, and to rise before rather than after four. Whilst searching the Scriptures with fervent prayer, a blessedly encouraging passage was applied to my mind, " If ye abide in Me, and My words abide in you, ye shall ask what ye will and it shall be done unto you." Why, Lord, I said, I want my father, my mother, my brothers, my sisters, the servant girls, all converting. I want a revival of Thy work in the world. Lord grant me my heart's desire. Increase my faith, and help me now to believe. This afternoon I am tried. Don't feel so near my Lord, and why ? because I do not, as fully as I ought, attend to the injunctions, " Rejoice evermore. Pray without ceasing. In every thing give thanks." Lord help me for the future. I shall certainly fall without continual prayer and watchfulness. Lord help me to pray more, and to strive for a greater height of grace.

January 3rd. Rose at six minutes after four, and feel determined, the Lord helping me, to get more faith, fire

and zeal, and every grace of God's Spirit. My faith this
day is not so strong; but I will not let the Saviour go.
Jesus help me and save me.

January 4th.   Rose a little before five.   I do not like
this.   I retired to rest late having had company.   This
has been a day of trial.   I do not realise the presence of
my Lord so fully.   There appears to be some controversy
between us.   What is the matter, Lord?   " Jesus the
hindrance show," and now revive my drooping, sinking
soul.   Now save me or I sink.   Uphold me Lord, I have
no help in myself.   Be Thou my help in this day of trouble.
Satan tempts and roars.   Grace repels and conquers.   My
soul still lives, though in a mist.   Lord shine; cheer Thy
servant, help him up and do him good.   Glory! glory!
glory!

> "I find Him lifting up my head,
> He brings salvation."

O the precious blood of Jesus.   May its cleansing power
ever rest upon my soul.

January 9th.   Rose between four and five.   O for a heart
to praise my God for His unbounded and unparalleled
mercy to me a poor, unworthy, unfaithful, unprofitable
being.   My soul has rejoiced this day in God my Saviour.
In visiting the church of Christ, from house to house, I
found some in a low fallen state.   Oh! how I feel for them.
How my soul breathed out in earnest prayer to Jesus, to
save His church.   O my God maintain Thine own cause
and prosper Zion.

January 10th.   Rose about five; have been much in the
world, but my soul has been calm and serene.   The Lord
is my portion saith my soul, therefore will I hope in Him.

January 11th.   Rose about five.   This has been a day
of rejoicing.   " What shall I render unto the Lord for all
His benefits ? "   I stand astonished and wonder at His

boundless grace. Glory! glory! glory! He has brought me into a wealthy place. He has put a new song of praise and thanksgiving into my mouth. Lord help me to do Thy will upon earth, as angels do it in heaven.

January 12th. Rose about five. This has been a day of trial. I find this evening upon strict examination, that I do not improve the grace already given, as I might and ought to do. This passage has struck my mind "The path of the just is as the shining light, that shineth more and more unto the perfect day." O what a depth do I see in this Scripture, that I have not yet fathomed, what a height that I have not yet reached. This day, however, has been a day of encouragement. Whilst visiting various families, at three different houses, I saw the power of God manifest in the awakening of sinners. Tears rolled from their cheeks. Here I see the goodness of God in the encouragement He gives me to go forward in His work. But this morning, I felt a little of the fear of man. This I have acknowledged to the Lord, and He has graciously delivered my poor unworthy and unfaithful soul. O for a heart to praise Him. May all my thoughts, words and actions, be one continual sacrifice through life.

January 13th. Rose about five-and-twenty minutes past four. A day of rejoicing in Jesus, my Prophet, Priest and King; my all and in all. The life that I now live is a life of faith in Him. Glory! Heaven is on earth begun. Glory! He still keeps me by His power. Not unto me, but unto His name be all the glory. Do I conquer? It is through Him. Do I enjoy a sweet calm and settled peace, which neither men nor devils can ruffle or disturb? It is through Him. Is my prospect clear in relation to the heavenly world? It is through Him. He is all and in all, the first and the last, the Alpha and the Omega, the beginning and the end. Glory! glory! glory! be to Him

for His saving power. He reigns, He reigns, He reigns,
the Lord of life and glory in my soul. His vital energy
is diffused through my whole being. In short, "I *live*."
O the depth of that word *live*. May I experience more of
His life in my soul.

January 20th. Rose between seven and eight in consequence of a severe cold. I intend going to Manchester
to see a friend. Lord, go with me. Set off to Manchester
by the coach, and arrived safe in the evening. I was
directed by a brother in Society, to Mr. Bambers, a
physician, who "lodged strangers," and found myself comfortable indeed. Wherever we are, if the Lord be present
all is well. Before we retired to rest we had family prayer,
and O, how I felt drawn out in holy, fervent, importunate,
believing prayer. My soul entered into the holy of holies,
by the blood of Jesus. I felt Him near to fill, enlarge and
fill. Glory! glory! glory be to God! He reigns supreme,
and heaven has all my heart. I can appeal to Him, and
say with Peter, "Lord Thou knowest all things, Thou
knowest that I love Thee."

January 21st (Sunday). Found myself very unwell.
Kept my bed till nearly twelve o'clock. Rose and went
down stairs, but was obliged to return to bed. However,
I felt happy, happy in Jesus' love. O how happy is the
man whose heart is fixed. Free from all sin. Free from
every worldly care. Free to hold converse with the whole
Trinity, Father, Son, and Spirit. Then all is light, life,
love, joy, peace, glory, heaven. May my soul feel more of
His love and power.

January 22nd. Went to see brother Holladay. Here I
saw a man like Barnabas, "a good man and full of the Holy
Ghost and of faith. Heaven beaming on his very countenance. O how abased, ashamed, and humbled before him,
did I feel. How I longed to enjoy the glory he appeared

to possess and feel. His very soul was love. In opening my mind to him, relative to various points of Christian experience, I found him to be a father to me. O my God what shall I render unto Thee for all Thy favours poured out upon me. Help me to give thee all. Amen, Lord Jesus, so let it be.

The diary of this date records a frightful dream, in which the sleeper imagined himself possessed by an evil spirit. The conflict was terrible. On awaking, Satan still seemed to rage, but Jesus spake to His servant's heart, saying, " I have prayed for Thee that thy faith fail not." For some time he was greatly distressed, and might have suffered spiritual loss, but for his nearness to his old friend, Holladay, to whom he instantly betook himself for counsel and help. The simplicity with which the youthful Christian told his trouble to his spiritual father, is most refreshing, and the strong common sense and spiritual wisdom, with which his adviser resolved the dream into its elements, and showed him that whilst the terrible oppression of the night arose from physical causes, and was simply an attack of night-mare, the devil was endeavouring to turn the dream to account, and get the advantage of him, prove the " primitive" Methodist preacher to have been a man of wise discernment, and well qualified for the cure of souls. His explanation and advice were of service to his young friend, who writes. Here we see that

> "Two are better far than one,
> For counsel or for fight."

Had I not unbosomed my mind to my friend Holladay, I might have been troubled for some time. Bless the Lord, I feel I love him. Jesus is mine, and I am His, and He assures me all is well. Glory ! glory ! glory ! He lives to intercede for me. He reigns supreme in my heart.

I

CHAPTER IX.

"Behold the servant of the Lord ;
I wait Thy guiding eye to feel,
To hear and keep Thy every word,
To prove and do Thy perfect will ;
Joyful from my own works to cease,
Glad to fulfil all righteousness."

MR. BROOKE'S change of residence and comparative rest told favourably upon his health ; and with recovered strength and spirits, he again threw himself into his beloved work of preaching from house to house, as well as in the pulpits of his own and neighbouring circuits, with surprising energy and devotion ; and he was honoured with success in the awakening and conversion of sinners not often witnessed. The fame of his ministrations spread and at length the squire was in such demand for special services and anniversary occasions, both far and near ; and the results of his preaching were so marked and marvellous, that the question was forced upon his consideration, whether, born as he was, to wealth, and having no need to work for gain, he ought not to relinquish his interest in the large and lucrative works at Armitage Bridge, and devote himself as a lay evangelist to the work of spreading scriptural holiness over the land. It was a question of grave responsibility, a question demanding much thought and earnest prayer for divine guidance. The pilgrim had reached one of those critical stages of life's journey, when a false step, bearing him into a wrong path, had given a false direction to his whole after life, and been followed by consequences most disastrous to himself and others; but Edward Brooke knew how to act at such a juncture. He had confidence in the Providence of God; a childlike and unfaltering confidence which his diary most beautifully illustrates at every stage of his career, and in relation to all the affairs of life. God was his father; his confidential friend, whom he consulted about everything; and whose manifested will determined his whole conduct. And what can be surer than God's guidance of His docile children? "The steps of a good man are ordered of the Lord, and he delighteth in His way." "The secret of the Lord is with them that fear Him and He will show them His covenant." No child of God, sincerely seeking and patiently awaiting direction from above, shall fail to hear the word behind him, saying, "this is the way, walk ye in it," when he turns to the right, and when he turns to the left,

> " By Thine unerring Spirit led,
>   We shall not in the desert stray ;
> We shall not full direction need,
>   Nor miss our providential way :
> As far from danger as from fear,
>   While love, almighty love, is near."

All this, Edward Brooke entirely believed, and with the simplicity and faith of a little child, he took this great perplexity to God, and spread his case before the Lord, and patiently awaited the indication of God's will.

At length, the answer came, explicitly directing, as he believed, the great sacrifice, when, at once, and with the same wonderful decision, with which, at the time of his conversion, he gave up his dogs and gun, he now relinquished his connection with the great money-making apparatus, by which his father and uncles had gained wealth, and which still enriches its possessors; and devoted

his best energies to Christian work. Some possibly may
question the wisdom of his conduct, but his motive was
pure. He made the sacrifice with a clear apprehension of
its greatness for the Lord's sake ; and shortly before his
decease, he was heard to say that, standing as he did, upon
the confines of eternity, and reviewing his past life in
prospect of his great account, he had not one regret in
relation to this step, but would repeat it, were he to begin
life again.

Released from the claims of business, Mr. Brooke's time
and strength were now still more largely given to evangelistic labours. Had he been officially appointed, and
maintained by the church, to do the work of a home
missionary, he could hardly have toiled with greater
assiduity than at this period. Night after night he
preached in village chapels, or in some poor man's cottage,
holding prayer-meetings, endeavouring to arouse the careless, and directing penitent sinners to the Saviour. The
following morning he often spent in visiting the people in
their homes, encouraging the awakened to seek the Lord
with all their heart, exhorting those who had believed, to
hold fast the beginning of their confidence unto the end ;
and urging all to avail themselves of Christian fellowship,
by joining the Society and meeting in class. A wonderful
helper of the circuit ministry, he must have been. Zeal
like his was contagious. The church was stirred up to
activity, and as the result of general and united labour,
" much people was added unto the Lord."

Preaching to a large congregation at Linthwaite, near
Huddersfield, on Sunday, April 15th, 1826, Mr. Brooke's
eye fell upon a young lady devoutly worshipping. Her
name was Martha, the second daughter of Mr. Smith, of
Greetland. Attracted by the preacher's popularity, and
by the fame of his usefulness, she had come to hear the

young squire preach; seeking only her soul's good, and
little dreaming that her visit to Linthwaite chapel on that
occasion would shape her destiny. The young lady was
unknown to the preacher, yet, as he looked upon her, he
felt a strange fascination, which somewhat embarrassed his
pulpit exercises, and constrained him at the close of the
service to make special inquiry respecting his fair auditor.
A powerful presentiment possessed him, that in that young
lady he had seen his future wife. Wishful, however, to be
rightly guided, in a matter so vastly important, as the
choice of a life-companion, he placed his impulsive nature
under stern restraint, and sought counsel of the Lord. His
prayers were not wilful, as prayers under such circumstances often are, the asking divine guidance in relation to
a choice already made, and a resolution unalterably formed;
they were the prayers of one sincerely wishful to be led by
wisdom higher than his own; for in his diary he writes,
"If it be not God's will, I feel determined, through His
grace, to give it up, and live as He would have me."

After further inquiry, much earnest prayer, and consultation with a Christian relative, in whose judgment he
confided, Mr. Brooke came to the conclusion, from which
he never swerved for a moment, either in judgment or
affection; that Martha Smith was the helpmeet whom God
had provided for him. He sought an early opportunity to
declare his love, and solicit reciprocation. At that first
interview, both parties engaged in prayer, and seemed
equally anxious to know the will of God; and their whole
subsequent courtship was conducted upon Christian principles, and in strict harmony with the law of Christ.

Courtship is a test, which sometimes discovers the weakness of good men. The intercourse and correspondence of
Christian lovers is not always free from folly; and such,
as if published to the world, would adorn their Christian

profession ; but this courtship, from first to last, was
exemplary, for it was sanctified, throughout all its stages,
by the word of God and prayer.

Succeeding interviews with his affianced, but served to
broaden the foundation of esteem, which is the only firm
basis of connubial happiness ; and to assure Mr. Brooke of
the wisdom of his choice. In his diary, he writes, "I went
to see Martha Smith, her conduct appears worthy of imitation. She manifests a Christian spirit throughout. I
feel fully satisfied that the Lord has pointed her out as
the very person to suit me. She loves God and longs to
enjoy a greater salvation. Lord grant her the desire of
her heart."

Having resolved to marry, Mr. Brooke had now to look
out and provide a suitable home. Brought up in the
country, a true child of nature, town life presented no
attractions. A comfortable country house, with a small
farm attached, where he might indulge, upon a small
scale, his taste for husbandry ; and so situated as to be
a convenient centre for evangelistic work, was the height
of his ambition. In this, as in every other engagement
of life, he confidently sought direction of the Lord.

Writing about a farm, which he had been to see, he
states, as one of its chief recommendations, "If I take this
farm, I shall have a fine opportunity of visiting five
different circuits. It is fifteen miles from Wakefield, eight
from Barnsley, thirteen from Sheffield, and thirteen from
Huddersfield." Of another place which he inspected, he
writes, "The appearance of it is too grand, the house is too
large, and the rent too high. I would rather have a little
comfortable house, than one of that kind. Lord find me
one. Thou knowest all about me. Help me in this affair."
Eventually he took a house and farm at Hoyland Swaine,
upon a lease of seven years. Recording his agreement, he

adds, " Lord, go with me there, or I shall be miserable. Help me, my Jesus, to do all Thy will."

Whilst perplexed in relation to his future residence, and occupied with various arrangements incident to his settlement in life, Mr. Brooke still maintained a close walk with God, and unabated devotion to Christian work. He writes,

May 15th. Set off to Manchester, to see Thomas Holladay, my mind being distressed, and wanting his advice upon some very particular points. Felt encouraged, whilst with him. O the piety and zeal of that blessed man of God. His souls dwells in the Trinity, breathes the pure celestial air, and lives in the suburbs of heaven.

May 16th. Rose a little before four. Set off home by the six o'clock coach. Felt comfortable. The Lord helped me to let my light shine in the coach. One man appeared a little affected, and promised to do his best in seeking for mercy.

May 19th. This has been a day of light, life, and comfort. I feel I love God with all my heart. He reigns without a rival. O may I never, never, never prove unfaithful.

May 20th (Sunday). Rose a little after five. Went to Skelmanthorp. Preached in the afternoon. Held a prayer-meeting, and two or three, it was said, found liberty, the liberty of God's dear children. Praise His name! He will save. He does save. He will save the world. In the evening went to Emley. Felt good liberty, and the people appeared blessed. Four or five, it was said, found salvation. Staid all night at brother Jackson's, and found the family very agreeable.

May 21st. Rose about six. Felt rather drowsy, not having had much rest. Preached at Emley again in the afternoon. Found the Lord to help and bless. Glory !

glory! I feel His service my delight. O for a heart to praise Him. Held a prayer-meeting, and two or three received good. One woman, with a child in her arms, wrestled hard, with sighs and groans and tears, and, thank God, she realised the fulfilment of the blessed promise, "They that sow in tears shall reap in joy."

June 15th. Rose about seven. My frame is weak, and rest is needful. I have not improved my time to-day, as I ought to have done. Lord help me, and bless me, with Thy great salvation. This evening I have felt much respecting the society at Honley. There appears a coldness. Prayer-meetings are not well attended. Some speak of our leading men being a hindrance. How this is, I cannot tell. Some of the young men appear dissatisfied, and, as it respects myself, I feel I have not laboured as I might have done amongst the people. However, I intend, if the Lord spares me, to do better, and labour for a revival at Honley. Lord send us one. Hasten Thy coming from above. Let not Satan reign, but let Thy kingdom come. Lord hear and answer. My complaint still hangs about me ; and, without much care, I shall never be fully cured. Visited four or five families, conversed with them about their souls, and prayed for the blessing of heaven to rest upon them. Lord grant it.

June 16th. Rose soon after five. Read and studied the word of life, and consulted various authors. Visited several families, and invited them to the band-meeting. I still feel athirst for salvation. Salvation by grace. Athirst for all that God can give. Lord help and bless me. We had a good meeting, and I trust that Jesus in answer to prayer will revive us again.

June 17th (Sunday). Rose about five. Went to the prayer-meeting at seven o'clock. Felt encouraged. Went to Burnplatts, and preached in the afternoon. Had liberty to speak, but little power. This will never do. O for faith in God. Lord increase my faith. Reclaim my soul. Preached at Honley in the evening. Felt much the same. Held a prayer-meeting, and four or five appeared to be seeking the Lord. One experienced the blessing whilst I was with them. I left the others in distress, wrestling for mercy. I am much discouraged. · I don't feel that holy wrestling with God for souls, which I have done. This won't do, Lord help me.

June 18th. This has been a day of severe trial. Lord save me. The smiles of men, if yielded to, will damn me. Lord save me. The frowns of men, if yielded to, will damn me. I stand in jeopardy every hour. Earth and hell are engaged to ruin me. Jesus baffle them. Undertake for me.

June 20th. Rose about six. This has been a day of good to my soul. The Lord has encouraged me, and blessed me with a stronger faith. Preached at Crosland Hill. Felt liberty and more power. We had a prayer-meeting, and there appeared to be five or six affected, and I think two found liberty. O for an increase of faith, and then souls would be saved.

June 22nd. This has been a good day. I have been attempting to purchase a horse. The one I have is weak, and, like myself, cannot stand much slavery. I see I might have given a word at many times, when I did not. Horse-dealing is no desirable trade, and no friend to religion; unless done with a pure intention and an eye to the glory of God. Lord help me to do Thy will. Glory be to God! I feel more for souls. This is all grace. O for a heart to praise my God. O for a heart to feel for sinners, and for courage to take up my daily cross. Lord help me.

June 24th (Sunday). Rose a little before six. Set off

to Gomersal to preach in the afternoon and evening. Preached out of doors, in a large field, to an immense congregation. Felt power from on high, but not that glory I wanted. O for the hallowed fire to burn with seraphic ardour on the altar of my heart. Preached in the evening in the Calvinist chapel, our place being too small. The Lord was there, and many felt, no doubt, His power. After preaching, we went to our own place and held a prayer-meeting. The Lord condescended to pour out His Spirit. Two boys and one young woman experienced salvation and rejoiced. Glory to God in the highest!

June 25th. Slept at Gomersal. Glory be to God! I feel He blesses and encourages me. Yesterday I had an impression, which I believe was from the Lord, respecting the propriety, nay, necessity, of our Gomersal friends having a chapel. I named it in the pulpit, and told them I should meet them in the morning. Accordingly, we met, considered and set to work, praying for the blessing of God to rest upon us, and, blessed be His name for ever, He appeared to go before us; for the people to whom we applied for land, seemed to acquiesce in our proposals, and there is to be another meeting, God willing, next Friday morning. Lord God let the work go forward. Thou hast the hearts of all people in Thy hands, and if Thou dost work, the desire of our hearts shall be granted. Having eleven classes, they stand in need of a chapel. Returned home. God Almighty was with me, blessing me. Praise Him for ever.

July 8th (Sunday). Preached at Gildersome, afternoon and evening. Felt great liberty. Several were saved, how many, I could not ascertain. Glory be to God! This has been a good day to my soul. Have gained, through grace, another victory over my stubborn will. O that Jesus may soon conquer and subdue me to Himself.

July 9th. Set off from Gildersome to Birstal. Called to see Mr. and Mrs. Clapham, and they and Mr. Almer wrestled with me for a greater salvation. Went to Gomersal, to see how they were proceeding with the chapel. I accompanied a friend, and agreed with Mr. Sigston, jun., for the purchase of the land at half-a-crown per yard. I think our Gomersal friends are now in a fair way to have a chapel; Lord grant it may be the case. I still feel dissatisfied with myself. I know, I feel, I am an unprofitable servant of Jesus.

July 15th. Glory be to God! I feel encouraged to trust in Him. I preached at Low Moor iron works, afternoon and evening. Felt the power of God, and many souls experienced salvation. Glory to God! He still works in spite of earth and hell.

July 19th. This has been a good day to my soul. When I look at the unbounded goodness of God to me in every sense, I stand astonished and amazed. Lord give me a heart to praise Thee more and serve Thee better. Went over to Huddersfield this afternoon, about some worldly business I have in hand. I find that whilst in the world, and in worldly company, I have much need of watchfulness and prayer, in order that my thoughts, words, and actions may be right in the sight of an omnipresent and omniscient God. Lord help me at all times to conduct myself as becometh Thy gospel. When I enter upon my farm I shall have to be more in the world, in all probability, and a thought has crossed my mind, when I sell off any of my stock, to put a fair market price upon it, and there abide, whether I sell or not. By so doing, those with whom I may have to transact business, will know at once, whether to purchase, and I shall be saved from that unprofitable conversation which frequently attends buying and selling. Solomon says, " In the multitude of words there wanteth not sin."

July 22nd (Sunday).   Went to Sheepridge : preached in the morning.   Felt liberty, but not the power I ought to have felt.   Heard a sermon in the afternoon.   Listened with attention and in faith, and the word was made profitable to my soul.   Afterwards went to Norland in the Sowerby-Bridge circuit, and preached for the benefit of the Sunday School.   The Chapel was too small to hold the immènse congregation, so I preached in the open air. Towards the latter part of the sermon especially, I felt a divine influence to go through my soul, and we had upon the whole a glorious meeting.   When the collection was made I put in a ring and breast pin, which I had begged at Sheepridge from two ladies, telling the people how I came by them.   After service we went into the chapel and held a prayer-meeting.   Immediately, the divine power went through the place.   Souls began crying for mercy.   Penitents were pardoned, Believers were quickened, and the Glory of God rested on the congregation. Glory to heaven! what a work is this!   A heavenly, glorious, happy work.   O for the fulness.   I long for this, to be filled with the Deity.

July 23rd.   Went to King Cross in the afternoon, and there I saw the power of God displayed as I never did before.   The promise was fulfilled, "Open thy mouth wide and I will fill it."   I have heard and read of souls being struck to the ground by the power of God.   Here I saw it.   One woman was so filled with God that she fell upon the floor, and lay gasping as if she were dying.   I asked her husband, a holy man, if he were not afraid of her dying in that state.   He replied, No.   She has been so filled and overpowered with the love of God scores and hundreds of times.   After this, we went to see a pious woman who was sick, and there the glory of God came down, and other two persons were filled and overpowered in the same manner. Never, never did I see such a work as this. But was it not all enthusiasm ? The devil would say so. Carnal reasoners would say so. Lukewarm professors would say so. The world would say so. But not the man or woman who has experienced the fulness of God. No, they see, they know, they feel it to be a reality. O that this work, this mighty work, may go forward in the hearts of professors. Lord carry it on. Sanctify believers. Fill, fill, fill my heart, and save me to the uttermost.

July 29th (Sunday). Rose a little before seven. This will not do. I lay too long. Seven hours are sufficient at all times for me. Lord help me to deny myself and take up my cross by rising earlier. Glory be to God ! He has been with me to day at Burnton and at Roydhouse. Many souls were seeking salvation, and some found. I had to preach out of doors at Roydhouse, and we held a prayer-meeting in a field. I longed to see souls converted out of doors, as I never had done, and the Lord condescendingly granted my heart's desire. Two or three found mercy, and rejoiced in a sin-pardoning God. O, for more power in preaching. Without divine influence, human efforts are ineffectual.

September 4th. Went to Wortley : preached in the afternoon. Felt wonderful liberty. The Lord took possession of my heart fully. Praise my Lord, I am His and He is mine. Praise Him for ever and ever and ever. Preached again in the evening. Felt wonderful liberty again, glory be to His name ! Prayer meetings were held after. It was supposed that fifteen souls were brought into glorious liberty, and two or three were sanctified. The glory is the Lord's. He shall have all of it. Lord help me to give Thee all : save me from self-exaltation, from thinking more highly of myself than I ought to think.

September 5th. Slept at Mr. Walker's, of Wortley. Felt at home with them, and longed to see them all saved. Lord save the whole family. Went to a prayer-meeting in the morning, and there the Lord again revealed His saving power. Four were blessed with pardoning mercy, and rejoiced in God their Saviour. Went to the Armley Missionary meeting, and there I felt His presence. Spoke a few words, but did not feel liberty. We held a prayer-meeting, and there were a few, I think, in distress. In the evening Mr. Dawson preached, and the power of God was again displayed, and souls were saved in the prayer-meeting. What cannot the Lord do? He can save a world. Lord ride on. Conquer the world. Glory! glory! glory! I feel Him in my soul! He reigns supreme. Lord keep me.

September 10th. Went to Leeds : preached in the Old Chapel. I had a mighty struggle before I ascended the pulpit, but in preaching I felt the Lord present to help. There appeared to be a good feeling amongst the people. A prayer-meeting was held, and several found liberty. I should suppose there must have been near thirty penitents. Some who had backslidden were crying for healing mercy, others for pardoning mercy, and others for full redemption. Slept at Mr. Sigston's, in the room good old Bramwell slept in. O may I possess as much of hallowed fire, and more, if possible. On Tuesday, the 11th, I returned home, called at Birstal to see Mr. and Mrs. Clapham, and there, glory be to God! I felt refreshed and strengthened, and renewed. The blood of Jesus was again applied. I felt it sensibly. Glory to Jesus! His blood can cleanse. My soul cries, it does cleanse.

September 16th (Sunday). Went to preach at Slaith-waite : felt discouraged because of the state of my mind. I felt little energy—little love to God and His cause.

Preached in the morning, or at least I may say talked a little. Felt little. Preached in the afternoon. Felt rather better. Went to Berry Brow in the evening and preached. Felt little again. This will not do. The hindrance must be in me. I have lost ground. I cannot rest here. At least, I would not. I want to feel sorrow and compunction of soul. Talking is not preaching. Lord have mercy upon me. I feel I can neither think, nor write, nor talk, nor preach, nor do anything but self rises. All self—all Brooke. I hate it. I abhor the very thought. I would rather be nothing, than want to take any praise to myself. I feel in a strange way. Lord help me. I feel low, dejected, cast down. I must pray, I must wait, I must strive to do better.

> " Tis worse than death my God to love,
> And not my God alone."

September 18th. Went to Morley, near Leeds. Felt discouraged on my journey, but as soon as I got into the pulpit my God delivered me. My fears were dispersed, and my soul was blessed. Glory be to God ! After preaching in the afternoon, several were pardoned and rejoiced in the salvation of God. Preached again in the evening. Felt the Lord wonderfully near to help. The power of the Spirit came upon my soul. I seemed to mount higher and higher, as in a chariot of fire. When the soul gets a divine touch of holy fire all is well. Held another prayer-meeting, and many more were saved. My soul praise the deity. How astonishing that he should thus condescend to bless me, even me. Amazing love ! Lord, I want more power to, do Thy will. More courage to face an infidel world. Now give Thy unworthy servant more of Thy fulness. After the prayer-meeting I returned to Birstal with Mr. Clapham. · Staid all night. Felt happy

with Mr. and Mrs. C.   Glory be to God !   O for a heart to
praise my God, and a heart to feel for sinners.

The Mr. and Mrs. Clapham referred to once and again in
the   daily   record   of   Mr. Brooke's   experience,   were   a
Christian couple of rare excellence.   Resident in Birstal,
the birthplace of John Nelson and the scene of his early
labours · and persecutions, their minds were richly stored
with the traditions of early Methodism.   They had enjoyed intimate fellowship with Bramwell, Stoner, and other
Methodist worthies, and were of kindred spirit.   Like
Zaccheus and Elizabeth, " they were both righteous before
God, walking in all· the commandments and ordinances of
the Lord blameless."   The writer well remembers his in-
troduction to Mr. Clapham, an elderly gentleman of middle
stature, somewhat stooping beneath the weight of years,
his calm face clean shaven, his thin locks combed down
and slightly covering a brow which they once concealed,
his throat enveloped in folds of snow-white cambric, his
suit of spotless black fashioned in severe accordance with
the recognised Methodist pattern of fifty years before, the
coat straight cut, the breeches and gaiters close-fitting.
He was a picture of primitive simplicity enough to awe a
young Methodist preacher attired in surtout and trousers,
and dressed after the style of his own generation.   But
when the old man spake, there was a frankness in his tone
and a savour of goodness in his speech, which at once proclaimed that beneath the antique and somewhat severe
exterior, there beat a heart in sympathy with youth, genial
and loving to all who loved his Lord.

Mr. Clapham was a most unworldly man.   Established
as a manufacturer of fine cloth, and possessed of capital
and energy, he had ample opportunity to gain wealth, had
he deemed it right to make wealth the great object of his
life.   But on principle, he preferred a small trade with few

anxieties, attendance on the means of grace, communion with God and a quiet heart, to the restless, all-absorbing, and successful pursuit of trade, which he witnessed in some about him. Memoirs have been written of Christian men who religiously made wealth. There have been Christian men who religiously refrained from wealth-seeking, cententing themselves with a moderate competence, whose lives equally deserve consideration in this age of Mammon-worship, but for whom no biographer is found.

Mr. Clapham's home was eminently a Christian home, where Mr. Brooke loved to pull up and spend an hour, or tarry for the night, when travelling that way upon his master's business. His visits were always welcome. Everything gave way on such occasions to spiritual intercourse and worship, and the young evangelist never left the Clapham's hospitable roof, without refreshment of soul as well as body, and a still firmer purpose to spend and be spent for God. Nor was the advantage all upon one side. After spending the night at Mr. Clapham's, Mr. Brooke writes, " The Lord appeared to work upon the eldest daughter of Mr. Clapham. She felt, she wept, and wanted the Lord to bless her. My God save her, bless her, do it now, just now, whilst I am writing. Lord save me. Hallelujah! Thou wilt save me. Thou dost save. Thou knowest that I want *all* Thou hast to give. Enlarge the vessel. Fill the vessel. Enlarge again. Fill again. Let the glory come. Hallelujah! It is coming. It will come. It does come. Now Lord, another touch. Glory! Glory! Glory! I am the Lord's, his free man, not a slave. No; at liberty. My chains are knocked off. The angel of the covenant has opened the prison doors, and by his power he has delivered me. Save me for ever and ever and ever. Thou wilt. Glory! Glory! Glory!"

Mr. and Mrs. Clapham have entered into rest, leaving

K

behind, the fragrance of a good name which still refreshes the Society at Birstal. But the daughter referred to by Mr. Brooke survives, and in reply to an inquiry relating to Mr. Brooke's visit to her father's house and its influence upon herself, thus writes :—

" I have a most distinct recollection of the event you mention. Many of my friends have heard me refer to it, when speaking about the conversion of children. I should then be nine years of age. Having been blessed with pious parents, I do not remember a time when I had not a desire to love and serve God. About that time, I had been led by the Spirit of God to see that without a change of heart I could not do this, and in this state of mind, on the morning referred to, I entered the sitting-room before breakfast. Mr. Brooke was there alone. He spoke to me very kindly, and inquired if I loved Jesus. I answered no, and burst into tears. He then put his arm round me and drew me to his side, and talked to me of the love which Christ had for Children, and tried to make me understand the way of salvation. We were interrupted by breakfast, but I could not eat any, and retired to my bedroom to weep and pray until called down to family prayer. While my father prayed Mr. Brooke came and knelt by me, and pointed me to Calvary. Then he prayed for me by name. I was very much excited, and did not then trust in Christ as my Saviour; but during the forenoon, while alone in prayer, I had a believing view of Jesus, and felt that He loved me and gave Himself for me. The blessedness of that happy day I shall never forget."

CHAPTER X.

INNER AND OUTER LIFE.

" If so poor a worm as I
    May to Thy great glory live,
All my actions sanctify,
    All my words and thoughts receive ;
Claim me for Thy service claim
    All I have, and all I am."

MR. BROOKE'S diary of this date appears to have been kept with singular care and exactness. Its records were not random or vague entries made for the mere sake of fulfilling, in some fashion, an acknowledged duty. In his closet he dealt faithfully with himself, communing with his own heart, searching his conscience, testing his life and recording the result for his subsequent profit. The following extracts may still further illustrate his experience of divine things, and his eager improvement of all opportunities of Christian usefulness :—

September 30th (Sunday). Preached at Brighouse in the morning. Before preaching we held a prayer-meeting. Two brothers were seeking salvation, and one found liberty. They had been seeking for some time. Felt good liberty in preaching, till toward the latter part of the discourse. I see and feel that I cannot preach without the Lord. Went to Ovenden, near Halifax, and preached in the afternoon and evening. Held a prayer-meeting after each discourse, and several found liberty and rejoiced in God their Saviour, Glory be to God! Not to man but to God.

October 1st. Went to Halifax, was invited to preach in the chapel. Accepted the invitation. Felt better than

when at Ovenden; but self prevailed. O, this cursed self.
I hate it. Lord help me to hate it more. Held a prayer-
meeting in the school-room, and several found redemption
in Jesu's blood, and others were filled with God.

October 2nd. Slept at Mr. Heaps', found him a very
pleasant man and a good man, a well-wisher to Zion.
Lord bless him and his dear wife. Left Halifax and returned home. Called at several places on my journey.
Went to my class-meeting, and there I felt encouraged to
press on. This morning I again felt self to rise. O, how
my soul did suffer. Lord save me from this cursed evil.
Make me an humble child.

October 3rd. Went to Huddersfield this afternoon, and
from thence to Birkby to look at a farm that is on sale.
Drank tea with ——. They want converting. My God,
undeceive them, and save them from the snares of the
devil. From thence I went to Mr. ——, and spoke to
him about his soul, and asked his permission to speak to
the family and pray with them, but he said they had company and it would not do. However, I felt that I was
clear. I long to see souls saved. From thence I went
to H—— House, and conversed and prayed with the
family. Returned home. I want saving from the fear of
man. Lord help me.

October 4th. Went to Hightown Missionary Meeting.
They pressed me to take the chair, and I at length con-
sented. Preached in the evening. Felt shackled. May
God save me, and make me willing to suffer His will as a
Christian, and leave all events to Him. A prayer-meeting
was held, and three or four found liberty and rejoiced in
God their Saviour. Slept at Mr. Parkin's, and felt happy
in my soul. Praise the Lord! I want a thankful heart.

October 5th. Glory to God and the Lamb! I feel
happy. My faith increases, my love abounds more and

more. I want perfect love. Glory to Jesus! He will perfect what is lacking, if I be faithful and do my part. Not that I can merit anything by doing. No. Salvation is a free gift, but bestowed on certain terms. Ask—seek—knock—in faith. Lord help me. I am Thine and Thou art mine. Returned home, then went to Hinchliffe Mill, near Holmfirth, to preach a sermon for the benefit of the Sunday School. Felt liberty and power, but I want to feel more, to pray and preach with power through God's Eternal Spirit, and then the walls of Jericho will fall; the strongholds of the devil will give way. Souls will be saved. Lord fill me with the Spirit just now. Hallelujah! the Lord is mine. My soul rises higher and higher and sinks deeper and deeper. O, for an increase of every grace, for burning love, a soul concerned for the glory of God and for the world's salvation. A prayer-meeting was held, and two souls were blessed with God's mercy and rejoiced in Him as their Saviour. One, if not both, were backsliders. Praise the name of our Lord! He does fulfil His ancient promise, "I will heal their backsliding, I will love them freely."

October 6th. This has been a strange day. Have not served the Lord as I might have done. Affliction of body presses down my soul, but after all, I might have been more faithful. I find I must take more care of my body. Lord help me.

October 7th (Sunday). I am going, the Lord willing, to preach at Meltham to-day, and at Honley in the evening. Lord save souls. Increase my faith, and help me to preach to-day. Glory be to God! He has helped me, but I have not always felt that holy influence I long to feel. Lord baptise me afresh. I lost ground on Saturday. I did not watch and pray as I ought to have done. When my soul has been happy, and when I have had good liberty in

preaching, I am in danger of thinking too highly of myself.
Nay, I frequently do.   Lord subdue me.   What a foolish,
weak creature I am to harbour any such thoughts, for I
have nothing, I am nothing, I can do nothing without my
God.   No souls saved to-day.   Lord, Lord, Lord have
mercy upon me.

October 8th.   This has been a good day, and yet a
strange day.   Went to Huddersfield.   Felt impressed to
call at Mr. T——'s to see Mrs. T., according to promise.
Spoke to her about her soul, and the necessity of seeking a
present salvation.   After taking tea with my Aunt ——
I went into the next house, and there we held a prayer-
meeting.   A few friends and one of their little boys cried
aloud for mercy.   O, how the Lord works when we work.
He is faithful and will fulfil his promises.   Left the boy
with the rest upon their knees.   Called on Mr. V——
to ask him to go with me to the sale of the Birkby Farm.
I prayed at Mr. V.'s, and a Miss G—— who was there
appeared to be much affected, and requested me to visit their
house.   Here I see the goodness of God in owning my labours,
and I record these facts as encouragements for the future.

The time was now approaching when Mr. Brooke was to
establish himself upon his farm at Hoyland Swaine, and
form new associations and meet new responsibilities.   The
separation from his old friends at Honley, with whom
hitherto his whole life had been so closely identified;
amongst whom he had found the Saviour, and for whose
welfare he had laboured with untiring and self-consuming
zeal, involved a wrench which made his heart ache; but he
believed himself to be acting under the sure direction of a
loving Providence, and he braced himself up to meet the
demands of the unknown future with a brave heart and
in humble dependence on God.

"I am now going," he writes, "to another field of action

and usefulness through God's blessing; may I give the Lord all my heart and ever faithful prove. Whilst in the world may I not be of the world. Whilst using it, may I not abuse it. Whilst passing through things seen and temporal, may I not forget the things which are not seen and eternal. Lord help me to do and suffer Thy will, to work out my own salvation with fear and trembling. Glory be to God! He still keeps me in the possession of His love. I feel I love Him supremely, and I long to follow Him fully and ardently. Lord help me. I find from past experience that sudden impressions are not always to be attended to. They may arise from a weak, debilitated, nervous state. This has been too mnch my case. I find that the *Word* is the rule by which we must regulate our lives. If we do nothing contrary to it we shall not err. We shall be led forth in the right way. It is the infallible truth of Jehovah, and it is the Word by which we shall be judged at the last day. Lord help me."

Again he writes: " I feel I want more power to take up my cross, to speak of Jesu's love wherever I go. Lord endow me with power from on high, that I may be bold and courageous, faithful and zealous for Thee and Thy cause. Glory be to God! for His unbounded goodness to me. He crowns me with his mercies and lovingkindnesses. O, for a heart to praise Him, to love, serve, and obey Him. I cannot be happy without Him. The world is an empty cistern, it can hold no water to satisfy my thirsty soul. Lord help me to come to Thee, the fountain of living waters; then, and only then, shall I be refreshed and satisfied. In consequence of having to furnish my new house and stock my farm, I cannot attend to reading and study, etc., as before, but I hope in a few days I shall be settled. O, for power to live to God at Hoyland Swaine. I am going if it be God's will. The language of my soul is, send me not up hence unless Thou, the God of Heaven, my Saviour, go with me, to comfort, direct, protect, and bless, and make me useful. Lord hear Thy servant's heart's desires, and according to Thy will grant him his request. Glory be to God! I feel the fire to burn "upon the mean altar of my heart." May it burn to the glory of God. I want to be a flame of fire, a son of thunder to the hardened and impenitent, and a son of consolation to the mourning penitent. I want to see Satan's kingdom fall. Souls saved under every sermon, believers encouraged, built up, sanctified. Lord ride on, conquer the world. Bow them to Thy sway. Reign supreme in every heart."

Before Mr. Brooke had well got through the bustle of removing, he bestirred himself to see what could be done to meet the spiritual wants of the locality in which he had resolved to make his home. The adjoining farm was in the occupation of Mr. Wigglesworth, an upright man of true respectability. He and his wife had given their hearts to God, and joined the Methodist Society. Another Methodist lived not far away, but there were no Methodist ordinances in the neighbourhood, and many of the people were sadly negligent of spiritual things. Mr. Brooke felt his responsibility in relation to his new neighbours. The cultivation of the few acres of land which he had leased, and on which he was in no sense dependent for a livelihood, he never meant to be his occupation, but simply a relief from the strain of higher and more arduous service. He had not retired upon his farm that, remote from large populations, he might the more readily forget the claims of his fellow-men, and take his ease, eating, drinking, sleeping, minding his own affairs, and seeking his own enjoyment, deluded by the vain thought that after this fashion he could fulfil life's responsibilities, find his way through the gates into the city, and secure an inheritance above. He had "not so learned Christ." Christianity to him meant work —unselfish, earnest, self-sacrificing work. He was God's servant, and wherever Providence might place him, his first thought was for his Master's interests ; his chief anxiety to find out what needed to be done for Christ and forthwith to do it. Hoyland Swaine he regarded as a neglected part of the great vineyard, and to bring it under cultivation and into full bearing, became now his first and laudable ambition ; and though eventually the management of his farm brought more care than he anticipated, and involved a heavier tax upon his time and thought than he felt desirable, the claims of God's work were still pre-eminent. The success of his spiritual husbandry, and a rich harvest of souls he coveted with immensely greater earnestness than increase of corn and wine ; and knowing that God works by means, he lost no time in putting the means in operation.

December 14th. Mr. Brooke writes : I find I need much grace to enable me to overcome myself, the world and all its cares, and the devil with all his schemes. Lord help me to conquer all. This day I have been down at brother Wigglesworth's, who has the next farm, to see what members live near, and to arrange, if possible, to have a class-meeting at a neighbour's house between his farm and mine. Mr. and Mrs. Wigglesworth are very much pleased with the plan, as they have no class-meeting nearer than Cawthorne, a distance of nearly two miles.

December 15th. Notwithstanding the pressure of home claims, Mr. Brooke set off for Low Moor, to be ready for two services upon the following Sabbath, concerning which he writes :

December 16th (Sunday). This has been a glorious day to my soul. Preached afternoon and evening, and felt the Lord wonderfully to help me. Held a prayer-meeting after

each service, and several, I know not how many, were justified and sanctified. Glory be to God ! He still owns me.
Praise Him for ever !

December 21st. I feel I want quickening, another baptism, a gale of grace to waft my soul in holy affection from
earth to heaven. Went to see a few friends who live near,
to consult about having a class-meeting. They appeared
very willing. We held a prayer-meeting at seven o'clock
instead of a class-meeting, as it was our first time of meeting. Lord help us and grant us Thy salvation. Revive
Thy work at Hoyland Swaine, and let the little one become
a thousand and the small one a great nation. O, for faith.
Lord increase my faith. Let me see Thine arm made bare.
Ride on. Bear down all opposition. Overturn, overturn,
overturn the kingdom of hell, and let Thy kingdom come.
Come quickly to every heart of man. Send us a revival.
The work is Thine. Cut it short and save the world.
Hallelujah ! God is my friend.

December 22nd. I have this day been helping the men
to make a few alterations about the house, but still, all
this will not do. I want *my* house altering, the floor of .
my soul sweeping, and my whole nature garnished with
the rich graces of God's eternal spirit. Lord increase my
faith and save me to the uttermost. I feel fear to overcome me frequently. This will not do. I must be faithful
and fear the face of no man. Lord help me to take up
my cross. I have wondered where I could have a comfortable room to preach in, and the schoolmaster of the
town has been to offer me his school-room. This is an
opening of Providence to all appearance. Lord help me
to follow Thee. Give me power to do and suffer Thy will.

December 25th. Christmas day. Went to my father's.
Dined with them. Visited a few of the members. Found
them still pursuing. Returned home to Hoyland Swaine.

I feel I want more grace. I had two or three invitations to preach this day, but have refused, owing to different things; but am I justifiable in thus doing? I doubt it. Lord help me to do better.

December 26th. Went to Denby-Dale with Mr. Wigglesworth. Staid tea at Mr. Wood's, and felt encouraged and quickened whilst conversing with Martha Burditt. I think her one of the excellent of the earth. She appears devout and heavenly : dead to the world and alive unto God. O for more of the mind that was in Christ.

January 1st, 1828. "Lord have mercy upon me and incline my heart to keep Thy law." Glory be to God! He has spared me to see the commencement of another year. May I live as I never have done before : live to His glory and for the good of souls.

January 6th (Sunday). Praise the Lamb! He has been present with me to day. A blessed passage was applied to my mind this morning, " Delight thyself also in the Lord, and He shall grant thee the desires of thine heart." I felt greatly encouraged to hope in God. Went to Thurgoland, in the Sheffield circuit, to preach ; and in the first prayer God visited my soul, and gave me power to plead and wrestle in mighty prayer. The people appeared moved. After preaching we held a prayer-meeting, and one or two received the pardoning mercy of God. Glory be to His eternal name! He still owns my labours. O what a fool I am, in the true sense of the word, that I do not enter more fully into this work. Lord help me to begin afresh. Preached again in the evening. Felt power in prayer and good liberty in preaching. O for more power. What is praying and preaching without the Spirit? I want to be mighty, full of faith and power, a flame of fire, a burning luminary, a polished shaft, a real workman, all light, life, love.

January 25th. Glory! glory! glory! Praise the Lamb! He has possession of my heart. I feel his love in my soul. Hallelujah to God and the Lamb! What shall I render unto the Lord for all His benefits? My heart, my heart, nothing less will do. Lord help me. When I entered the farm yard this morning, this thought crossed my mind, write on every cow and horse, etc., "Set not your affections on things on the earth." Lord help me, for Thou knowest I have been slain here many a time.

January 26th (Sunday). As my day, so is my strength, "He is faithful that promised." O for ten thousand tongues to praise Him. He has helped me at Huddersfield to-day. He has owned my labours. Souls, immortal blood-bought souls have been saved. Glory! Hallelujah! Praise the Lord! O for a gust of praise to my redeeming God. How is it that I should be so noticed by Him. O my God, help me to praise Thee. After the sermon in the afternoon we held a prayer-meeting, and if ever I saw the kingdom of heaven suffer violence and the violent take it by force, it was in Huddersfield vestry. The penitents mourned, and sighed, and groaned, and wept, and prayed and sweat in an agony, and many realised salvation and rejoiced in a reconciled God. What cannot God Almighty do? When He works the mountains and hills flow down before Him : the strongholds of hell give way.

January 30th. This has been a good day, and yet a trying one. I have had the farm valued by two persons; and as I had them to dinner, I felt it my duty to have prayer with them, notwithstanding any reflections they might cast upon me afterwards. I was blessed in the duty and hope they will be led to seek for the favour and peace of God. I see and feel myself an unworthy and unprofitable servant. I want more faith, more love, more courage, more zeal. Lord help me to do better.

February 11th. Glory! glory! glory be to God! He is my salvation. But, alas, this day I have not been faithful. I felt an impression from His Spirit to call my new man into the room and speak to him about his soul, and exhort him to live to God; but alas! I did not, and in consequence I have suffered loss; but I have promised to do it if the Lord will help me; and help me He will, I know, if I am faithful in making the attempt. The Lord is reviving His work about Hoyland Swaine. Many are receiving His pardoning mercy. The language of my soul is—

> "O Jesus, ride on, Till all are subdued;
> Thy mercy make known, And sprinkle Thy blood.
> Display Thy salvation, And teach the new song,
> To every nation, And people, and tongue."

February 12th. Praise the Lord for His goodness. He is my rock, my fortress, my defence, in Him will I trust. This day I have been at Honley to see my parents. Prayed with the servants, and felt wonderful liberty and power. O to be faithful, to take up my daily cross—to be a man of God, all light, love, praise, obedience. Lord help me. I feel I want more courage. Lord give me more. I often think that the people who pronounce me courageous and valiant for the truth know little of my heart.

February 13th. Glory be to God! for all I enjoy. I am surrounded with favours. I swim in the goodness, the bounty of heaven. Where, I often wonder, is the man who is more blest than myself? Without doubt there are many who enjoy more grace, and this is the greatest blessing heaven can bestow; but taking temporal things into account, I don't know one so blest, so favoured. Lord, what am I and what my Father's house to Thee, that Thou should'st have such special regard for me? Make me thankful and help me to praise Thee.

March 9th. (Sunday). Preached at Stanningley, in the
Bramley circuit, to an immense congregation. A few
windows were broken, intentionally or not, I leave. We
held a prayer-meeting after each service, and in the
afternoon the glory of God descended, and cries from
the penitent were heard both in the bottom and the
lofts. Several experienced a glorious deliverance, and
my soul rejoiced in God my Saviour.

March 10th. Set off from Stanningley to Scholes, in
the Cleckheaton circuit. Called at Westgate-hill, near
Gomersal, to see old Mrs. Bramwell. I dined with her,
and she told me she believed Mr. Bramwell never lost
the blessing of perfect love, but held it fast to the day of
his death. O for Bramwell's spirit, to be filled with God :
to enjoy all that God has to impart. Went forward to
Gomersal, called upon a friend or two, and went to see the
new chapel. I thought the plan good. Lord grant that
thousands may be born there. Set off to Hightown :
called to see Mr. and Mrs. —— : found them well ; but
Mrs. —— does not fully give up all. She wants deeply
awakening. Lord God convince, convert, and comfort her.
From thence I went to Mr. Parkin's, and found the family
well, and doing well in the best of things. O that they
may ever live to God, and their tribe after them. From
thence I went to Scholes chapel, and there I tried to
preach from " Speak to the children of Israel that they go
forward." I felt pretty well, but not much power. O my
God clothe me with power, and let my preaching be " not
with enticing words of man's wisdom, but in demonstration of the spirit and of power." O for the faith of
Abraham, and the zeal and power of the Apostle Paul.
Lord endue me with power from on high. Held a prayer-
meeting, and one or two I think found deliverance. One
woman in the lofts cried aloud, and wrestled hard for

salvation. She declared that she came on purpose to be saved.

"O that the world might taste and see
The riches of His grace."

March 16th (Sunday). This has been a good day, and yet a day of trial. Preached at Rothwell in the afternoon and evening. Harassed by fiery temptations. The devil appeared to be let loose upon me. He sought to persuade me that in the afternoon, I had preached in a devilish spirit. Before entering the pulpit in the evening, I felt what tongue cannot describe, but, praise the Lord! when engaged in the work, the Lord came to my relief and His glory was revealed. It was supposed that nearly twenty souls found salvation. O, what a work is the work of saving of souls. Every time the Gospel trumpet is blown the sound carries life or death. O, my God, lay souls upon my heart.

March 17th. Glory be to God! He is mine, and I am His. Left Rothwell this morning, accompanied by two local preachers. Called to see a friend or two upon the road. Held a prayer-meeting in one house, and to my surprise many wept, and two were in deep distress. A woman about thirty years of age wrestled till she appeared to find salvation. A young man promised to go to class, and I hope will lead a new life. Lord help him. After this, we pursued our way to Wakefield. I felt wonderfully blest. The Lord was eminently with me and round about me, as a wall of fire. Arrived safe in Wakefield, and went to see the superintendent, and felt encouraged. Lord save the preachers. Fire their souls. From softening the truth, Lord save them. There is a danger I see and feel of our not declaring plainly and faithfully the whole counsel of God. Lord help me: quicken me. Save me. Let Thy glory be all my aim. Fearless of the frowns of dying men and women, may I do Thy will, and preach and live Thy word. Preaching, and praying, and winning souls is my work. Farming and going to fairs is not my work, at least I feel no real satisfaction in it.

After dinner I left Wakefield for Hoyland Swaine, and on the road conversed with several people about their souls and felt for them. When about half way home, I was strongly impressed to talk and pray with a bar-keeper, with whom I had had conversation on the previous Saturday, and who then told me that he felt a desire to be saved. When I reached the bar I hung my pony to the gate, went into the barhouse (it was a small wood house put up as a "catch-bar"), and talked with the man about the salvation of his soul. He began to feel, and expressed a strong desire to be saved. Now, said I, don't you think God can save you now? And is He not willing? Yes, said the barman, I believe He is. Then, said I, let us kneel down. He consented, and we both began to wrestle with the Lord. I prayed and he prayed, but still the blessing did not come. I felt I wanted an increase of faith, and I earnestly prayed Lord increase my faith. The Lord did increase it, and my soul felt his sacred power. Now, said I to the man, try again; and with guilt upon his conscience and tears flowing from his eyes, he struggled again. Such was the agony of his soul that he took little notice of what was passing on the road. He continued to pray and wrestle, and I continued to exhort him to believe in the Lord Jesus Christ for a present salvation. After a long struggle, the Lord in answer to prayer delivered his soul and made him happy.. We rose from our knees, and sang,—

"Praise God from whom all blessings flow."

I exhorted him to go to class. He promised me he would. I then left him, got on to my pony and rode home. O my God, what canst Thou not do? This has been a day of wonders.   Lord save me from thinking anything of myself.   The work is Thine.   The glory is Thine.   Help me to give it Thee.

March 23rd (Sunday).   Praise the Lord for all His mercies.   He still helps me.   Preached at Outlane, near Huddersfield, in the afternoon, and at Lindley in the evening.   Felt liberty but not much power.   I want to be filled. Lord fill me.   Several were crying for mercy, one or two at Outlane, and a few at Lindley.   One young woman at Lindley was clearly saved.   Slept at Mrs. D——'s, of Lindley.   She still keeps by the way side.   Lord help her another step.

March 24th.   Lord Jesus have mercy upon me.   I want more love.   Went to breakfast at Brother Firth's.   We held a prayer-meeting, and to the glory of God three souls were seeking salvation, and one experienced the blessing. Went to Dudley Hill, near Bradford, and preached for the benefit of the chapel : felt rather shackled, but still had power.   Glory be to God !   Shackled or not, the work is God's, and the glory is God's.   Lord help me to give it Thee.   Held a prayer-meeting, and several were seeking : how many, I know not.   Slept at a friend's, and found a very agreeable family.   Lord bless and save them for ever.

March 25th.   Glory be to God !   I still feel a hungering and thirsting after righteousness.   Left Dudley Hill and went to Great Horton, and there I felt the presence of the Lord.   Went to John Thornton's, a pious man.   There my God talked with me and gave me a sermon.   After this we went to see a few friends.   We called at a collier's cabin, and poured out our souls in fervent prayer.   The Lord God of Elijah answered by the baptismal fire of His spirit.   From thence we returned to John Thornton's, and held a prayer-meeting, and many were blessed and fired.

L

O for more faith. After the meeting we went to the chapel, and there I tried to preach from the text my God had given me in the afternoon. He sent His spirit—the spirit of liberty and power. We had a shout throughout the congregation. Glory be to God! for His great condescension in visiting worms of the earth. After preaching we held a prayer-meeting, and several were seeking. One young man was pardoned. Lord ride on at Horton. Send them a great revival. Staid all night at Thomas Myer's, and felt God's presence there. Lord bless Thomas and his wife.

March 26th. Glory be to God! I feel nearer and nearer His beloved embrace. I feel Him drawing me to Himself. The devil, the world, and the flesh are giving way. Through God's blessing arrived safely at home, and found all going on well. Praise the Lord! when I work for Him and cast my care on Him, He can and He does take care of my home. O for a thankful heart.

April 6th (Sunday). Went to Elland and preached in the afternoon and evening. I felt liberty, and Jesus revealed His saving power. Lord let Thy kingdom come. Many were crying for mercy, and several, I believe, experienced the desire of their heart.

April 7th. Glory be to God, my soul is rising. I am His and He is mine. Set off from Elland to Brighouse. Preached at Brighouse, and felt the power of God. Jesus revealed Himself, and many, it was supposed a score, experienced salvation. How long they had been seeking I know not. Where or how they were wounded I know not ; but wounded they were, and healed, killed, and made alive. Lord save the world.

April 21st. This has been a day of good, and also a day of trial. My friend Parkin and I have been considering what is the duty of a Christian respecting charity ? How much of his property a Christian ought to give to the Lord ? I think, as far as we can learn from Scripture, that he ought to give at least one tenth of his income.

It is gratifying to find these two Christian friends, at the outset of life, occupying themselves with the serious discussion of Christian economics ; testing their views by Scripture, and reaching a conclusion upon the important question, what proportion of his income should a Christian give to God ? Not less than a tenth for God, they both accepted as a principle of general application, and forth-with, they gave it a place in the code by which they ruled their life.

A man after Mr. Brooke's own heart was William Parkin. Endowed by nature with immense physical strength and force of character; in his earlier life, he was a rare champion of the devil. But he, too, was a chosen vessel. Under the awakening ministry of David Stoner, he received a soul-wound that filled him with agony un-utterable. After a mighty struggle he found peace through believing, and his energies before prostituted to iniquity, were now consecrated to Christ with that complete un-reservedness, which made his Christian life an absolute contrast to his former course, and convinced all who knew him that he had become "a new creature in Christ Jesus." Soon after his conversion he began to preach, and in and out of the pulpit was a true Boanerges, and bold as a lion in his master's service. With kindred natures and similar experience, and engaged in the same great work, Edward Brooke and William Parkin were friends well met, and cherished for each other undying respect and love.

About the time of the conversation before referred to, William Parkin prepared a ledger and opened a charity

account, which he kept with business-like exactness until
his sudden translation from earth to heaven, and which
no eye saw till it passed, with his other papers and effects,
into the hands of his executors.   At the commencement
of the ledger appears the entry, " From this time I intend
to devote a certain proportion of my gains to God."   The
ledger shows how God honoured His servant's vow.   With
few exceptions, year after year increased funds were placed
at his disposal, followed, and sometimes preceded by
corresponding increase of gifts.   With a delicate suppression of names, the ledger tells of hundreds succoured by
his bounty; poor supernumerary ministers and local
preachers supplied with suits of black befitting their
vocation; widows and orphans cheered in winter with
coals and blankets and necessary food.   Were the principle of systematic and proportionate giving generally
adopted by Christian people, there would be little un-
relieved necessity around them; none of the Christian
brotherhood would suffer want, nor would any good cause
languish for want of help.   " What proportion of his
income should a Christian give to God?" is a question
which claims consideration from all, and which none can
evade without criminal neglect and an inevitable penalty.

No ledgers are forthcoming in proof of Mr. Brooke's
fidelity to the convictions of his early life in relation to
Christian stewardship.   His habits were not so minutely
exact as were his friend Parkin's, but that he gave on
principle and with large liberality is unquestionable.   Soon
after his conversion, with doubtful wisdom, he appointed
a time to meet the poor of his neighbourhood and relieve
their necessities.   As may be supposed, these levees were
largely attended, the numbers still swelling as weeks rolled
on.   They attracted the attention of persons not person-
ally interested, and a neighbour felt it to be his duty to

acquaint the young squire's father with his son's singular and lavish distribution of alms. Tradition reports that the old gentleman asked his informant how much he supposed Mr. Edward was giving away. Was he distributing so much per week? mentioning a large amount. O, no, replied the man, surprised that so heavy a sum should be named. "Then mind your own business,". said the father," "and let Mr. Edward mind his, for he cost me more than that before he went amongst the Methodists."

Whenever Mr. Brooke saw misery and want, his heart instantly sympathised, and his hand went into his pocket as by instinct; shillings, half-crowns, and in special cases, sovereigns and five-pound notes were given to lift poor wretched creatures out of their distress. In visiting remote places to preach and make collections for chapels, schools, and local interests, he invariably bore his own expenses, and where the cause was low and needed help was commonly a liberal contributor. When tea-meetings were held, he would often ask how many widows and old folk were connected with the place, and hand over a sovereign or two to supply them with tickets for the festival. On returning home from preaching expeditions he would sometimes go into his larder, which was usually well stored, and to the consternation of the cook order a distribution of the good things he met with, amongst his poor and sick neighbours, gladdening many a household by his bounty. When fat pigs were slaughtered on his farm, not content with distributing the "sparerib" and broken pieces, he would have a carcass cut up and deal out ribs well fleshed, and substantial joints, on which a poor family might live for days, and the memory of which was an abiding gratitude. He has been known to clear out his wardrobe, reserving only the clothes upon his back, that he might cover the nakedness of others. To his servants he gave that which is generous, as well as "just and equal." Cabmen liked well to take a fare to the squire's, for they were sure of good fare at their journey's end. · It was a large heart that beat in his bosom. He loved to share his good things with others, and to make the world happier by his bounty. His travelling companion who witnessed his daily benefactions, was met by a gentleman who said to him, "The Methodists will get all Mr. Brooke has, and make a poor man of him." Informing Mr. Brooke what he had heard, and seriously suggesting the curtailment of his bounty, Mr. Brooke said to his friend, do you think I am a fool ? I only give out of my income, and if I do not touch the capital I cannot beggar myself, can I ?

Conversing with the writer upon the subject of Christian giving, Mr. Brooke stated that for the first fifteen years of his married life he gave away all his income, after meeting family expenses, and never saved a shilling ; and then, scraping up the soil with his foot, he said, with a look of ineffable scorn, " See, I don't care for money any more than I care for that dirt."

Advancing years and increasing family responsibilities led, without doubt, to the more cautious distribution of his bounty ; and the wide sphere over which his liberalities were scattered, might sometimes reduce his giving to objects on which others concentrated their generosity, but to the last, he remained true to the principles which he espoused in early life. In later years, when pressed by numerous claims, it was his acknowledged rule never to give less than from ten to fifteen per cent. upon his income. He felt himself to be a steward placed in trust, and held responsible for the right disposal of his Lord's goods, and he acted in relation to the great account.

CHAPTER XI.

MARRIAGE.

" Nothing lovelier can be found
In woman, than to study household good,
And good works in her husband to promote."

ON Saturday, May 3rd, 1828, exactly twelve months after Edward Brooke's first declaration of love to Martha Smith, he consummated the engagement by marriage. The event came off at Halifax. It was a quiet wedding, for bridegroom and bride were equally averse to the gaities of life. A considerable portion of the wedding day was devoted to the Master's work, and the diary contains the following record, " I have just entered upon a fresh line of life, and I feel I want a fresh supply of grace, so that with a Christian spirit I may live as I ought, and honour God with my all. Lord grant me this power. I am fully and scripturally satisfied that in taking this step I have done the will of God."

With most men whose daily bread is not dependent upon daily toil, the honeymoon brings joyous release from ordinary occupations. The happy pair escape from the claims of life and from their circle of acquaintance, and hide themselves in sweet seclusion, where, devoted to each other, they gain, by uninterrupted companionship and intercourse, that deeper insight into each other's character which tends to broaden and establish the basis of a life-long happiness. By undisturbed and loving communion, they rivet more closely the new-formed link, to withstand

life's afterstrain. It was a wise provision of the stern law
of Moses which, when dealing with the newly married,
relaxes into gentleness and loving-kindness, " When a
man hath taken a new wife he shall not go out to war,
neither shall he be charged with any business, but he shall
be free at home one year, and shall cheer up his wife
which he hath taken." Under sanctions, both human and
divine, Mr. Brooke, on the occasion of his marriage, might
have interrupted his arduous labours and taken the indulgence of a long honeymoon. His ample income placed
such indulgence within easy reach, and he had a taste
for the beautiful in nature which a month's wandering
in fellowship with his young bride, amid fair scenes at
home or in other lands, must have immensely gratified ;
but he had such intensely realising views of the responsibilities of life and of the nearness of eternity, that he
could brook no interruption of his Christian work. His
honeymoon was to do the will of his Father in heaven.
Souls were perishing—souls for whom Christ died, and
he must haste to the rescue. His opportunity, in relation
to many, might be now or never ; and how could he
forgive himself, or face the great judge of all, if one soul
perished through his neglect. The day following his
wedding found him twice in the pulpit and busy in the
prayer-meetings, and through the week he was labouring
with unremitting earnestness, cheered by the sympathy
and approval of his bride.

A Christian help-meet Mr. Brooke wanted, when he rode
over to Greetland and sought his first interview with
Martha Smith. Smitten by the charm of her fair woman-
hood he undoubtedly had been, when he first saw her in
Linthwaite chapel ; but though his heart was conquered,
his Christian judgment asserted its supremacy, and held
his affections under a just control, for after making Miss

Smith's acquaintance, he wrote in his diary, " I feel all is
well respecting her : I believe my God intends her to
become a help-meet for me in the way to heaven.   If
this were not the case. I would not have her, if she were
weighted with gold.   My Lord thou knowest I would not.
Lord save her fully.   Make her a Mrs. Fletcher." And
now that Martha Smith had given herself to Edward
Brooke and become his own wife, he found her all that
heart and judgment could desire.

Mrs. Brooke was an " elect lady" whom nature and grace
combined to fashion into a character of unwonted attractiveness and beauty.   Her strong sense was chastened
by womanly refinement.   Her manners were simple and
dignified.   Christian principle pervaded and governed her
conduct.   " The beauty of the Lord our God" was upon
her, and when at length family responsibilities increased,
and owing to her husband's frequent absence from home,
the burden of such responsibilities fell mainly upon herself, her matronly bearing and wise domestic management won universal admiration.   " Her husband praised
her, and her children arise and call her blessed."   As a
class-leader Mrs. Brooke rendered invaluable service to
the church of her early choice.   Old and young, of her
own sex, equally delighted in her counsels, and her
removal in the midst of her usefulness was mysterious
discipline, and inflicted a great loss, for which no subsequent additions to the church have, as yet, made compensation.

But the greatest service which Mrs. Brooke rendered to
the church, was her unselfish and generous relinquishment
of her husband for God's work.   To say that she never
felt the almost continuous sacrifice of domestic comfort
which her husband's devotion to evangelistic work involved would be utterly untrue, and if true, would be

small praise. It was a great trial to a young wife to be
left for successive days alone; a trial greatly intensified
when the young wife became a mother, and looked upon
her little ones, and felt that the responsibility of training
those wayward natures,—weighty and solemn, if shared by
the father,—must be almost exclusively borne by herself;
but with a brave heart, and in humble dependence on
God, she faced and fulfilled the demands of her position.
She was far too noble and too richly imbued with her
husband's spirit, with love to Christ and to the souls of
men, to assert her domestic rights in opposition to her
husband's sense of duty and the paramount claims of the
work of God. She accepted Edward Brooke when he
went wooing, as a consecrated man, and she now bade
him God speed in his great Master's work.

The intimacy of married life sometimes discovers imper-
fections and weaknesses which before escaped observation,
and the husband becomes a less ardent admirer and lies
under a lighter spell than the lover. In this case it was
not so. Beauties of character, and not defects, were
developed by familiar intercourse, until at length Mr.
Brooke's high estimate of his wife's Christianity gave her
an almost unbounded influence over him, which she ever
wielded for good. Happy the man who after experience
of married life, and in the calm sobriety of devotional
retirement could write, " This day I have felt thankful to
the Lord for my dear wife. She is just the woman I
wanted. The Lord has done all things well. O my God
help me to praise Thee for this gift. My wife lives nearer
to God than I do, breathes a sweeter, richer air, drinks
more deeply of the wells of salvation, dives into the fulness
of God, and brings Him more glory than I do. She is a
pattern of piety. Her words, her actions, her whole
deportment prove her to be " an Israelite indeed in whom

is no guile." She lives in God. And must I rest where I am ? God forbid. Strive I must,—strive,—Lord help me to say in the strength of grace I will."

Sustained by a help-meet so devoted, and encouraged by wonderful manifestations of saving power in connection with his preaching, Mr. Brooke began to feel even the oversight of his small farm to be an irksome interference with his great work. He longed to escape from all worldly entanglements, and to live only for the salvation of souls. He had previously written, " I felt determined to give up all for religion, and I prayed that the Lord would use me in His way, and not my own. He condescended to reason with me, and I clearly saw, at least, as far as I could understand, that worldly business is not for me, and I do believe that I shall never prosper as I ought, until I give up all. I am almost ready to conclude I erred in taking Hoyland Swaine farm. Farming does nothing for me. It shackles me from hand to foot. My work is saving souls; and I feel determined to sit loose from the world, the Lord helping me. I have a seven years lease, and without a wonderful turn of Providence, I expect to continue till the term expires. However, thank God, I have a pious man who can manage the farm, and I can trust him with it. Lord help me. When on my knees, weeping and praying, these passages were applied to my mind, 'In all thy ways acknowledge Him, and He shall direct thy paths.' 'This is the will of God, even your sanctification.' 'Follow Me, and let the dead bury their dead,' that is, I suppose, let the men of the world have it, but follow thou Me. My Lord what condescension. O for a heart to praise Him. My work is saving souls. My care is, or ought to be, the church, my all, in the Lord's vineyard." Shortly after his marriage, he writes in the same strain, "This has been a strange day. Lord, Lord, Lord. I am

like Noah's dove. I find no rest for the sole of my foot.
And why? Because my heart is divided. The things of
the world take up my attention, and too much engage my
affections. Help me to reform. I see I must give the
world more up, and let my man Thomas take it off my
hands. Preaching and cow-jobbing do not go together:
Lord help me. Show me Thy will, and give me inclina-
tion and power to do it." Again, he writes about the same
date, "Lord have mercy upon me. I am wrong. I carry
a blaze of light in my soul which shows me my duty, but
I do not fully do it. Lord help me. I firmly believe that
the Lord never intended me to be a farmer, and now I
suffer. Were it in my power, I would give it up to-day.
O what anxiety, what trouble, what misery have I
suffered."

The conviction that worldly business should entirely
give place to evangelistic work still gathered strength, and
Mr. Brooke seriously contemplated the transfer of his lease
of the farm at Hoyland Swaine. Difficulties interposed to
delay the fulfilment of his purpose, and in the meantime
the management of the farm was largely committed to
trusty Thomas. The diary of this period shows, how
almost entirely Mr. Brooke dismissed all care of horses,
cows, farm stock and produce, and how earnestly he
laboured for the spiritual good of his own neighbourhood,
as well as of towns and villages remote. Not content
with exhausting his own strength in the work of God, he
called in the help of others. In his home, evangelists
whom God had honoured found hearty hospitality, and a
centre of Christian work affording abundant opportunity
for the expenditure of their utmost power. Whoever
stayed there, might build up his strength with generous
fare, for the squire's table knew no stint, but he must give
his full quota of prayer and service in return, and might

rely, that when he retired at night, sleep would not be absent for want of weariness to court it.   In fact, lassitude could not livé where the squire was.   The energy of his nature seemed infectious.   It communicated itself to guests and co-workers.   Under his influence, phlegmatic natures often kindled into enthusiasm, and the religious services of Hoyland Swaine were characterised by animation and spiritual power which made them wondrously attractive.

Just at this time Mr. Brooke made the acquaintance of an untutored genius, baptized with the spirit of holiness and power, and who, despite the disadvantages of neglected education, uncouth manners, and a lowly calling, made a wonderful impression upon men, and won for himself a name still held in wide honour and which "shall be had in everlasting remembrance."

Amongst the worthies of Methodism, Samuel Hick, the village blacksmith, holds an unchallenged place.   Samuel's conversion was remarkable, and though often told will bear repetition.   He lived in carelessness and sin till after his marriage to a young woman careless as himself; when, scared one night by a dream, in which a heavenly visitor warned him to flee from the wrath to come, he jumped out of bed in wild affright.   Terror gave instant place to the agony of conviction, and he cried out for fear.   His wife, alarmed by her husband's anguish, and supposing him to be seized by some serious ailment, was hastening to the door to rouse the neighbours, when Samuel sobbed out the words, "I want Jesus,—Jesus, to pardon all my sins." This was evidently no case for the neighbours' interference, for though kindly disposed, they were all worldly people ; so his wife returned, to witness through the long night hours, her husband's agony without power to help. Samuel knelt upon the cold flag, confronted by the sins

of his past life, which all rushed upon his view, and
threatened to crush him into hell, praying as he never
prayed before. No human teacher was at hand; but in
his boyhood the penitent had heard John Nelson, the
Birstal stone-mason, preach Jesus from the market-cross at
Aberford, and in his youth he had heard the venerable
Wesley "preach like an angel" upon saving faith in the old
chapel at Leeds, and now, truths long since forgotten, were
brought to his remembrance, unfolded, and applied by the
Divine Spirit. Great sinner though he felt himself to be,
he saw in Jesus the propitiation for his sins, and· trusted
in Jesus for salvation. "I believed," said he, "that the
blood of Christ was shed for me. The moment I believed,
I found peace, and could say with the poet,—

> ' My God is reconciled,
>   His pardoning voice I hear,
> He owns me for His child,
>   I can no longer fear ;
> With confidence I now draw nigh,
> And Father, Abba, Father, cry.' "

So assured was Samuel of the reality of the great
change then wrought within him, and of his covenant
relationship to God at that time established, that the flag-
stone on which he kneeled through that long night, and on
which he still knelt, when God spake peace to his soul,
became a sacred memorial of the most important transac-
tion of his life. He looked upon it with feelings akin to
Jacob's when rising from the place where God met him in
a dream, the patriarch "took the stone which he had put
for his pillow, and set it up for a pillar, and poured oil
upon the top of it," and called it God's house, investing it
with perpetual sanctity. Often, when relating his religious
experience, Samuel referred to the very "flag" where God
blessed him. At his decease, Mr. Brooke, partly from

respect for the good man's memory, and, perhaps, chiefly as a delicate manner of ministering to the widow's comfort, purchased the memorable flag-stone at a great price, and often humorously referred to his acquisition of the cumbrous relic.

After his conversion, Samuel Hick soon felt the obligation to make Christ known to others, and his testimony was followed by remarkable results. Few churches could have found a sphere for the exercise of the blacksmith's peculiar gifts; but Methodism at once assigned him his position, and gave him congenial work. His simple, artless teachings illumined by homely illustrations which all could appreciate, delivered in the broad dialect of Yorkshire, with unction both human and divine, fell on many a hard heart with the force of a sledge-hammer breaking the rock in pieces. The blacksmith's preaching won wide and not undeserved popularity. There were "signs following," and where these are, Methodists are not nicely critical. Success covers a multitude of faults. He is the best workman, who, however uncouth the process, turns out the best work; and, judged by results, Samuel was a workman that needed not to be ashamed. Having heard of the old blacksmith's fame, Mr. Brooke invited him to Hoyland Swaine, where he spent some time under the squire's hospitable roof, discoursing and praying in the family and preaching in hamlets and villages around.

June 20th. Mr. Brooke writes, "My brother, Samuel Hick, has been praying with us, and whilst thus engaged the Lord blessed me with another baptism." He then records their joint labours in various places, on successive days, when they had "precious times" and "wonderful influence and power," sinners seeking and finding mercy. "Old brother Hick" cherished so lively and lasting a remembrance of the labours "more abundant" to which

the squire's zeal committed him, during his sojourn at
Hoyland Swaine, that notwithstanding his grateful recollection of generous hospitality, and the gift of a new suit
of clothes, he anticipated his next visit with fear of
consequences approaching almost to dread.   When Mr.
Brooke's conveyance pulled up at the house where he was
staying, the tears started in the old man's eyes, and,
turning to his hostess, he falteringly exclaimed, "He will
kill me."

The blacksmith's fears were not realised. He survived
his visit to the squire, and suffered no serious damage ; but
the squire well nigh killed himself, for though a young
man just entering upon his best days, he writes "I am
like a man of sixty or seventy. I cannot walk far without much labour. When I have walked a mile or two I
feel myself weak. Lord help me to do better."

Mr. Brooke's strength was so broken by excessive labours
that he was compelled, at length, to take rest. Acting
under medical advice he visited Buxton, long famed for
its fine scenery and salubrious and bracing air, and at
that time thronged with visitors. Unable to preach Mr.
Brooke still sought opportunity of usefulness. His first
thought was for the visitors lodging under the same roof
with himself, and though with shattered nerves he shrank
from intercourse with strangers, and craved seclusion, he
felt pressed in spirit to conduct family devotion and invite
the visitors to join him. In this way he might let His
light shine, and possibly guide the feet of some weary
one into the way of peace. His invitation met with an
encouraging response. "I felt it a cross," he writes, "but
have taken it up through grace. Several of the friends have
come in to prayer. O, my God, this is all through grace ;
help me to give Thee the glory. I see there is nothing
like taking up the cross. Every cross taken up in Jesus'

name and in Jesus' strength, proves a blessing. Lord help me to be more faithful and to follow Thee fully."

July 15th (Tuesday). This has been on the whole, a good day, but I find that without constant watchfulness I shall be overcome. The world is an enemy to religion, at least, when the Christian sets his affections upon it. Lord save me from the love of the world. Thank God I feel better in health. With rest and proper care, I think, through God's blessing, I shall recover to pursue my wonted labours. O that I may spend and be spent for God. Went to chapel this evening, and heard Mr. Hardy from these words, "Will ye also be His disciples?" Felt instructed and encouraged. I see I am not yet as I should be, but with the Apostle I can say, "I press toward the mark for the prize of the high calling of God in Christ Jesus." Lord help me to do it with all my heart.

Some professedly Christian people, when taking well-earned and necessary relaxation in gay watering places, throw off in some measure, the restraints of piety; observe the Sabbath less sacredly than when they are at home, are less faithful to religious duties, and less scrupulous in their amusements. Mr. Brooke remarked this during his brief sojourn at Buxton, and was so deeply affected, especially by the Sabbath desecration which obtained, that he penned and printed his thoughts upon the subject, in the form of a leaflet tract, which he circulated in hope of lessening the evil. The result of his appeal through the press is unknown; but the fact, that when debarred from preaching, he adopted this means of displaying a banner for truth, is an additional proof of the steady intensity of his zeal, and that in strength and weakness, in every place and under every circumstance, he felt that he must be about his "Father's business."

Having returned from Buxton to his happy home, with

M

but small advantage from the change, he writes in his diary :

July 26th. I feel I have not derived much good. I want care and less labour. Lord help me to conquer my spirit. Have I been as faithful as I ought to have been at Buxton? No. Lord have mercy upon me. Fear is one of my greatest besetments. Lord deliver me from the fear of man.

July 30th. This has been, upon the whole, an encouraging day; but I see how I have missed it. I want more grace to conquer Edward Brooke. A little will not suffice. Lord conquer and subdue him ; kill and make alive.

July 31st. This day I have been visiting my poor neighbours. I have found much distress. O my Lord, what am I? that I should be so favoured and blessed;—a worm of the earth. I have felt for the poor to day, as I ought always to feel. Lord bless the poor.

August 5th. Went to Doncaster fair. What work I have had to day in reproving sin. My God has helped me. Fear has been removed and my soul has been blessed. Some received my reproofs. Others turned again, and raged furiously like their father the devil. But this I expect. Lord help me to be faithful. The word of God says, "Warn them, whether they will hear or whether they will forbear." Lord help me.

August 31st. Glory be to God ! for His rich, superabounding, overflowing mercies. I cannot tell how to praise Him. When I look at His providential mercies, how He prospers me in my farm, sends me good crops and fine weather to get them in, and above all pours the riches of Paradise into my soul, I cannot tell what to think or what to say respecting His goodness. Whilst writing, I feel His love springing up in my soul. Lord bless me with a thankful, loving, and obedient heart. I want to be

Thine, O Lord, Thou knowest, and have Thee all mine own.

> "Take my body, spirit, soul,
> Only Thou possess the whole."

Thou hast redeemed me by Thy blood, sanctified me by Thy grace, and made me an heir of glory. What a privilege, what a glory, to be a child of God. Lord keep me Thine for ever and ever. I am better in health, but I want more grace. I have daily crosses to take up, and self to deny. Lord help me to do better. I feel ashamed when I contrast myself with the primitive Christians. They seemed to live more fully to God, to have more love, courage, patience, zeal, etc., than ever I possessed; but why? Their God is my God, and He is no respecter of persons, and therefore, why should not I be as zealous as Daniel or Paul or Barnabas? Lord again baptize me. Send the hallowed fire, the divine glory, the burning love, the ardent zeal, the undaunted courage, the heavenly mindedness, the purity of intention and singleness of aim which Thy servants of old had. Lord hear and answer prayer. Hallelujah!

> "I find Him lifting up my head,
> He brings salvation near."

November 31st (Sunday). Glory be to God! for the unparalleled mercies He bestows upon me. I stand astonished and amazed. How is it that I should be thus blest? This evening, I preached at Norfolk Street chapel, Sheffield, and felt the presence of my God. After preaching, we held a prayer-meeting. The Lord wonderfully poured out His Spirit. Many, it was supposed upwards of twenty souls were saved, and many believers were re-baptized. The glory is and shall be the Lord's.

In the spring of 1839, Mr. Brooke's health having greatly improved, he spent a few days in the Snaith circuit, preaching and holding protracted prayer-meetings on successive evenings. His labours were signally owned of God, in the awakening and conversion of sinners, and he was still further strengthened in his purpose to relinquish his farm and everything that might interfere with his full consecration to spiritual work.

March 7th (Sunday). Preached at Rawcliffe, near Snaith, and there I felt the glory of God. Many wept. In the prayer-meeting, nearly half-a-score were seeking mercy, and two found the pardon of their sins. In the evening I preached at Snaith, and there I felt liberty and power. One more found peace and several others were in deep distress.

March 8th (Monday). Preached at Snaith again, and felt the power of God. In the prayer-meeting, there were about thirty in distress, and eight found peace with God. The Lord here appears to be working in a most powerful manner. Praise His holy name! The work is His. The glory also. O may I ever sit at His feet.

March 9th (Tuesday). I preached at Temple Hirst, near Snaith, and there the power of God descended upon the congregation, and many were in distress and earnestly sought the Lord. Six or seven found peace. Glory be to God! This is the way. O may I ever walk in it. I see more than ever the will of God concerning me. I see my work is to visit first one circuit and then another. Lord help me thus to do.

March 10th (Wednesday). Preached at Rawcliffe again, and there I felt the divine unction and power with God. In the prayer-meeting nearly forty souls were in distress, and about twenty found peace and rejoiced in the pardoning mercy of God. Glory! glory! glory! O may I be more and more humble, watchful, zealous, loving, obedient. Lord make me so. Amen and Amen.

CHAPTER XII.

EVANGELISM (I).

"My talents, gifts, and graces, Lord,
   Into Thy blessed hands receive ;
And let me live to preach Thy word ;
   And let me to Thy glory live ;
My every sacred moment spend
   In publishing the sinner's friend."

TWELVE months passed over before Mr. Brooke's ardent wish to be released from secular engagements, and entirely given up to spiritual work, was realised.

April 17th, 1831. He writes, since I last wrote my experience, various have been my trials, blessings, and mercies. I am going to quit my farm. Farming is not my work. I must give up all. Souls are perishing. Time is short. Eternity is at hand, an eternity of bliss or misery. O to be ready, always ready. Lord help me.

May 13th. I feel troubled on account of my unfaithfulness. O how soon I swerve. I speak too much. I offend with my tongue. Lord help me to keep the door of my lips, and live alone for Thee. O how I feel pride striving to hold up its infernal head. Lord save me from this demon pride. On Wednesday evening, whilst conversing with a friend about giving Jesus my whole heart, the Lord baptized my soul with holy fire. The heaven I felt was indescribable. On Thursday morning I felt the same divine power, but, alas, in the after part of the day, I was off my guard, and felt something within which I think was not of the root of holiness. I must come again. Lord help me. I have given up my land, my farm, my all, in order to serve Jesus, and now, having again forsaken all, if He does not comfort me, I am left comfortless. But glory be to God! He is loving, compassionate, and tender. He says, and I believe it, I will not leave you comfortless, I will come again unto you. O that word, I *will*, I *will*. " Lord help my unbelief."

Having given up his farm at Hoyland Swaine, Mr. Brooke now established himself at Sheepridge, near Huddersfield, where he resided for many years, and in the immediate vicinity of which village, he spent his later life and ended his career. Adjoining his house, was the Methodist chapel, which he took under his special care, sustaining its varied interests, showing unbounded hospitality to all who served its pulpit, and preaching whenever opportunity presented. Within easy reach, lay Honley, the place where he was twice born, the scene of his early life, and the residence of numerous relatives and friends. Mr. Brooke seemed now to have a settled conviction that he had found his right place, and been directed to a residence in all respects favourable to the great purpose of his life, and, freed from all secular distractions, he gave himself to his life-work with renewed consecration.

August 7th (Sunday). Preached at Lindley. Felt happy in the morning, but had no liberty in the afternoon. I believe the Lord was punishing me for my past unfaithfulness. O how unfaithful am I. Reproving sin is a very little cross. Confessing Christ before the poor and amongst my own members is a very little cross ; but to confess Christ before my own rich and unconverted friends, relations, and neighbours, is a cross. O my Lord help me to deny myself. Make me willing to become a fool for Christ. I must be singular, or I must be damned. Notwithstanding my unfaithfulness, the Lord saves souls. Within the last few weeks, I have seen a vast number in distress in various circuits. The Lord has wonderfully owned my poor labours. To-day, at Lindley, a few were in distress, and one or two, I think, got good. But here I must not rest. I want and must have a great salvation, more power in preaching, more love for souls, more zeal for God's glory. Lord come and baptize and fill me. I want a visit Lord from Thee. May heaven commission me afresh.

September 11th (Sunday). Preached at Lindley in the morning, and at Almondbury in the afternoon. Felt little. A barren day. Lord have mercy upon me. I must rise. I see where I miss it. I do not keep the eye of my faith continually fixed on Jesus. I eat and drink too much. I often sleep too long. I talk too much about myself. I am too wishful to know what others think of me. I don't feel that love to the poor I ought. I might save more and give more. Of late I have been much exercised respecting my providential path, that is, to know where I shall be most useful. I feel a great desire to see a revival in Huddersfield circuit. We are very low. The people are formal. I seldom hear of any good being done. Oh my God undertake for us. But why do I not believe? God hath said "according to your faith be it unto you." Where is my faith? "When the Son of Man cometh shall He find faith on the earth?" Lord increase our faith. Save us as preachers, leaders, members. Send the fire into all our hearts, and make us all a flame. Amen and Amen.

September 18th (Sunday). Rose a few minutes past five. Went to the prayer-meeting in the school-room. Felt happy, happy. Hallelujah! Jesus is bringing lost sinners to God at Sheepridge. One or two in distress. Went to the Houses chapel, and there I felt the divine presence. Preached morning and afternoon, and felt an increase of power and love for souls. O I should be a miserable man if souls were not saved. I feel sometimes I could almost lay down my life for them. Held two prayer-meetings, but not a soul in distress that I saw. Came home with brother Philips from Leeds, and in the evening he preached in Sheepridge chapel. I felt happy to hear him. We held a prayer-meeting, and O how Jesus did baptize and fill my soul. Souls were in distress, and one or two, if not more, found peace. Hallelujah! I believe I am just where my Lord would have me to be. O may I now do what He would have me to do.

The six o'clock prayer-meeting on the Sabbath morning, was a means of grace to which the squire attached special importance, as a blessed preparation for services to follow. When preaching in his own circuit and able to attend, his presence might always be depended on. Mrs. Brooke and family were regularly found in their places. On dark, cold winter mornings, the little children felt it a somewhat rigorous rule, that withdrew them, at so early an hour, and whilst nature was still asleep, from their warm beds, and took them through the raw air into the adjoining school-room, to worship God with the villagers; but their father was an implacable enemy to all softness, and on principle required their attendance.

The squire's preaching and house-to-house visitation at Sheepridge were followed, at this time, by marked results. The Methodist chapel was thronged by worshippers of various classes. The young ladies connected with a flourishing boarding-school located at Sheepridge were regular hearers. One now advanced in life, looks back with lively interest and gratitude to her school days, and tells of a wonderful service which the squire conducted. The congregation was mightily impressed. The young ladies were deeply affected and cried for mercy, several found peace through believing, and this Christian matron dates from that occasion her consecration to God and the commencement of a happy Christian life.

One of the members of the Sheepridge Society unhappily tampered with strong drink, till his enemy got the advantage of him. He was found one day, in a public-house, indulging in free potations; and his wife's persuasions failing to bring him out, she came to the squire to ask his interference.

Away went the squire forthwith, conducted by the sorrowing woman, and reaching the house, he walked straight into the bar, where a number of old topers were soaking according to their custom; and there in their midst, was the fallen man. "What art thou doing here?" said the squire, fixing his eyes upon the poor backslider, "this is no place for thee." Disconcerted by Mr. Brooke's unexpected appearance, and conscience-stricken, the man gave no reply, and seemed as though he would fain have dropped through the floor to escape the terrible gaze of the squire's reproving eyes. "Come out with thee and come home with me," said the squire, and as the culprit still kept his seat, he seized him by his coat-collar and pulled him out into the street.

The topers, exasperated by such infringement of the "liberty of the subject," sprang to their feet and rushed to the rescue. The squire turned himself about, looked his opponents in the face, and raising his big, powerful arm, said, "There is not a man in the lot dare lay a finger on me." He then walked off his captive, gave him good counsel, and there is reason to believe that he never fell into the snare again.

September 19th. Rose about five. This has been a day of exercise. I have not improved every moment as I might have done. Friends coming to see me interrupted work I ought to have done. This will not do. I must do my work come who will. Lord help me. Time is flying. Death is approaching, and the judgment with its all-important realities will soon be here, and then it will be Life or Death for ever; Heaven or Hell for ever. Lord help me to secure a lot amongst the blessed. This night we have had a prayer-meeting in the school-room, Sheep-ridge. Nearly two hundred men, women, and children were present, and one or two found peace, I think. Glory be to God! O, may I pray with all prayer, watch with all watchfulness, labour with all diligence. "The harvest truly is plenteous, but the labourers are few." Lord increase the number. Amen. Amen.

September 29th. Went to Bramley, near Leeds, and felt wonderfully blessed in preaching. Held a prayer-meeting, and several found peace with God. Retired to rest, and left the people praying. O my God carry on Thy work.

September 30th. Glory be to God! Assisted the people in holding a prayer-meeting early this morning. A few were in distress, groaning for mercy. Went again at the dinner hour, and the factory people, men and women, came. The Lord poured out his spirit in a most wonderful manner, and fourteen or fifteen were crying for mercy, and several found peace. O what a field of usefulness. The Lord appears to be about to do a great work. From Bramley I rode to Batley, in the Birstal circuit, and there I felt the presence of my Lord. He touched my heart with holy fire. In the prayer-meeting several were seeking mercy.

October 2nd (Sunday). Praise the Lord! Preached at Brampton, near Chesterfield, in the afternoon and evening. Souls were crying for mercy, and Jesus pardoned first one and then another.

October 3rd. Preached at Chesterfield in the evening, and felt pretty good liberty, but not what I want to feel. In the prayer-meeting there were from ten to fifteen in distress, and some found mercy. The work is the Lord's, and the glory is His.

October 4th. Preached at Staveley, in the Chesterfield circuit. In the afternoon there were six or seven in distress, and in the evening I should think nearly twenty.

October 9th (Sunday). Preached at Luddenden, in the Todmorden circuit, and felt the presence of the Lord. Souls were crying for mercy, and nearly twenty found peace with God. To Jesus be all the glory. His blood was spilt for them, and by His power they were saved. The Lord spake in power to my soul. " Now are ye clean." Glory !

October 23rd (Sunday). Glory be to God ! This has been a glorious day, a day of power, liberty, feeling, success. Preached at Brotherton, near Ferrybridge. Held a prayer-meeting, and two or three were saved. I see more than ever the necessity of talking to all I come in contact with. The Lord often blesses it. Soon after entering the house of Mr. Jackson, with whom I staid, I spoke to the servant girl about her soul. It seemed useless, for she laughed at what I said. However, at the evening service she cried aloud for mercy, and through faith in Jesus found salvation. Hallelujah ! The glory is the Lord's. O, may I labour yet more and more.

October 24th. Preached at Whitley, in the Snaith circuit, in the new chapel just opened. Felt rather shackled, but the Lord in mercy saved one soul, and it was worth all.

November 20th (Sunday). Preached at Royton, in the Oldham circuit. Jesus was powerfully near. Cries for mercy went through many parts of the chapel. Salvation was imparted, the glory revealed, and many were happily saved. Glory be to Him that sitteth upon the throne !

November 21st. Preached at Rochdale in the evening. I felt wonderfully blest. Jesus was near to save, and I think nearly twenty found peace. Hallelujah ! Jesus reigns. O, may He reign till all are subdued.

November 27th (Sunday.) Preached at Mount Tabor, near Halifax. Felt the presence of Jesus. Held two prayer-meetings after each service. Souls were crying for mercy, and the power of the Lord was present to heal. Many were saved.

November 28th. Preached at Luddenden Foot, in the Todmorden circuit. We felt happy, and rejoiced in the power of Jesus. Some of the congregation were stricken, and fell almost as dead. After awhile they came round, and shouted for joy, their very countenances beaming and flaming with the glory of God. Some object to this work, but if they read their Bible they will see that such manifestations obtained hundreds and thousands of years ago.

The squire's celebrity as a successful evangelist was now becoming connexional. Invitations to preach poured in upon him from circuits not only near but remote. To answer the numerous letters which the postman day by day left at his door, was no small tax upon his scant leisure when he returned home upon the Friday, to set off again upon the morrow. The extent of his correspondence necessitated the cultivation of an epistolary style, always laconic, and sometimes provokingly abrupt. To an earnest superintendent, who, pressed by burdened trustees, had indited a long letter of elaborate statement and powerful appeal to induce the squire to serve some struggling interest, and who considered his letter irresistible, the curt answer :

Dear Brother,

I cannot.

Yours, etc.,

EDWARD BROOKE,

was not the most satisfactory reply ; and yet after each day for long months to come was pledged, negative replies, more or less brief, to pressing applications were reluctantly despatched by scores.

As already intimated, one of Mr. Brooke's great difficulties lay in the selection of spheres most suitable to his peculiar gifts, and where, by God's blessing, he might expect to reap most success. In this he sought guidance from above, and he seldom left his home without first obtaining the assurance that his Master would go with him. Many a time when he mounted his gig before break of day, to drive to some distant place in a neighbouring county, he would crack his whip and, with jubilant confidence, say to his companion, "We shall have souls," and playfully referring to the expenses of the journey, would add, " a sovereign a soul." Whilst driving along the road the burden of souls seemed ever on his heart and how to win them, the problem which he longed to solve. All day long he seemed intent upon his Father's business; and remembering how he was awakened by the casual remark addressed to him by Thomas Holladay as he passed him on the moor, he cultivated the habit of improving incidental opportunities, till he acquired a wonderful facility of sowing beside all waters. A word in season seemed always at command, and the result often illustrated and verified the inspired aphorism, "A word spoken in season, how good it is."

His travelling companion, still living, tells how as the

squire pulled up at toll-gates more numerous then than
now, he had always a suggestive remark for the gate-
keeper, "So you are going to leave," said the squire, as
he passed through a gate and held out the toll. The
barman, startled by the unanticipated news, exclaimed,
"Well! that is the first word I have heard about it. The
Master was here the other day, and he said nothing."
"Yes, you are going to leave," repeated Mr. Brooke, with
an emphasis which intimated that his information was
reliable ;—" and the man that comes after you wont stay
long, 'For what is your life? It is even a vapour that
appeareth for a little time and then vanisheth away.'
Mind you are ready John, when your great Master calls
you," and on drove the traveller, leaving John more
thoughtful than he found him.

"Do you ever think of the bar of God, and what is to
pay there?" said the squire to a gate-keeper who held
out his hand for the accustomed toll. The man looked
thunderstruck. It was a new idea. "The bar of God."
He was familiar enough with toll-bars, and with the toll
to be demanded for every variety of beast and vehicle,
but "the bar of God," what could it mean? The traveller
preached him a short homily upon the judgment which
led to the awakening of both man and wife.

. On many occasions when the squire saw that impression was made, he prolonged the conversation, tied up
his horse, and entering the toll-house, endeavoured by
exhortation and prayer, to lead the sinner forthwith to
Christ.

Stone-breakers on the highway, who seldom receive
kind words from passers by, he often accosted. "Now
John," he would say, as he reined up his horse, "You
have hard work here. You don't get much for this job.
Religion is a good thing man. Godliness is profitable

unto all things. You must begin to pray and you will soon get out of your poverty. Now John, I will pray for you," and getting out of his gig the squire would kneel down upon the stone heap, heedless of passers by, and pray, till in many a case the stone-breaker's heart of stone was broken, and the big tears fell, and the cry for mercy rose, and then slipping a piece of silver into the poor fellow's hand, and giving a few last words of loving exhortation, he left him wondering whether it were man or angel he had met with. One stone-breaker whom the squire prayed with was miserably clad, so after putting a half-crown into his hand, the squire stripped off his own coat and put it on his half naked brother saying, "I have two coats with me to-day, and I will give you one;" and we may be sure that counsels and prayers sustained by such kind deeds would not be readily forgotten.

Driving to an appointment on a fine Sabbath morning in spring, with Mr. D. Smith, a Sheffield local preacher and a colleague in labour, Mr. Brooke suddenly said "Pull up Smith." Mr. Brooke then stood up in the conveyance and shouted to a man in a distant part of a field by the way-side, who was gathering nettles, "Here I want thee," beckoning with his hand at the same time for the man to come to him. When he came up to the fence Mr. Brooke said, "Thou poor foolish sinner, art thou going to sell thy precious soul to the devil on a Sunday morning for a few paltry nettles!" and looking earnestly into his face, he prayed with great solemnity, "the Lord have mercy on thy soul. Amen." Then, quick as thought, he said "drive on, Smith." When fairly on the way again, he said, "I could not let that man sell his soul for nettles without warning him."

The squire sometimes told to his friends.. with quaint humour and a twinkling of the eye, an incident which

occurred when he was driving to Skipton to fulfil a
preaching engagement. It was a bright frosty day, and
the ice upon the road made travelling perilous to those
who had not looked well to their horses' shoes. Descend-
ing a hill, near Bingley, the squire caught sight of a
catastrophe in front. A horse ascending the hill with a
load of coals had lost footing, and was down upon the
road. The carter was vainly struggling to raise the shafts
and extricate the poor beast from its distress. Said the
squire to his companion, "John, we shall have to act the
good Samaritan here." Reaching the spot the squire and
John got out of the gig. The squire tucked up his coat
sleeves, helped to unstrap the gears, and putting his strong
shoulder to the cart the difficulty was presently got over.
Addicted to profanity, the carter rapped out an oath.
"Thy horse may well be down," said the squire, "when
thou swearest in that way; down upon thy knees man,
and ask God to forgive thee, or we won't help thee any
more." There was no alternative. The squire spake with
authority. The shafts of the loaded cart were beyond the
man's power to lift. So to his knees he went. "Pray,"
said the squire. "I don't know how," replied the swearer ;
and then laying hold of a sentence of the church service
which opportunely came to his remembrance, he said, "We
have left undone those things which we ought to have
done, and we have done those things which we ought not
to have done." "Thou must pray differently to that,"
said the squire. "What must I say ?" replied the carter.
Say, "God be merciful to me a sinner." "God be merciful to me a sinner," repeated the submissive man, still
kneeling on the road, "God be merciful to me a sinner."

Taking a bag of hay from the cart, for the protection
of his knees, the squire knelt by the swearer's side, and
implored God to have mercy on the poor blasphemer. As

the squire made intercession, the man became deeply affected and cried out for mercy. A gentleman driving past at the time, was attracted by the strange scene upon the road, and observing the man's evident distress, interposed, saying " What are you doing with the man ?" John answered, "you must come and see." The gentleman approached, no doubt with humane intentions, but catching the words of the praying carter, " God be merciful to me a sinner," followed by the squire's loud " Amen," he quickly divined the nature of the case, and judging that discretion was the better part of valour, he remounted his gig and effected his escape. The penitent man prayed on for half an hour or more, the squire pointing him to Jesus, the sinner's friend. At length he found comfort through believing, and rising from his knees, exclaimed, " Bless the Lord ! I will never swear any more as long as I live." The squire spake words of encouragement, and the man went on his way rejoicing.

The following Sabbath, Mr. Brooke conducted a lovefeast near Bradford. Obeying the instincts of his new nature and the promptings of the good Spirit, the converted carter had found his way to the house of God and obtained a note of admission to the lovefeast. He at once recognised Mr. Brooke as the instrument of his salvation, and rising, he narrated the circumstance of his wonderful conversion, to the unbounded delight of his astonished auditory. This man joined the Methodist Society, held fast the profession of his faith, and ultimately became a respected and useful local preacher.

Taking long journeys, Mr. Brooke had sometimes to bait his horse at the inn, or to wait the arrival of the coach. Under these circumstances he watched his opportunity to sow the " good seed." Calling on one occasion for refreshment, the landlady showed him into a long room, at one

N

end of which he observed three young gentlemen playing
at cards. He approached them, put his hand upon the
shoulder of one, and said, " Young man, you have a mother
that is praying for you." A chord was struck, which
vibrated through the young man's soul. He flung down
the cards, listened to the squire's exhortation, left the room
conscience-stricken, thought upon his ways, and sought and
found mercy.

Driving to some village in Derbyshire, where he was
expected to preach in the after part of the day, the squire
pulled up at a way-side inn. Having seen his horse fed, he
ordered his usual refreshment of ham and eggs. A fine,
healthy-looking young countryman entered the room and
sat down to rest. The squire made some friendly observations, and when his repast was spread, invited the young
man to join him. The offer was gratefully accepted.
Whilst enjoying their savoury dish, the youth's heart
opened, and there was a pleasant flow of conversation.
"We are expecting a very strange preacher," said he, "at
our village to night. He is a great man for prayer-meetings, and tries to convert all the folks into Methodists."
"Indeed," replied the squire, with evident interest in the
topic, "have you ever heard him?" "No, I havn't," said
the youth, "but my brother has." "Well. What did your
brother say about him?" inquired the squire. "O he
told me he never heard such a queer chap in his life;
indeed, he didn't know if he were quite right in his head;
but," said the young man, "I intend to go and hear for
myself." "That is right, my lad," said the squire, "and
get your brother to go too, he may have a word to suit you
both." They did go, and greatly to the young man's surprise, as the preacher mounted the pulpit, he recognised
his friendly entertainer at the way-side inn. As the squire
proceeded with the service, the young man's heart was

touched, and his brother's also. At the prayer-meeting, they were found amongst the penitent seekers of salvation, and were both converted not merely into Methodists but into Christian believers.

Mr. Brooke's presence at the wayside inn, writes Mr. S. Taylor, "was more like the pastoral visit of a clergy-man than the call of a gentleman on travel. On arriving, his first business was to arrange about his horse, and as he was a great admirer of a good horse his orders were given in a very particular manner. His own refreshment would then be ordered. On being shown the best room, a polite refusal and a preference for the kitchen would be given. This was done that he might have a better opportunity for conversing with the family. After some inquiries and observations of a general character, he would throw out some words bearing on religion, and which often had reference to his own experience. . Having paid his bill, he would then ask if he might pray with them. The family would be called together, and the voice of prayer and praise be heard, where noisy inebriation much oftener resounded. His horse being ready, the ostler's fee was handed to him along with a word about his soul," and the traveller resumed his journey.

On one occasion, the squire fell in with a navvy, a big, powerful fellow, and a somewhat famous pugilist. He humoured his man, and lured him at length into free conversation. Rejoicing in his strength, the boxer boasted that he was a match for any one. Mr. Brooke challenged him to fight, and was met with the answer, " I'll take thee up and down or all round." " I'll take you any way you like," said Mr. Brooke. Disdaining to make a choice, the pugilist replied, " I'm a better man than thee any day, and I'll take thee any way." The affair seemed critical, when, gently addressing his antagonist, who, confident of an easy triumph, appeared eager for the fray; Mr. Brooke said, "Well, I always ask God's blessing before I commence any undertaking, so we must kneel down and pray." The eyes of the big navvy opened, and he said, "What, you're Squire Brooke I reckon." "I believe," says the narrator, "that this incident resulted in the man's conversion."

Travelling by rail upon a day of unusual traffic, when there was insufficient accommodation for third class passengers, Mr. Brooke was asked by the guard, if he would object to admit two or three poor women into his first-class compartment. Pleasantly assenting, the women took their places, and when seated, began to expatiate in amusing phrase upon the size and comfort of the carriage, and to enumerate the stations they must pass ere reaching their destination. With his usual aptitude for improving an opportunity, Mr. Brooke remarked that he had travelled in a much larger carriage than the one they occupied,—a carriage so commodious and expansive, that it would hold as many as ever would come in, that not one who wished to enter was ever refused admission, and that there was nothing to pay. The women were all attention, while he spoke to them of entering the carriage at the first station called Repentance, and travelling to the next station which was Faith, and thence to Justification and Sanctification, till they at length reached the terminus called Heaven; and he invited and urged them all to take their places in this heaven-bound carriage, and join him in his journey to the skies. The women listened with beaming eyes, and on parting, thanked him for his conversation, and said, "Aint you Squire Brooke?"

To a ticket collector, who asked him for his ticket, Mr. Brooke on showing it said, "Have you got *your* ticket?" The man stared in surprise, when Mr. Brooke added, "I mean your ticket for heaven; mind you have that all right, my man."

Detained at the Chester station, at the time of the races, a gentleman playfully accosted him, saying, "have you come to the races, Mr. Brooke?" "Have you not heard," replied Mr. Brooke, "that I have won a hundred?" "Indeed!" said the gentleman, looking much surprised, "I did not know that you were in the habit of betting." "Ah!" said Mr. Brooke, "then you don't know that I set out in a race more than twenty years ago, which I am still running, and I then received a promise which has been fully verified. 'Every one that hath forsaken houses, or brethren, or sisters, or father, or mother, or wife, or children, or lands, for my name's sake, shall receive *an hundred fold*, and shall inherit everlasting life.'" The gentleman looked serious and said, "you are in the right, sir."

To a station-master, he has been heard to say, "Can any of your men tell me what I must do to be saved?" thus delicately directing his attention to the things belonging to his peace.

To a hotel waiter, who answered his call, he said, "can you tell me what I must do to be happy?" The young man burst into tears. The question had brought up memories of happy days, when walking in the light, it was better with him than now.

Entering the houses of his friends, Mr. Brooke had commonly a kind word for the domestics. "You are very busy," he said, to a servant girl who opened the door and ushered him into a room where the furniture was in disorder, she replied, "Yes, sir, we should have been straight, but we have been waiting for the whitewashers." Mr. Brooke looked her in the face, and said with solemn earnestness, "My girl, has your soul been washed and made white in the blood of the Lamb?"

Sometimes, in his eagerness to bless the families which showed him hospitality, the squire was somewhat erratic

in the course which he pursued, and ran no small risk
of offending those who were unable to appreciate his
motives. This danger, however, was commonly escaped
by the result.

It was placarded in a certain neighbourhood, that
Edward Brooke, Esq., would preach in the Methodist
chapel, on a given day. A family of some consideration,
whose doors were not open for the entertainment of
Methodist preachers in general, signified their readiness
to receive the preacher whose social position, indicated
by the Esq. appended to his name, precluded all pain of
condescension. It was accordingly agreed that the squire
should take up his quarters at the hall, and he was duly
apprised of the arrangement. Humbler accommodation
had been more to Mr. Brooke's liking, for he knew enough
of the temptations of wealth, to be aware that style and
grandeur and sumptuous entertainments by no means
favoured the great object of his mission. As the squire
and his companion John drew near their destination, it
was apparent that the squire's mind was considerably
exercised, and that he was meditating how he might be
useful to his *elite* host and family. Addressing his companion, he said, "we will pray as soon as we have got in,
John." They drove up to the hall and were received with
due ceremony and a kindly welcome. The host, supposing
John to be the squire's servant, and not a co-worker, was
directing him to the servant's quarters, when the squire
interposed, saying, "John goes with me." John, however,
was not wanting in discretion, and at once perceived that
he should best consult his comfort by taking "the lower
room," so the squire passed into the drawing room, where
gentlemen and ladies were assembled in his honour, and
John found his way into the kitchen, where great preparations were in progress for the squire's hospitable entertainment.

John, who was like-minded with the squire, well trained in evangelistic work, and an invaluable helper, soon got into conversation with the servants, and quickly found that they had small interest in spiritual things. The squire in the drawing room, by a like process, had arrived at a similar conclusion in relation to his host, hostess, and company, and, as their best occupation till dinner time, proposed prayer; and remarking, that at home, he always called in the servants, he requested that the domestics might be summoned. His host, though somewhat startled by the unworldly bearing and unusual proposition of his guest, gracefully assented, and John and several of the servants joined the party in the drawing room. " Let us pray," said the squire, and offering brief and earnest intercession, John followed in kindred strain. Seven times each they prayed, the squire exhorting the company at intervals to pray for themselves. Finding all silent, the squire rose from his knees, walked out into the hall, saying, " where is my horse? I will not stay here if none of you will pray." Taking his top-coat, he was making for the door, when the lady of the house followed him, exclaiming, " O Mr. Brooke, do not go away; if you will come back, I will pray." With a glad heart the squire returned into the drawing room, when the lady began to pray with a simplicity and earnestness that touched all hearts. The dinner was forgotten. The prayer-meeting was continued till service time, when, with a drink of water and piece of bread for refreshment, the squire hurried to the chapel to preach according to announcement.

The public services which followed this drawing-room engagement were memorable. In the afternoon, the squire took for his text, " O Lord revive Thy work." As he proceeded with the sermon, the congregation was greatly moved, and in the prayer-meeting that followed, many were seeking mercy. After a brief interval, the squire was again in the pulpit. He announced the text, "It is time for Thee, Lord, to work." There was a wonderful impression. At the prayer-meeting, the squire mounted a form, and exhorted the people to turn from sin and flee for refuge, to lay hold upon the hope set before them, and wound up by saying, "as many of you as are resolved to live in sin and go to the devil hold up your hands and show yourselves like men." Not a hand was uplifted. He then said, "All of you that mean to give up your sins and live to God, hold up your hands;" and raising his hands high above his head, he said, "I will hold up both mine." Here and there throughout the chapel, hands went up, impelled, in many a case by holy purpose, and indicating the sincere resolve of a contrite heart. Rejoicing with great joy over "the multitudes in the valley of decision," the preacher cried, "all you that hold up your hands come here," pointing to "the penitent forms" arranged in order ; and as he and his fellow-helpers sang,

" Come to Jesus,"

up streamed men and women, old and young, and cries for mercy rose, which ever and anon gave place to shouts of joy and songs of praise.

CHAPTER XIII.

"The mercy I feel, To others I show,
    I set to my seal That Jesus is true :
    Ye all may find favour, Who come at His call ;
    O come to my Saviour, His grace is for all."

THE destruction of the diary kept by Mr. Brooke during
the greater part of his public life ; abounding, as it is
known to have done, in stirring and strange incident,
remarkable providences and astonishing triumphs of divine
grace, is greatly to be regretted, and prevents anything
beyond a cursory glance at evangelistic labours extending
over a full quarter of a century, and resulting in the turning of thousands "from disobedience to the wisdom of the
just." A few reminiscences supplied by various friends,
with hurried letters of Mr. Brooke, are almost the only
available material for the further illustration of a most
remarkable career, which, if fully depicted by a skilled
pen, had doubtless stirred the hearts of multitudes.

In the summer of 1831, Mr. Brooke preached twice in
the old Hunslet chapel, Leeds. The announcement of his
name attracted vast crowds of people. Pews, aisles, and
all available spaces within the walls were packed to the
uttermost, and hundreds were unable to press in. A
young man, just breaking loose from the restraints of a
godly home, found his way to the chapel, and obtained a
place in the crowd within; and now, in mature life, he looks

back upon that service as the grand crisis of his being.
The squire preached in the morning, from "O Lord revive
Thy work," and in the evening from "Nevertheless when
the Son of Man cometh, shall He find faith on the earth ?"
A wonderful influence accompanied the word.   In the
evening, especially, a gust of divine power swept over the
vast mass of humanity, bowing all before it like ripe corn
before the blast.   During the sermon, the people in all
parts of the chapel cried out for mercy, as if confronted by
the terrors of death and judgment.   Young Samuel Milnes
was amongst the stricken, and at nine o'clock that night,
in the prayer-meeting which followed the discourse, he
"obtained mercy," and received the witness of his adoption
into God's family clear as the sunlight.   A brother also
was saved, and numbers of young people, many of whom
still live, occupying positions of influence in the world and
church.   A revival broke out under Squire Brooke's preaching that day, which continued for some time, and resulted
in the conversion of hundreds.

Having been invited to spend a few days in the Colne
circuit, Mr. Brooke preached at Barnoldswick.   The chapel
was crowded to excess.   The word was "quick and powerful."   Numbers "were pricked in their heart," and in the
agony of conviction cried mightily for mercy.   The sermon
was followed by a prayer-meeting.   Midnight arrived, and
the penitents were still upon their knees, resolved to plead
till they prevailed.   As one and another found peace through
believing and withdrew, others whose hearts were stricken
filled their places.   So intense was the awakening, that
though the squire had retired, the alarmed and sorrowing
people could not be induced to leave the chapel, but all night
through, and all through the following day and night, the
prayer-meeting continued without intermission.   It was
supposed that above one hundred persons were converted,

whilst many an old professor received quickening, and gave himself to God by a fuller consecration. Some of the quiet sort, who witnessed this wonderful work of grace, no doubt raised the alarm of "wild fire," and predicted that such excitement would be followed by reaction, that would place the church in a worse position than before; but they were false prophets. With few exceptions, the converts of that revival held on their course. Some became local preachers and office bearers of the church, and still serve their generation by the will of God, whilst others are fallen asleep.

A few weeks after this great revival at Barnoldswick, Mr. Brooke spent a week in the Clitheroe circuit. On Sunday he preached at Waddington. Great numbers came from Barnoldswick to hear, once more, the man whom now they loved and honoured as their spiritual father, and not only to hear, but to help him by their prayers. Here the old scenes were repeated. Had the preacher fired upon the congregation with grape shot, the wounded had not been more numerous, or the cry of anguish more bitter. It was simply impossible to proceed with the discourse; leaving the pulpit, the squire came down amongst the people, to gather the praying men for intercession, whilst he conversed with the penitents and endeavoured to help them to the Saviour. A lady who had suffered the amputation of a limb was amongst the sorrowing. She found peace and shouted for joy, and triumphing over her infirmity, in the fulness of her love, she passed from pew to pew to encourage others by relating how she had found the Lord. Scores of persons on the occasion of this visit professed to find peace and joined the Society.

Visiting Doncaster, the squire's fame as a revivalist attracted large congregations. Two Quakers (so called), respectable tradesmen of the town, pressed through the

crowd into the chapel. The preacher's style of procedure
ill comported with the severe notions of propriety which
regulate the worship of the "meeting house," and it might
be supposed that prejudice would have fortified the hearts
of the two "Friends" against impression; but as the
service proceeded, a strange influence came over them, and
at the squire's invitation, with great self-violence, they
walked up to the penitent form, and finding peace through
faith in our Lord Jesus Christ, they confessed that though
"Friends" all their life long, and possessed of the form of
godliness, they had till then been destitute of the saving
power, and they glorified God in the great congregation.   '

Having preached at Hull on a Sunday and Monday with
the usual result, Mr. Brooke crossed the Humber, and held
services at Barton on the Tuesday and Wednesday following. Amongst the penitents were two young gentlemen,
students of law and medicine, who both found peace. The
young doctor had an unmistakable weakness for jewelry.
His fingers were bedecked with rings, the glitter of which
soon caught the squire's keen eye. Attaching a literal
meaning and general application to the inspired prohibition
relating to the wearing of gold and pearls and costly array,
the squire could brook no outward adorning. He regarded
finery upon a Christian man or woman as a desecration of
the temple of the Holy Ghost, and contended, as he
believed, on Christian principles, for a severe simplicity.

> "Silken coats, and caps, and golden rings;
>   With ruffs, and cuffs, and farthingales, and things,
>   With scarfs, and fans, and double change of bravery,
>   With amber bracelets, beads, and all this knavery,"

he held in absolute abhorrence, as the devil's livery, and
he at once urged upon the penitent youth the surrender of
his cherished ornaments for Christ's sake. The next evening, when conducting a service at Barton, the young gentle-

man presented himself, his face beaming with gladness, and his fingers beautiful in their natural simplicity,

"When unadorned, adorned the most."

Being asked what he had done with his rings, he said he had sold them to a jeweller, and distributed the money to his poor patients in making his morning rounds, a sacrifice which the squire gratefully regarded as an evidence of his convert's sincerity.

Visiting the Newark circuit, it was arranged for the squire to preach in a distant village, where the Society was feeble and the cause low. The night was severely cold, and fearing the exposure of the drive after the steaming evening service, he determined to sleep in the village and return to Newark the following day. To find a lodging, however, was the difficulty, for the people were of the labouring class, and their cottages afforded scant accommodation. There was a village public house, but the squire objected to take up his quarters at an inn, except under an absolute necessity, The old man at whose house the squire took tea was a pauper, who broke stones upon the road, but he was a good man and the leader of a class. His wife was a member of forty years' standing, a godly and thrifty woman who struggled to eke out her husband's slender earnings by selling smallwares, which were exposed for sale in the cottage window. The old folks had no family, but a nephew lodged with them and occupied a rude chamber open to the tiles, and containing a bed which was simply a bed by courtesy. Feathers or flocks were a luxury, to which the weary bones in that rustic home were strangers. Said the squire, as his host and hostess declared the impossibility of finding accommodation for a gentleman like him, " you must get your nephew to sleep with a neighbour, and his bed will do for John and me." The old woman devoutly protested against the squire's humiliation ; but he insisted that such arrangement would meet the case, so she stripped off the sheets, and with wondrous celerity washed, mangled, and aired them before bed-time.

After a hard day's work and a light supper, the evangelists retired to rest, the squire and John dividing the chaff bed between them, and pillowing their heads on chaff as best they could. The squire, with his great coat for a coverlet, composed himself to rest, thanking God for His mercies. As John looked up to the tiles, he saw the stars twinkling through rifts in the roof, and feeling as if the squire's zeal had brought him almost to a level with his Lord, who said " the foxes have holes and the birds of the air have nests, but the son of man hath not where to lay his head," he ventured some word of sympathy. "Are souls saved ? John," said the squire, abruptly shutting him up, and went off into sleep, sweet as the sleep of childhood.

In the morning they rose with the lark, and offered a sacrifice of praise as grateful as if they had been lodged in a palace. Whilst taking their frugal breakfast the old woman went into the squire's chamber to make the bed, and on the chaff pillow found a five pound note, which she quickly brought to her guest. "I know all about that," said the squire, "That is for you. We are not going to stay here all night and give you nothing. We don't do in that way." After breakfast the squire said to his hostess, "Now, you go and invite the neighbours to come in. You can pray old mother, and John can pray, and I can pray, and we can have a good prayer-meeting." The cottage door was thrown wide open. The old woman went round from house to house. The squire, sustained by his companion, struck up a lively tune, and the neighbours came trooping in. First one prayed and then another. The prayer-meeting was continued till far into the afternoon, when the squire was obliged to leave to preach at Newark in the evening. It was supposed that twenty persons found peace with God, and the feeble Society received an impetus, the influence of which was felt for many years.

The extravagant musical performances which often desecrated the Sunday-school anniversaries of the past generation, transforming the service of sacred song into an entertainment, in painful dissonance with the efforts of the preacher, and almost precluding the hope of spiritual impression, had so often grieved the squire, who, in all preaching, aimed at the immediate conversion of his hearers, that it became a question whether he should not uniformly decline invitations to preach anniversary sermons.

Better taste, if not Christian principle, has exerted a chastening influence upon these services of later years, and congregations of the present day, can hardly imagine the combined effect of organ, trumpet, trombone, and serpent, clarionet, bass-viol, and violin, and other instruments too numerous to mention, all labouring together upon a grand piece, specially composed for the occasion by some village amateur, whilst hundreds of voices joined to swell the oft-repeated chorus, which threatened to lift the chapel roof. No music is so befitting a school anniversary as the concord of trained children's voices, guided and steadied by some simple instrumental accompaniment, subdued to allow the sweet voices of the little ones to exert their full play upon fathers' and mothers' hearts.

Preaching school anniversary sermons in a village near Lincoln, the squire found, to his sorrow, the orchestral arrangements of the usual elaborate character. After singing the first hymn he called upon his companion, John, to pray. Whilst the congregation were supposed to be engaged in worship, the squire's attention was attracted by the rustling of book-leaves, and glancing at the orchestra, he observed the choir turning over their books and busily preparing for their next performance. John having concluded his supplications, the squire broke out in earnest prayer, "Lord have mercy upon that fiddler, Lord have mercy upon that trumpeter, who have been turning over their tune-books instead of praying to Thee." Rising from his knees he gave out the second hymn, but quickly found that the choir, having taken offence, had struck work, and that he was thrown upon his own resources. But the squire had a well-tuned organ, whose pipes seldom failed him, and lifting up his voice he raised the tune and carried the congregation with him in song, if less artistic, not less devotional and effective than the congregation had anticipated. He took for his text, "The Lord hath made bare his holy arm in the sight of all the nations, and all the ends of the earth shall see the salvation of our God." In no wise disconcerted by his collision with the choir, he preached with his usual power. As he proceeded with his sermon, the mortification of the singers gave place to better feelings, and when the squire called his prayer-meeting and exhorted penitents to come forward, most of the choir responded to his call, and came conscience-stricken and trembling to the form, where the Saviour met them. The next evening the squire preached in the same chapel. The choir were present in full force, and having found their voices sang as they never sang before, heart and voice in unison, making melody unto the Lord.

In the spring of 1837, Mr. Brooke, accompanied by John Hudson, visited the Epworth circuit and preached at Crowle, on a week-day afternoon. At the close of the sermon, he announced a prayer-meeting; when a local preacher informed John that a young actress, belonging to a company of strolling players then visiting the village, was in the gallery and apparently in deep distress. John at once went to the girl, and finding that she was " sorrowing after a godly sort," he invited her to come to the penitent form below. Yielding to persuasion, she came down into the body of the chapel, and avowed her sincerity and earnestness, by taking her place amongst those who were kneeling at the form and crying for mercy. The poor girl was deeply convinced of sin, and after a long struggle was enabled to believe in Jesus for salvation. Her mourning was turned into joy, and her lamentation gave place to praise.

Mr. Brooke, finding that she was an actress, told her that her calling was inconsistent with a Christian profession, and that she must forthwith relinquish it, or give up her interest in Christ; at the same time slipping a sovereign into her hand for the supply of her immediate necessities. The girl professed her readiness to give up all for Christ, but intimated that as her father was manager, she feared he would insist upon her maintaining her relations to the company.

To bring matters to an issue, John offered to escort the new convert to her quarters and act the mediator, with the understanding that during the interview with the father, both of them should pray. When they arrived at the lodgings, they found the manager surrounded by his company, rehearsing their parts and preparing for their next performance. Taking "the bull by the horns," John said to the father, "I have brought you a brannew daughter. God has converted her in the Methodist chapel," and added, "I will pray with you." Without waiting for permission, down went John upon his knees, the actors all keeping their seats, wondering at the novel scene, and no doubt vastly amused by John's simplicity.

o

John having concluded, the young actress broke out in prayer, and with all the fervour of her new-born soul, she pleaded for the conversion of her father, and then, one by one, and mentioning each member of the company by name, she pleaded with God for their salvation. As the girl proceeded, tears started in their eyes, and melted and overcome, one after another, they dropped off their seats on to their knees.

The time of the evening service was approaching, and John invited his new acquaintance to come and hear the squire preach. The manager declared that he would find his way to the chapel, and that his people should all come with him. The squire was always better than punctual, but that evening, earlier than their wont, he and John took their places in the pulpit, watching the congregation enter, and wondering if the actors would be faithful to their promise. At length, the squire's keen eye, recognised the girl as she approached the door, and he said to John, "She is coming;" and John replied, "And there is her father and the whole set of them." The service proceeded. The squire preached with his might, and as he appealed to the people, the manager broke down and the company seemed all affected. At the conclusion of the sermon, seekers of mercy were invited to the penitent form. The girl led up her weeping father. The company all followed, and instead of amusing the villagers that night by comedy or farce, the whole company of actors were on their knees in the Methodist chapel, crying for mercy, and one after another professing to find liberty.

Twenty years after this remarkable occurrence, John attended a lovefeast in the Guisborough circuit, when, after relating his experience, a well-dressed matron rose and said, "That is the man who twenty years ago led me to the penitent form," and then related her wonderful conversion.

At the conclusion of the lovefeast, John accompanied his old friend to her home to partake of her hospitality. He found that she was the wife of a Methodist local preacher, and occupying a respectable position in society. She informed John that her father never lost the blessing that he found under the squire's ministry, that he abandoned theatricals, became a teetotal lecturer, and lived and died a happy Christian man. She further stated, that so far as she knew, the members of the company not only commenced but had continued to serve God.

The Rev. Martin Jubb, amongst other reminiscences, writes : "In 1839 I was stationed at Alford, when Mr. Brooke paid a visit to that place. The Society was in a happy state of preparation for his visit. He preached that good sermon of his, on 'Sanctify them through Thy truth.' He spent two evenings, and on one of those memorable nights no fewer than fifty souls professed to find peace. It is a frequent complaint that converts made in seasons of excitement turn again to the world, that their goodness is like the morning cloud and the early dew that pass away ; but in this instance, I can bear testimony to their stability, and to the permanency of the work. Some remain unto this day, and others have fallen asleep in Jesus. I do not think that half a dozen of that number fell away."

No wonder that labours which told with such powerful effect upon the devil's kingdom, should stir up Satan's rage and provoke persecution. Had the squire lived a century earlier, rotten eggs, brickbats, the horse-pond, and the common gaol had tested the fidelity of this remarkable evangelist, as in the case of the first Methodist preachers. Happily, however, the days of religious toleration had dawned upon our land, and the enmity of the carnal mind was held in check by law. The squire could traverse the country and preach in town or village without risk to life or liberty. But "the tongue can no man tame." Restrained from violence by fear of consequences, bad men still say, "With our tongue will we prevail, our lips are our own ; who is Lord over us ?" and they "say all manner of evil—falsely ;" and insult, misrepresentation, reproach, and calumny fell sometimes to the lot of this pure lover of mankind. When preaching in the neighbourhood of Huddersfield, in the midst of his discourse, a low fellow whose enmity was roused by the faithful application of the truth, took his black pipe out of his pocket and flung it at the preacher. The insult, though felt, was not resented. The squire ruled his spirit, bore the affront with Christian meekness, and went on with his sermon as though nothing had occurred. At the close of the service, some of the congregation urged him to prosecute the öffender for misdemeanour, and by well-deserved punishment teach him good manners for the future; but as the insult was offered for the Master's sake, so, for the Master's sake, he would endure it. The next day the man, affected, as much it may be, by the squire's forbearance, as he had been by fear of consequences, went to his house and asked forgiveness.

In the year 1839, Mr. Brooke visited Northamptonshire, and conducted revival services at Higham Ferrers. There, as elsewhere, he attracted large congregations, aud his preaching was followed by remarkable results. After his departure from Higham Ferrers, the *Northampton Herald*, an intolerant and ill-mannered newspaper, regaled its readers, week by week, with letters (believed to have been written by a clergyman having the cure of souls in a neighbouring village,) which contained a most false and scurrilous attack upon the squire and his evangelistic work. Amongst other vile slanders, the correspondent affirmed " that some of the squire's congregation were smoking, some swearing, some singing ' Jim Crow,' etc. That a woman's fainting would be accepted as a proof of conversion, and that for the life of him he could not find anything in the Bible resembling the Higham ranting, unless it were the conduct of Baal's worshippers on Mount Carmel," etc.

Visiting Stamford a few weeks afterwards, the papers containing the scurrilous attack were put into Mr. Brooke's hand. Grieved by the falsehoods of the correspondence, and fearing, lest, if unchallenged, the cause of God might suffer, Mr. Brooke addressed the following letter to the *Northampton Herald*, which the editor, with unblushing and insolent unfairness, refused to insert in his delicately conducted journal, but which appeared in the *Northampton Mercury* :

To the Editor of the *Northampton Herald.*

Sir,—

Being on a visit in Northamptonshire this week, two or three of your papers have been put into my hands, in which are found some barefaced untruths, and some truths distorted and misrepresented in relation to myself and a friend of mine, which, not for my own sake chiefly, but for the sake of others, I feel it right to notice.

In the first place, it is stated that " I represented myself as a Yorkshire squire." *That*, I never did, and by the grace of God I never shall. John is not my man, and never was, but is a person in business for himself, as a bookseller in Lancashire. He has occasionally accompanied me in my journeys, and is, in my estimation, one of the best men in existence.

I never said, as your correspondent states, that " I had sent my dogs and gun to the devil," but I have said on many occasions, something like the following : " I gave up my dogs, gun, and all for Christ, and the devil might have them all for me." I never in my life said, that I could

convert any one in five minutes." I know too much of
human nature, of the Bible, and of my own insufficiency,
for such arrogant boasting. I do frequently say, that if the
sinner will repent and believe the Gospel, as God com-
mands him to do, he may have salvation in five minutes or
less, and so may your correspondent and his informant.

Sir, the Holy Scriptures and long observation have
taught me to believe in what some people call "instan-
taneous conversions." In reading the Acts of the Apostles,
your correspondent will find that conversions were ordi-
narily sudden under their ministry. The three thousand
conversions on the day of Pentecost appear all to have
taken place during the sittings of one assembly. It is
true, Saul of Tarsus was three days in seeking the Lord
before he obtained comfort, yet the jailor of Philippi and
all his house were converted in one night, and the Old
Testament prophecies teach us that thus it will be, when
the Spirit shall be abundantly poured out from on high.
See Isaiah xliv. 3-4; xlix. 18-22; lxvi. 8, etc. Your correspondent seems to sneer at all excitement in religion. I
dare say he has no objection to excitement in worldly and
political matters, but any excitement in the most momen-
tous of all concerns, with him, is enthusiasm. Let him
read his Bible prayerfully, and Church history carefully,
and he will find that in all Christian churches, when there
has been any special divine visitation, it has been attended
by corresponding excitement. And as to my proceedings
"increasing instead of lessening the immorality of mankind, and Satan reaping an awful harvest from them," it
will be known in the day of eternity, whether the cause
of Christ or the kingdom of Satan has been promoted by
them.

I pass by other scurrilous remarks of your correspondent
as not worth my time or notice. Now sir, let it be under-

stood that I am not going to enter into a paper war or controversy with your correspondent. No ! with Nehemiah,
when persecuted by his enemies, I would exclaim, "I am
doing a great work so that I cannot come down," a work
which, I doubt not, by the blessing of God, will tell when
eternity with all its important realities is ushered in. . . .
But O sir, my heart bleeds for your correspondent and his
informant. They must take care that the hand that made
them does not smite them. O sir, my bowels yearn over
them, and nothing would give me greater satisfaction than
to have the honour of pointing them to the once dying,
but now risen, exalted, and interceding Saviour, and seeing
them like the once persecuting Saul of Tarsus, weeping,
praying, believing, and receiving salvation. O how I
should, as I have done a thousand times, shout the praises
of my God. I wish them all well, throughout life, in
death, judgment, and eternity. They shall have an interest in my prayers, notwithstanding I am represented as
a fool by them. . . . As your correspondent has occupied
part of three papers with his tales and lucubrations,
though this letter is rather long, I expect, in all fairness
and honesty, that you will insert the whole of it.

I am, yours,

Stamford, March 13th, 1839.   EDWD. BROOKE.

A few envenomed words in his notices to correspondents, were the only attention which the editor of the
Northampton Herald bestowed upon this letter. He
reindorsed the slanders to which his journal had given
currency, and advertised Mr. Brooke's expected return as
follows,

Important ! The Yorkshire squire and his man are
expected at Higham Ferrers shortly, to revive the Wes-
leyans again.

In quiet rural districts, away from observation, where squire and parson hold joint supremacy, a spiritual tyranny sometimes asserts itself, which dares not show its face elsewhere. Still more was this the case when intolerance stood in no wholesome dread of exposure by a liberal press. Whilst Mr. Brooke had sometimes to suffer persecution, his converts did not always escape. A respectable farmer, who was awakened under the squire's preaching at Settle, and gave his heart to God and joined the Methodist Society, received a prompt intimation that his landlord would endure no Methodist tenant, and that he must give up his Methodism or his farm. Had this man's conversion been spurious, and his Christianity nothing more than religious excitement, such alternative had quickly revealed the deception, and with sobered views, he had clung to his homestead and acres ; but he had found the pearl of great price, and he was not disposed to risk its loss, by deserting the people amongst whom he had obtained it. His landlord's threat was carried into execution. In due course, he received " notice to quit." For conscience sake, he gave up his home and livelihood, but God opened his way, and he at length found a " quiet habitation " in Australia, where he served God and his generation as a Wesleyan local preacher.

The following testimony to Mr. Brooke's usefulness in the Grimsby circuit, where he conducted revival services about this time, is borne in *Hocken's History of Wesleyan Methodism in the Grimsby circuit.* " In the early part of this year (1839), the Lord has been graciously pleased to pour out his Holy Spirit on the circuit, and to bless the recent visit of Edward Brooke, Esq. Scores of persons have been savingly converted, and 213 were admitted on trial for admission into the society at the March visitation of the classes. May all their names be written in the Lamb's book of life, and never be blotted out."

Mr. Brooke's helper in evangelistic work had settled as a town missionary in Sunderland, and now restricted his labours to that locality ; but when the squire happened to be within easy reach, he generally communicated with his old co-worker, and John, by consent of his committee, sometimes arranged to join him for a brief campaign, to their mutual joy and to the advantage of their common object.

Visiting Shotley Bridge circuit in the year 1841, where he gave a week's hard labour, the squire sent for John. On the Sunday afternoon, the squire had a large congregation, and had commenced his sermon, when John, who had walked from Sunderland and was late in reaching the chapel, was struggling to press through the crowd which surrounded the open door. The squire caught sight of the old familiar face, and said, "There is my old friend John, the town missionary, trying to get in : make way for him, I have sent for him to help me. Come here, John :" and waiting till John had pushed his way through the crowded aisles and effected an entrance into the pulpit, the squire shook him by the hand, and said, "I am glad you have come. We are going to have a great revival." The congregation sympathised. The preacher resumed his sermon and besought the people to be reconciled to God. Coming down from the pulpit he held a prayer-meeting, inviting all who wanted salvation to come forward. Many responded, and penitents were pleading for mercy, and would not desist till the time of the evening service. The squire slipped out for a few minutes to take refreshment, and then re-entered the pulpit, and preached from "sanctify them through thy truth," and again worked in the prayer-meeting with no more consideration for his mortal frame, than if it were an engine driven by steam power.

A notorious sinner, whom the squire's name had allured to the chapel, was convinced of sin, the sorrows of death compassed him, the pains of hell gat hold upon him, and crying for mercy, he found pardon and peace through faith in Christ, and subsequently became a local preacher. The services were continued night after night, and numbers professed to find salvation. Some years afterwards, John was appointed by his committee to spend six months in the locality as a town missionary, and visiting from house to house he met with many who dated their Christian life from the week of the squire's visit to Shotley Bridge; and three of the local preachers upon the circuit plan, claimed him as their father in the gospel.

Mr. Brooke's congregations commonly tested the stability of the structures in which they assembled, and in some cases the testing amounted to actual peril. Preaching in a country chapel in the Holmfirth circuit, to a packed congregation, a side gallery showed signs of weakness, and the alarm was raised that the chapel was falling. A scene of excitement and wild disorder followed. The people, eager to escape, leaped one upon another. Some of those in the galleries jumped out of the windows. In the midst of the confusion and danger, Mr. Brooke, after vainly endeavouring to calm the agitation, stood with his feet upon the Bible-board, and at the top of his voice shouted, " Sudden death will be sudden glory." One man in the body of the chapel was heard to say, " Yes, it may be so with you, but what shall I do ? " In the rush to escape, several persons were badly crushed. No lives, however, were lost; but hats, bonnets, and apparel suffered sad damage. When all the congregation had withdrawn, the preacher followed, and with perfect self-possession finished his sermon in the open air.

A like scene transpired at Birstall, though in this instance, the alarm was false and malicious. The old chapel was crowded to excess; every seat and available standing place being occupied. In the midst of the sermon, a large piece of plaster previously detached from the ceiling dropped upon the bonnet of an old-fashioned Methodist sister, to her no small consternation. A cry arose that the building was falling, and the dense congregation was thrown into a tumult of excitement which threatened disastrous results. Mr. Brooke sprang on to the Bible-board, and with outstretched arms, and with his utmost power of voice, shouted, once and again, "It is only the devil that wants to come in, and we won't have him." The congregation was reassured, aud the preacher continued his discourse.

On Sunday, January 15th, 1843, Mr. Brooke preached the anniversary sermons of the Kilburn chapel, near Derby. An aged saint, still living, cherishes a lively recollection of the power which accompanied the word upon that occasion. A young woman had such a vivid discovery of her guilt and danger, that dreading instant death and damnation, she roared, "God be merciful to me a sinner," and encouraged by the divine assurance that "if we confess our sins, He is faithful and just to forgive us our sins, and to cleanse us from all unrighteousness," she trusted in Jesus, and was enabled to rejoice in the God of her salvation.

An old man upon the verge of seventy, who had been a true church-goer all his days, and had a self-complacent sense of safety, based upon the regularity of his attendance at church services, and his stated reception of the Sacrament of the Lord's Supper, was startled out of his vain dream. God showed him that all his righteousnesses in which he trusted were as filthy rags, and feeling that if he died as he was, his soul would be lost, the old man cried for mercy and found peace through believing, joined the class, and lived and died a happy Christian. Numbers from all parts of the circuit were "deeply wounded by the Spirit's sword," a large proportion of whom found mercy and became "new creatures in Christ Jesus."

The Rev. Martin Jubb has kindly supplied the following communication :—

"When, in 1843, I was stationed at Doncaster, Mr. Brooke was invited for special services at Tickhill. He kindly promised to come, but as the time drew near, from the pressure of local arrangements, it was decided that he should conduct a service in the afternoon at Wadworth, and proceed to Tickhill in the evening. He had a very uncomfortable time of it at Wadworth, and expressed strong dissatisfaction with the arrangement. At Tickhill on Sunday and Monday evenings he was happy and successful, and I had the pleasure of being with him both evenings. On the Monday evening, he called me aside in the prayer-meeting, and pointing out an individual he asked me if I knew that man. I answered, Yes.

B. "What do you call him?"

J. "W——."

B. "What is he?"

J. "Relieving officer."

B. "Do you know anything about him?"

J. "Yes, he has been seeking mercy for about two months."

B. "He says he has found peace, but he is good for nought."

"We then proceeded to take our respective parts in the prayer-meeting, and this conversation I should have forgotten, but for the fact of meeting Mr. B. at the Masbro' station about five or six weeks afterwards. We alighted on the platform, and after the usual civilities, Mr. B. asked, "Well, how are you getting on?"

J. "Thank you, sir, very well indeed."

B. "How are you getting on at that place on the top of the hill? What do you call it?"

J. "Wadworth."

B. "Yes, Wadworth. The Lord sent me to Tickhill, and the devil and you chaps sent me to Wadworth. How are you getting on at Wadworth ?"

J. "Not very well. Sinners are hard there."

B. "How are you getting on at Tickhill ?"

J. "Joyfully. The good work continues there."

B. "How is that big fellow getting on ?"

J. "All right, sir."

Just then the railway whistle sounded, and we had to pursue our respective journeys apart, but while in the act of shaking hands, Mr. B. said with great emphasis, "*He is good for nought.*"

I wondered that Mr. B. should remember this man so well, but I wondered more, when in about two months after, there was such a disclosure of the man's wickedness, that left no doubt on the minds of those who knew the case, that he had been sinning grossly all the time that he was professing to be penitent and to become a Christian. To me this appeared a case of discernment of the spirit of the man, and to this day I can come to no other conclusion. How is it that this discernment was given to a stranger, when the man's neighbours were rejoicing over him as a sincere penitent and a true believer ? There are designing men in all departments, religion not excepted. Such cases furnish painful confirmation of the truth of the Scriptures. "Satan himself is transformed into an angel of light."

A kindred circumstance to the above, transpired at Newchurch, near Bacup, where Mr. Brooke had preached, and was holding a prayer-meeting, according to his custom. After several had engaged in prayer, he startled the people by exclaiming, "There is something wrong here, or the Spirit would descend in answer to prayer." Very shortly after Mr. Brooke's visit, one who held office in the Society was expelled for immorality of conduct, which was proved to have existed at the time referred to.

In the year 1845, Mr. Brooke paid two visits to the
Watlington circuit, and was hospitably entertained by
Mr. John Paine, one of the circuit stewards, then residing
at Haddenham.

On Sunday, February 23rd, Mr. Brooke preached twice
at Thame.   The Divine Spirit was present to convince of
sin, and in the prayer-meeting which followed, rich and
poor kneeled side by side at the penitent form, and several
were saved.   On the following day he preached the chapel
anniversary sermons at Haddenham.   In the afternoon, he
took for his text, Micah ii. 7, " Is the Spirit of the Lord
straitened ?" and in the evening, John xvii. 17, " Sanctify
them through Thy truth."   The congregations were large
and a blessed influence pervaded them.   Many groaned
under the bondage of sin, and were brought into the
glorious liberty of the sons of God.   A revival dated from
these services, which spread week after week.   Morning
prayer-meetings were held at half-past five o'clock, and in
the evenings, cottage services were conducted.   The whole
village felt the influence.   The Holy Spirit worked marvellously upon the people.   Sinners were awakened in
their houses, and apart from outward and visible instrumentality.   Whole families were saved, and in a short
time, the number of members in the Methodist Society was
nearly doubled.

On Tuesday, the 25th, Mr. Brooke preached at Long
Crendon, from Psalm cxviii. 25, " Send now prosperity."
Here the same signs followed.   A man and his wife, who
were amongst the penitents, found liberty together, and
five in one family were brought into the fold.

Wednesday, the 26th.   Mr. Brooke again preached at
Thame.   His text was Isaiah lxii. 11, " His reward is with
Him, and His work before Him."   Again, God honoured
His servant with seals to his ministry, and not only at

Thame, but at Cuddington, Ashendon, and other places in the circuit, a good work commenced, which lasted for some months, and resulted in numerous conversions.

Soon after this visit, Mr. Paine wrote to Mr. Brooke, informing him how greatly his visit had been blessed, and how the good work was still going on, and received the following characteristic answer :—

Dear Brother,

Go on and prosper. Live and die in and for Christ. Verily I say unto you, you shall not lose your reward.

In your prayers,
Remember

April 19th, 1845.   EDWARD BROOKE.

In July of the same year, Mr. Brooke revisited the Watlington circuit. On Sunday, July 29th, he preached twice at Watlington, and again, on Monday evening, with great impression. On Tuesday, he preached at Ewelme, in a large barn, lent for the occasion. His text was Zephaniah iii. 17, "The Lord thy God in the midst of thee is mighty." It was a season never to be forgotten. A mighty influence fell upon the people. Between thirty and forty persons were in deep distress. Men notorious for their ungodliness were amongst the stricken, and several were made happy in the pardoning love of God.

Mr. Brooke's host, who had full opportunity closely to observe his guest during these visits, writes, " I found that Mr. Brooke lived in close fellowship with God. He was happy and cheerful in company, but of few words. His habits were very retiring. He spent much time in prayer, and generally had in hand a book of a devotional character, and never remained long at a time in the same company. His favourite themes in the pulpit seemed to be present pardon and holiness."

Mr. John Rose, a respected local preacher of Aylesbury, writes in relation to these visits, "The name of Squire Brooke has become a household word amongst Methodists, in the sylvan vale of Aylesbury. The services which he conducted were marked by divine unction, and many gems were won for the Redeemer's crown. Moreover, churches were revived, indifferent members were quickened, and God's cause was blessed during his labours here. True, some of the more quiet sort, objected to these revival services, because of their attendant noise. Yet among such, there was an after rejoicing in the religious prosperity resulting. Mr. Brooke was a living testimony to the possibility of praying without ceasing; and his labours evinced a daring trust in the promise, "According to your faith be it unto you." His life was an illustration of "the pure religion and undefiled before God and the Father," which St. James so beautifully describes. After preaching on one occasion, he was invited by a widow of slender means, to partake of her hospitality. The wealthy preacher complied, and, ere his departure, he secreted a piece of gold under a turned down tea-cup to cheer the widow in her affliction."

In this case, it would seem, the squire was an invited guest. It was, however, no uncommon circumstance for him to select his own quarters at the close of a public service, in some instances, to the disappointment of *elite* friends, who, unacquainted with his tastes, had got up a large party and sumptuous entertainment in his honour. The excitement of public work left the squire small strength for social intercourse. He dreaded parties and entertainments, especially in prospect of services to follow. He felt the need of comparative retirement, and partly on this ground, and partly from his strong sympathy with the poor, and his desire to lighten their adversity, he often looked out for some clean tidy old woman attired in widow's weeds, or in garments which indicated poverty; and beckoning to her, as he left the pulpit, astonished her no less than others, by saying, "Mother, I'll go home with you to-day, you'll give me a cup of tea, won't you?" And then promptly repressing all apology for the lowliness of the abode and the plainness of the fare, he walked off with the favoured one. On entering her cottage, the squire at once put the old woman at her ease, by taking the old arm-chair, and saying a few kind words, and as the kettle upon the hob sang its version of

"Home, sweet home,"

and the busy hostess spread the white cloth upon the well scrubbed table, brought out and burnished her best crockery, put an extra spoonful of tea into the pot, and produced the best fare which her house afforded, the squire looked the picture of content, the humble repast was sweetened with kind inquiries and pleasant intercourse, and, on taking his departure, the guest, welcome for his own sake, always contrived to leave a handsome acknowl-edgment of the hospitality received.

When distant from home, preaching in outlying districts, the squire's accommodation was sometimes of the humblest order, involving hardships and privations which to one accustomed to the comforts and luxuries of life, must have been trying, and, but for his abounding zeal, had been simply intolerable; but though in the freedom of confi-dential intercourse, he occasionally made playful allusion to rude hospitalities, his diaries contain not the slightest reference to discomfort, except in one instance, when having been kindly entertained by some rich man, and, perhaps, somewhat overdone with style and ceremony, he appends to the simple record of his work and quarters, the prayer, "Save me from great folk."

P

CHAPTER XIV.

"O let us still proceed
In Jesu's work below ;
And, following our triumphant Head,
To farther conquests go.
The vineyard of their Lord
Before his labourers lies ;
And lo ! we see the vast reward
Which waits us in the skies."

MR. BROOKE was now in the full vigour of manhood, and in the midst of his usefulness. Reserving occasional Sabbaths for his own circuit, his labours were spread over the land, yielding fruit which remains to this day. Many of his converts are found in the ranks of the ministry, and others serving the various offices of the church at home and abroad, helping to carry on the great work of the world's evangelisation. A few of his letters, happily preserved, may serve to illustrate his unabated zeal and devotion. The letters immediately following were addressed to Mr. John Hudson, the squire's former companion in labour :

Dear John,

I received yours, and felt thankful for your success. Oh ! let us labour. I see wonders. You would be delighted were you with me at some of the places. But I want more grace, more of the Spirit's power. A full blaze. Give my respects to Mr. and Mrs. Brown, and Mr. Muschamp, etc. Tell Mr. Capp he must strike home, and get 500 souls before Conference. . . . Go on, John, the devil will roar. Sinners will kick. Half-hearted professors will sneer behind your back and look shy before your face. Well, remember Jesus. The devil tempted Him. The Jewish rabble persecuted Him, and His own disciples " forsook Him and fled." Keep to it, John. Play the man. Never expect peace while you proclaim war. My respects to your family and all friends, and in your prayers remember

EDWARD BROOKE.

November 19th, 1841.

Dear John,

I received yours, and am glad you are doing well. I have seen wonders in Cheshire, and at Liverpool, and at various other places. I am still fighting, and am determined to be a better man than ever, and preach such sermons, through grace, as I never did. Oh ! Hallelujah to Jesus ! I bless the day that ever I was born. Write soon, and give my respects to all friends, and in your prayers remember

EDWARD BROOKE.

March 10th, 1842.

Dear John,

In answer to your kindness, I beg to say that I am fully engaged north, east, south, and west. Pray for me. I see wonders in all directions. I have been in London again, and the power of God was there, awakening and converting them on all sides. Hallelujah ! My respects to all friends,

And believe me, the same as ever,

Your unwavering friend,

May 19th, 1842. EDWARD BROOKE.

Dear John,

I have just returned out of the south. Sinners fell
under the power of God, wept, prayed, believed, and got
saved. Hallelujah ! Go on, John. The devil will roar.
Half-hearted professors will look shy. Sinners will perse-
cute, but God reigns and His kingdom must come. Play
the man. Go your own way, it is the best. I shall be
glad to have a pull with you. When I am within ten
or twenty miles, I purpose writing. My respects to your
preachers and family.

I am, yours, as ever,

EDWARD BROOKE,

A poor, bruised reed—half asleep.

December 17th, 1842.

To the Rev. Samuel Simpson, who, having recently left
Huddersfield, was stationed at Nottingham, and had invited
Mr. Brooke to visit his circuit, Mr. Brooke addressed the
following letter :

My dear Sir,

Had I received yours a few days sooner, I could
have given our Quarter-day folks a little of its contents.
Heaven seems to smile upon your borders, and there is
peace and prosperity. Oh, that we could, in return, say,
so is it with Huddersfield circuit. We have a few signs of
better days, and are going to have a few more extra meetings to see what can be done. Pray for us. But to the
point.

Your invitation to Nottingham is clear and full, scriptural and Methodistical, and I could not refuse had I been
disengaged. But I have not one Sabbath at liberty on this
side August. North, east, south, and west lie before me.
In Somersetshire, Cumberland, Lancashire, the borders of

Scotland, etc., etc. My voice, God willing, will be heard according to promise.

I think we have done wrong in not dividing our circuit. We are a vast number of human beings, leaders, stewards, local preachers, etc., looking at one another, and apparently doing nothing. Lord help us, and put us into a better way. Our kind respects to Mrs. S., and goodwill and success increasingly to yourself.

Yours, as ever, in Christ,

March 31st, 1843.   EDWARD BROOKE.

To Mr. John Hudson.
Dear John,

Hundreds and thousands are getting saved in Yorkshire, and I am labouring on. When I visit North Shields, (but at present I do not know when), I will write and let you know. Pray on. Believe on. Love on. Persevere, and I will try to meet you in heaven in a short time. I have been very unwell this spring. The influenza has shaken my constitution, but I am better. My respects to all friends. In your prayers, remember

EDWARD BROOKE.

May 27th, 1843.

To Mr. John Hudson.
Dear John,

In answer to yours, I beg leave to say that I am not coming your way; but should I engage, I shall be glad to see you. I still see wonders, and expect to see. Hallelujah! In your last letter you say nothing about Sunderland,—how may souls have been saved,—or backsliders healed,—or believers cleansed. Now we must see the glory come; and you cannot live without souls. What are chapels, sermons, meetings, etc., without souls? Souls,

John, nothing but souls. Go to it again, and with your shattered frame play the man, and tell heaven, earth, hell, and the church, you will have souls. Amen. My God, give John souls.

Give my kind respects to your preachers and all inquiring friends, and write soon. I am always glad to receive a letter from John Hudson. In your prayers, remember a poor slow runner to Zion,

EDWARD BROOKE.

August 22nd, 1843.

To Mr. John Hudson.

Dear John,

My affectionate and best wishes towards you remain unabated. I thought you owed me a letter. I am, through mercy, passing from county to county, seeking the wandering souls of men. I often think about our travelling together in the gig, the happy seasons we had, and the souls saved. Oh, John, let us live for God, and souls and eternity. My kindest regards to your super., and Mr. and Mrs. Browne, whose kindness I have not forgotten.

Yours, as ever,

April 3rd, 1845.   EDWARD BROOKE.

I am going to Cornwall this month, pray for me.

To Mr. John Hudson.

Dear John,

It is better and better with me than ever. Oh, the boundless goodness of God to me. I am now swimming in the river of mercy, lost in wonder, love, and praise. The Eternal God is my refuge, and underneath are the everlasting arms. I am travelling, and preaching, and fighting, and winning souls as ever. I have now fought the devil almost in every county in England, and I tell

him I shall not yield. Give my kind respects to Mr.
Brown and Mrs., and all friends. Mr. Caughey, the Ameri-
can, would do you good. Go on, John, and never yield.
I gave the devil a broadside in Lancashire, last Sunday,
about curls, and artificial flowers, and gold rings, etc., etc.
You may depend upon it, this is rough work. There is a
great deal of pride among Methodists, John; I say Methodists. It is a shame, a sin, a bad example. We see it
awfully in our chapels. I feel determined to lift up my
voice against it Lord help me. My kind respects to your
family and the preachers, and in your prayers, remember

EDWARD BROOKE.

November 26th, 1845.

To Mr. John Hudson.
Dear John,

God willing, I am off for near London to-morrow
morning. Pray for me, that I may have a single eye, a
clear head, a lively imagination, a warm heart, a sanctified
soul, a voluble tongue, the fulness of the Spirit, and mighty
success. Amen: my Lord, let it be so.

John, I say, John, I am for heaven, for souls, for God's
glory, and for the salvation of the world. I have a con-
straining power within me; the great love of God. Oh,
Hallelujah! Praise the Lord! My kind regards to the
preachers, people, friends, enemies, the church and world,
and in your prayers, remember

EDWARD BROOKE.

I am not coming your way, and therefore I cannot have
a regular set struggle with you for souls. I see them saved
on all sides; north, east, south, and west. John, though
distant from you, I respect you as much as ever.
Hallelujah! I have not forgotten Yorkshire and Derbyshire hills and vales, where we travelled together.

The following letter was addressed by Mr. Brooke to Mr.
E. Brown, now the leader of a large class in connection
with the Mildmay Park chapel, Highbury. Mr. Brown
found peace with God during the revival services which
Mr. Brooke conducted at City Road chapel, in 1842, and
had written to Mr. Brooke informing him of his steadfast
Christian profession, and that he was attempting to speak
to sinners.

Dear Edward,

   I am glad you have got to work. Don't be discouraged when you have not all the liberty you want. Go
on. Preach a present, free, full, increasing, everlasting
salvation, and the Lord will bless you and make you a
blessing. Let not men or devils shackle you.

   In your prayers, remember
April 26th, 1846.   EDWARD BROOKE.

Mr. Brooke was remarkable for his punctual fulfilment
of engagements at whatever inconvenience to himself.
Unless disaster or sickness interposed, congregations might
calculate on finding the preacher at his post, and probably
at work before the appointed time. The pain of disappointment or suspense was, in his case, of rare occurrence.
It seems, however, that at Birstall on one occasion, a congregation gathered to hear the squire, and anxiously
awaited his appearance, but no preacher came, and the
people dispersed with reflections and animadversions more
or less severe, according to the measure of their charity.
A letter of inquiry brought the following reply :

Mr. Clapham.
Respected Friend,

   1st. Believe me when I say, I had entirely forgotten
my promise made to you.

2nd. Whether Mr. Robson, your super, invited me to his house or not I really cannot recollect. I am sending hundreds of letters north, east, south, and west, and I just open and answer.

3rd. My affection and respect for Mr. and Mrs. Clapham, of Brownhill, remain unabated, and never have deviated from my first acquaintance.

4th. Should I visit Birstall, Mr. Clapham's house shall ever be my home.

5th. But how could I forget? I attribute it, first, to carelessness. Secondly, to not putting it down in writing. Thirdly, to so many such like interviews in chapels, when I am excited. Fourthly, to my multiplicity of invitations and engagements. I am off to-morrow morning for Cheshire, and the next fortnight I am travelling and preaching ten days in the fourteen. My kind respects to all, and please to ask pardon for me. If some of your leaders are grieved, please read them this letter, and say, when I see my way clear for Birstall, I am their servant; but they must forgive,

Yours,

EDWARD BROOKE.

CHAPTER XV.

SORROWS.

"To Thy blessed will resign'd,
  And stay'd on that alone,
I Thy perfect strength shall find,
  Thy faithful mercies own ;
Compass'd round with songs of praise,
  My all to my Redeemer give ;
Spread Thy miracles of grace,
  And to Thy glory live."

A CAST-IRON constitution had been severely tested by the labours indicated in the foregoing correspondence, and glanced at in former chapters; and the squire's robust manhood, built up amid the wild moor-breezes of his native Honley, at length gave way under the excessive strain.

The brain work involved in his perpetual appearance before the public was not inconsiderable, for though the squire sometimes spoke at random, and gave the impression of negligent preparation for his pulpit work, his manuscript sermons and the testimony of those well acquainted with his habits, show that he was not accustomed to offer to God that which cost him nothing. The word of God was his study. The commentaries of Henry, Clarke, and Benson, were his closet companions, and go where he might, he had commonly some text of Scripture in hand, endeavouring to analyse and master its teachings with relation to the instruction of others.

Mr. Brooke's wonderful equipment of holy unction,— the secret of his remarkable success,—was not accidental.

It cost him, as his diary testifies, much agony of soul and secret wrestling with God in the still hours of night, when others took rest in sleep. He well understood the lesson which Christ taught His disciples, when foiled in their attempt to eject the dumb spirit, they came disheartened to their Lord, with the inquiry, "why could not we .cast him out?" and received the answer, "This kind can come forth by nothing but by prayer and fasting;" and he not only understood the lesson, but he turned it to practical account, abstaining not merely from pleasant but from necessary food, and wrestling for power from on high till faith waxed mighty and triumphant, but frail nature sank exhausted.

The exposure of long journeys performed on horseback or in his open gig, at all seasons of the year and in all states of weather; preaching twice and three times on the Sabbath, and preaching on successive week nights in old-fashioned chapels and preaching-rooms with low ceilings, packed congregations and bad ventilation, where, to use his own words, he was "stewed in the hot breath of the people;" the conducting of prayer-meetings, sometimes prolonged till near the midnight hour, amid the excitement of sinners crying for mercy, and reluctant to depart; and when weary and exhausted by the labours of the day, lodging not unfrequently in homes which strangely contrasted with his own comfortable mansion, and where, occasionally, from want of consideration, he had less generous fare than work so exhausting demanded :— all these things combined to break down his strength and to necessitate temporary cessation from public work, and an eventual restriction most painful to his ardent nature.

Acting under professional advice, in the Autumn of 1852, Mr. Brooke visited Buxton, in company with Mrs. Brooke,

and remained for some time, taking the baths and sub-
mitting to medical treatment. It was painful to see the
strong man eager to work, crippled by disease, and
so completely broken that he moved with the utmost
difficulty, and largely depended on the help of others.
Still, he was able to drive through the romantic country
to which Buxton owes so much of its attractiveness, to
feast his eyes upon the glorious scenery and breathe the
exhilarating air; and the following beautiful letter, addressed to one of his daughters soon after his arrival
at Buxton, shows that whatever the prostration of his
body, both intellect and heart retained their vigour.

. . . . Mother and I arrived safely, after a long
drive over the Derbyshire hills and dales : all beautiful,
romantic, grand, majestic, displaying the wonders of an
all-creating, preserving, upholding hand.

The hand that made them is divine. "Thou hast created
all things, and for thy pleasure they are and were created."
We have just come in from a very beautiful drive; the
rocks on either hand splendid, majestic, hanging over,
with small shrubs and trees interspersed. It is supposed
to be one of the finest drives in the British empire. At
the bottom of the valley there runs a clear trout-stream,
where the fishes swim and leap to catch the flies. There
is nothing like it at Blackpool, Scarborough, Harrogate,
or any other place I have ever seen. During the drive
we saw a beautiful cottage, grown over with ivy and
shrubs, just under a wood, the trees of which were of
varied autumnal colours. We intend going to the top
of a little mountain, where there is an old building of
castellated form. From the top is a splendid view of
the surrounding country. But what are all the sights
throughout the world, and the grandeur of nature, to

heavenly, spiritual, ever-enduring, boundless realities ? *Nothing!* All dwindle into perfect insignificance.

We said the rocks were splendid and the scenery grand ; but what compared to the "Rock of Ages," "the Stone cut out of the mountain." We said the river was beautiful, winding its way through the hills; but what is that to the "pure river of water of life clear as crystal, proceeding out of the throne of God and of the Lamb," ever flowing, everlasting. The saints of the Most High drink of that river, "the streams whereof shall make glad the city of God." We said the cottage was neat, antique, and very beautiful ; but what compared to the house above, "not made with hands, eternal in the heavens." That sweet little cottage will crumble into dust, but the house above will outweather all storms, and stand secure through unending ages, and will be the shelter, the refuge of the redeemed, when the storm of God's wrath is poured out upon an unthinking, careless, sinful world ; and when millions shall say "to the mountains and rocks fall on us, and hide us from the face of Him that sitteth on the throne and from the wrath of the Lamb;" and the redeemed and saved, all who have died in the Lord, shall sing the song of the Lamb. Oh, my child, I hope that you and I and all our family, unbroken, will be there.

We said the trees were lovely, but what compared with the tree of life, bearing twelve manner of fruits, and yielding her fruit every month, and the leaves of which are for the healing of the nations.

Yesterday we were at the house of God, the temple of the Lord. I heard of Jesu's saving, hallowing mercy, and there we prayed, and sung, and believed, loved and adored. But O when we get to the new Jerusalem above, paved with gold, and see Jesus in all His dignity, grandeur, and glory, and worship at His feet, to what heights of rapture and amazement shall we be carried, and wonder at His bleeding, dying love, and be astonished at His unparalleled condescension in bringing us there from a world of sin, misery, and death. There all is light, holiness, and happiness, life and glory! Now after all this glory I am seeking and praying; believing that if I conquer through His blood, I shall the glory win. Jesus often whispers in my ear, " Be thou faithful unto death, and I will give thee a crown of life." You must pray for me. I have been travelling on the road to heaven nearly thirty years. I left the road of sin and misery and disappointment when I was about twenty-two. Happy man! Happy change! to leave the dominion of sin and Satan and enter the liberty and kingdom of Jesus, who is the King of kings and Lord of lords. I feel now that my body is worn, weak, breaking down; but the hand that formed it will rebuild it at the resurrection morn, and fashion it like unto His glorious body, stamped with incorruptibility and immortality; and thus rebuilt and glorified, I expect to shine as the sun in the kingdom of God. What a work,—salvation! What an end,—Glory! Heaven! the Presence of God! I intend bringing you a present. Leave it to me. Your father knows the best. But go you to Jesus and ask Him for the " Pearl of great price," "the White Stone," the pardon of all your sins, the favour and peace of God. And having thus secured heaven's smile, life will pass away sweetly, death will be met triumphantly, and heaven's riches will be yours. Write again and tell me all news.

Your very loving Father.

Buxton, October 4th, 1852.

About this time, came the additional pressure of domestic affliction. The increase of Mr. Brooke's family having made a change of residence desirable, he removed to Boston

Spa, and subsequently to Thornton Lodge, in the vicinity of Huddersfield. Thornton Lodge was beautifully situated on gently rising ground, and nestled among trees, which afforded pleasant and salubrious shelter. It was a spot where health might be supposed to make its home, but from some cause, at the time inexplicable, typhoid fever made its appearance and lingered about the place, and would not be driven away, prostrating Mrs. Brooke and one and another of the family, and imperilling lives most precious.

Church troubles also caused Mr. Brooke no small anxiety. Huddersfield became the great stronghold of the "Reform Agitation." Long after other churches had found rest, misguided men kept the Huddersfield Societies in continuous excitement most damaging to religious life, resulting in the separation of numbers from the church of their fathers, and in the alienation of many from all Christian fellowship, and inflicting a blight, the effect of which is sadly visible at this day. It were unwise to uplift the veil which time has thrown over that dark past. Let it be hoped that such scenes as Huddersfield Methodists witnessed may never recur, and that whatever adaptations of the Methodist economy to altered times and circumstances, appear desirable, may be sought by constitutional means, and in harmony with "the gentleness of Christ."

The following letters addressed to the Rev. John McOwan, the superintendent of the Huddersfield Buxton Road circuit, may serve to illustrate the Christian spirit with which Mr. Brooke bore the severe trials of this period, as also the interest which, notwithstanding his extensive itinerancy, he took in the affairs of his own circuit, and his steadfast attachment to the principles and economy of Methodism, at that time assailed with unexampled persistency and bitterness.

Buxton, September 17th, 1852.

Mr. McOwan,

Dear Sir,

Yet troubles come. Yes, and will come. I hope, however, things will go well in Judah, in Huddersfield, on the Quarter-day, and also at the great local preacher's demonstration. I am now an invalid. The doctor here, says, as my own, that my constitution has been overwrought, and that I must give up, till brought round, through mercy. I now write to ask this favour, to get me a supply at the Quarter-day, for my appointments at Slaithwaite. I am taking the hot bath, and have had much difficulty to crawl along. However, I think upon the whole, that I am better.' God is good to me. I "have not followed cunningly devised fables," but divine realities. I see in Christ all fulness dwells, and that for me. I cling here, rest here. I feel peace. We think and talk of you, and say again and again, poor Mr. McOwan. Unwell, overdone, too much work, jaded, looks so, is so. Eyes sunk. Rest, rest, rest, he wants. But when and where is he to have it? Our kind respect to self, etc.

In your prayers, remember

EDWARD BROOKE.

Buxton, September 25th, 1852.

Mr. McOwan,

Dear Sir,

Yours came safe to hand, with thanks. I am a little better, but still weak, and cannot walk far. Sciatica is a complaint not easily got rid of, unless touched by the divine hand; then fevers fly and death starts into life. May He who healed all manner of sickness and disease among the people, heal my shattered frame. I think He will. I am going on, praying, looking, believing, loving, enduring, suffering, conquering. All is well. To God be all the praise. I am going to heaven, to rest, to glory, where all will be calm and peace, without *agitation* and disunion.

We were glad, my wife as well as myself, that you got over your Quarter-day business so well. The old man still survives, prejudice still exists, bad feelings still* break out; but I think things are coming round to a more settled point of rest and quiet. To God be all the praise. I am glad you met Mr. ——'s arguments or assertions. He is too hasty in his conclusions and may be easily confuted. . . . Time and mercy will, I hope, bring us to our desired haven. "My people shall dwell in a peaceable habitation, and in sure dwellings and in quiet resting places." But as Moses said to the Israelites, "Ye are not as yet come to the rest and to the inheritance which the Lord your God giveth you." Still, I think, we are marching towards it, and I see the land in the distance, and hope ere long to enter, and there live and die with a full assurance of a rest which will be undisturbed and eternal. "There remaineth therefore a rest to the people of God."

I shall be some time before I can get fully into work, and I purpose staying here a few more weeks, trying to regain health and vigour. My kind respects to Mrs. McOwan. Tell her she must overlook all my eccentricities when she visits our humble home. I know my singularities, and disapprove of them altogether; but still, I think I am sincere in my profession of Christianity, and I wish to be put right when wrong. Give my respects to Miss McOwan, and tell her she must rise in every grace, be a pattern of all good works, and a praise in the gate; none more holy, none more useful,—all light, all love, all praise, a woman in a thousand. Give my respects to son John. Tell him that though affliction

Q

is not joyous but grievous, it is his Father's hand that
chastens whom He loves.   Perhaps he may yet rise to
health, and labour, and usefulness in God's great church
and work.   He must, however, get here, however hard
to flesh and blood,—"Thy will be done." As for yourself, you know the way.   You feel the power.   You
rejoice in the Saviour's love; and, when touched by His
hand, you preach, and pray, and sing, and shout, and
love, and adore.   Oh ! to God be all the praise.   There
is nothing like preaching yet.   It is of God.   The Gospel
is His.   It must prosper.   Antichrist must fall, and the
world be saved.

Mrs. Brooke is coming over to the missionary sale.
She looks pretty well, rides, and walks out with me, and
encourages me to look up when I am cast down ; a help-
meet, a partner of my joys and sorrows : but you know
these things.   My respects to Messrs. George Brooke
and Keighley and Lockwood, and all such friends,—
I say such, and remain the same strange, undeviating
friend,

EDWARD BROOKE.

To the same,

Thornton Lodge,

October 23rd, 1852.

Dear Sir,

Affliction for the present is not joyous.   I am very
unwell, suffering from influenza.   The doctor has ordered
me to bed to-day, but I cannot submit.   My poor dear
Jane, we are afraid is in the typhus fever, and therefore
it will not be wise in you to come here.   We have sent
Mr. Bond word to procure a home for Mr. Punshon, as of
course we cannot entertain him.

But there is a trustee's meeting, according to a notice

sent me, next Thursday. What is to be done? Please
see Mr. ——, and tell him there does not want much consideration about the matter. Mr. Jacomb, the solicitor,
advertises to lend money. See him at once; or the bank
will lend it us, and be glad. Get a promissory note drawn
up in the usual form; send it to me, and I will sign it at
once. Then get Mr. ——, Mr. ——, Mr. ——, Mr. ——
to sign it, if you can; if not, four of us will be quite
sufficient. Tell Mr. —— to go about the business in a
manly way, as he knows how to do, and say to Mr. ——,
now Mr. —— when will you have the money. It is quite
ready. Get it paid at once and have done with them, and
all such like trustees. God will help us, and we shall
prosper. Pray for us, and especially for the Lord to spare
my wife, if in His wisdom, He has determined to take
some; but I hope not.

In your prayers, remember

EDWARD BROOKE.

P.S. I write this apparently authoritative note under
feverish excitement, but have expressed the sentiments of
my heart. Whatever you or Mr. George Brooke have to
propose, a line from either shall have my prompt attention.

Happy the superintendent minister, who in the troublous
times referred to in these letters, had a wise counsellor and
an able and ready helper like Mr. Brooke to lean upon.
All through those weary years of strife, Mr. Brooke remained the same staunch supporter of constitutional
authority. Whoever wavered, he stood firm. When the
hearts of many well-disposed men failed for fear, and
numbers thought that Methodism had received her death-
blow, and shrank from accepting obligations, and placing
their shoulder beneath burdens which they feared might

gather weight and prove too heavy for them, he was ready
to take his full share of responsibility and work, and, if
need be, his neighbour's also.   Sustained by Mr. Brooke
and men of kindred spirit, and favoured from above, Mr.
McOwan, the judicious superintendent of the Huddersfield
Buxton Road circuit, saw his circuit brought through the
fiery ordeal with little damage, and enter upon a career of
material and spiritual prosperity, which has continued with
small check unto the present.

To Mr. McOwan, who on removing from Huddersfield,
was appointed to Leeds Brunswick, Mr. Brooke writes :

Thornton Lodge,
December 30th, 1853.

Dear Sir,

Our Quarter-day is past, and we have peace and
prosperity.   We have about twenty-eight on trial, and I
think a few added.   Mr. Tindall and Mr. Smith are
straightforward men, prudent, careful, firm, unflinching,
different in talent, but both received.   Honley is low, but
there is a little prospect of better days there.   As for the
Morrisonians, I hear very little of them, only that they
have separated.   What next ?   When will men learn
wisdom ?   We shall be glad to see you at our fireside, I do
assure you.   When you have a day or two at liberty, and
your nerves are shaken, come, and we will nurse you.   I
intend calling when I come to Leeds.   I have passed
through many conflicts since I last saw you, but still keep
the prize in view.   Our kind regards to Mrs. and Miss, and
in your prayers, remember

EDWARD BROOKE.

The Rev. John Holmes, at this date a student at Dids-
bury College, having paid a brief visit to Thornton Lodge,

and rendered service at Honley, received shortly afterwards, the following letter :

Dear John,

In reply to yours, I beg leave to say that our labour at Honley was not in vain. A new class has been formed, and about a dozen have gone to it. Two found peace. Praise the Lord ! We shall rise. All hell is on the move, but we must go round about the bulwarks of our Zion, and mark well her palaces, and we shall ultimately and finally triumph over all. I say all. Go on, John, in the work. Live near to God. Be a giant in religion ; one of the first and best men in your day. Plead with God. Live in the glory. "Advance" is the Christian's motto. Onward to certain victory over sin, the world, and hell. Trample down worldly, fashionable conformity. Know the will of God and do it. Do it heartily, cheerfully, fully, eternally, and heaven will be your guide, defence, all and in all. Our kind respects,

And in your prayers, remember

Thornton Lodge,   EDWARD BROOKE.
December 22nd, 1853.

To his esteemed friend, the Rev. Samuel Tindall, the superintendent of the Huddersfield Buxton Road circuit, who was attending Conference, Mr. Brooke addressed the following letter :

August 1st, 1854.

Dear Sir,

Thanks for your repeated kindness flowing in upon me, letter after letter, information upon information. I am glad things go well in Judah. Oh for a baptism of fire, love, joy, peace. I have felt well lately in preaching, praying, labouring in different parts. Heaven still smiles. Salvation still comes. Ichabod is not yet written upon us. The Lord of Hosts is with us, and will be, whilst we maintain character, prudence, discipline. I am sorry for poor ———. Oh! how needful to watch. See Abraham's prevarication, see Aaron's making the calf, see David's fall, see Solomon's idolatry, see Peter's cowardice. Lord help me. I see more than ever I stand by faith and good works. Lord help me and you. We have and shall have our trials; but the Lord reigneth. Let us be up and doing. I think the circuit is rising, and hope we shall see better days.

Yours affectionately,

EDWARD BROOKE.

CHAPTER XVI.

" The things impossible to men
    Thou canst for Thine own people do :
  Thy strength be in our weakness seen ;
    Thy wisdom in our folly show ;
  Prevent, accompany, and bless,
    And crown the whole with full success."

IN his earlier life, Mr. Brooke, as already stated, felt justified in relinquishing his interest in the mills at Armitage
Bridge, that, released from all worldly care, he might do
the work of an evangelist; but, as family responsibilities
increased, and sons were fast rising into manhood, he
became wishful to embark a portion of his capital in such
way as to provide some of his family with occupation and
income suitable to their social status.   Reading his Bible,
Mr. Brooke often remarked the simplicity with which the
patriarchs acknowledged God in the ordinary business of
life, and how entirely they relied upon God's promised
guidance and help in relation to their earthly affairs.   In
his judgment, the teachings of the New Testament war-
rant an equally simple trust in God's providence on the
part of Christians in these days; and from a very early
period of his Christian life, he was accustomed to consult
God about his worldly concerns, and to expect an answer
in some form.   In this habit he seems to have been con-
firmed by reading a letter of the Rev. John Wesley, the
following extract from which he copied into his journal.

"For many years I had a kind of scruple with regard to
praying for temporal things, but three or four years ago, I

was thoroughly persuaded that the scruple was unneces-
sary. Being then straitened much, I made it matter of
prayer, and I had an immediate answer. It is true we can
only ask outward blessings with reserve. If this is best,
if it be Thy will, and in this manner, we may certainly
plead the promise, 'all these things shall be added unto
you.' "

An estate was offered for sale in the neighbourhood of
Huddersfield, which Mr. Brooke, after due consideration
and prayer, was encouraged to purchase. Reading one day
in his closet, the fifteenth Chapter of Joshua, which records
Caleb's gift of a portion to Achsah, his daughter, and
musing upon God's fatherly care over himself and family,
it was suddenly impressed upon his mind that the land he
had purchased was rich in mineral treasure. The more he
prayed, the more assured he became that the impression
was divine, and in the confidence of faith he at once instituted search. Whilst the result was apparently uncertain,
and each surmounted difficulty was followed by another,
he was encouraged by the application of passages of Scripture, which he accepted as from God. One of these was
the promise, " I will instruct thee and teach thee in the
way which thou shalt go, I will guide thee with mine eye."
On another occasion, when severely exercised, there came
with singular impressiveness and power, the words—" The
Almighty shall bless thee with blessings of heaven above,
and blessings of the deep that lieth under." Thus strengthened, he persevered with an unfaltering conviction of
ultimate success.

Returning from Leeds by train one day, the impression
came clear and strong upon him as though a voice had
spoken in his ear, they have found coal. Stepping on to
the platform, as the train drew up at Huddersfield, the first
men he met with were his borers, who greeted his return

with the welcome intelligence, " We have found coal."
Recording in his journal this discovery of coal, Mr. Brooke
adds in relation to his trust in Providential guidance, " I
believe yet I am right."

Men who live remote from God, or who have no clear
sense of their adoption into God's family, and are strangers
to the habitual, simple, childlike intercourse with God im-
plied by sonship, and encouraged by the command, " in
everything, by prayer and supplication with thanksgiving,
let your request be made known unto God," may attach
small importance to the impressions of which Mr. Brooke
was not unfrequently the subject ; or may possibly regard
them as the offspring and evidence of an ill-balanced mind.
We are far from contending that all impressions which
good men upon their knees receive, and at the time consider a divine response to their petitions, are really so.
Good men may be mistaken. Their impressions may,
in some cases, be the mere offspring of desire. The
wish may be " father to the thought," and he who hastily
acts upon impressions is very likely to be misled. Still,
in some way or other, God will answer the sincere and
believing prayers of his perplexed and bewildered children
who go to Him for counsel. He saith, who cannot lie, " I
will instruct thee and teach thee in the way which thou
shalt go, I will guide thee with mine eye ;" and undoubtedly the answer to believing prayer sometimes comes in
the form of an impression, deep, powerful, irresistible,
abiding, and which the event proves to have been from
God for His child's guidance, as was again and again the
case with Mr. Brooke.

The seam of coal to which Mr. Brooke always believed
himself providentially directed, lay in close proximity to a
bed of fire-clay, to which it gave heightened value, and the
discovery was soon turned to practical account in the

establishment of extensive works for the manufacture of
sanitary tubes, fire-bricks, etc., which for years past have
been profitably conducted by members of the family.

To this and other striking manifestations of Providence
on his behalf, Mr. Brooke often adverted in the pulpit and
elsewhere, in proof that God still directs the steps of those
who acknowledge Him in all their ways, and that whatever
sacrifices God's children make for His sake, shall not be
forgotten or unrecompensed.

Influenced partly by business considerations, and partly
by the impression that a change of residence might promote the health of his family; Mr. Brooke enlarged the
farmhouse which stood on his newly-acquired estate to
meet the requirements of his household, and removed from
Thornton Lodge to Fieldhouse. He also adapted a house
which stood close by the entrance gates of his new home,
for Christian worship, that the old people and others unable to reach Huddersfield, might hear the gospel on Sabbath evenings, and enjoy week-night ordinances. In this
room associated with precious memories, Mr. Brooke established and conducted a class-meeting, and here he delighted
to preach when free from weightier responsibilities ; here,
too, he at length wound up his public work by preaching
his last sermon a few days before his departure. Once a
month upon a week-night, the circuit ministers were expected to officiate in this consecrated room, when the
neighbours, duly apprised, not only by announcement on
the circuit plan, but by house to house visitation, commonly
mustered in strong force, and with the members of the
squire's family, constituted a congregation of unusual interest. The squire availed himself of this monthly
appointment of the circuit ministers, to show hospitality
to them and their families, testifying by the most con-
siderate and courteous treatment, that he " esteemed them

very highly in love for their works' sake." When accompanying the preacher to the little sanctuary, he would playfully remark, "Now don't give us one of your great sermons to-night, such as you give at Buxton Road, for we are plain people here, and we want it short and to the point." His responses throughout the service showed how heartily he appreciated the simplest ministrations which had Jesus for their theme, and dealt experimentally and practically with truths bearing upon " the common salvation."

Business involves care, and the development of the Fieldhouse works in their earlier stage occasioned Mr. Brooke no small anxiety. Springs of water were tapped as the miners proceeded with their work, and constant pumping became necessary to prevent the mine being flooded. Wishful, if possible, to avoid all Sabbath labour, Mr. Brooke expended a large sum of money in making sufficiently capacious water levels to hold twenty-four hours' flow of water, so that pumping might be suspended on the Sabbath, without damaging the interests of master or men.

Explosive gas was generated in the coal-mine, requiring the continuous use of an underground furnace, to ensure adequate ventilation and safety. Not realising the greatness of the risk, Mr. Brooke released the firemen from their posts upon the Sabbath ; the result was a serious explosion, which greatly distressed and compelled him, however reluctantly, to rescind his regulation forbidding *all* work upon the Sabbath, in favour of one less rigorous, and more in harmony with the spirit of the Gospel, which distinctly recognises the lawfulness of necessary labour.

The colliers also were explosive. Great consideration is due to men who earn their bread under conditions involving physical discomfort and risk of life ; and coal-

miners, whose severe and perilous industry lies at the basis
of our national wealth and domestic comfort, deserve
generous treatment. None, surely, would grudge them
short hours and good wages. On the other hand,
employers and the public have rights which are entitled
to respect, but which are sometimes unwisely overlooked.
"Trade's unions" may, in some cases, serve the interests
of a particular class, but the union of a common brotherhood which seeks to harmonise the interests of all classes
and promote the general good, is the great want of the
times. Presenting demands, which, being deemed "un-
reasonable and unjust," were resisted, Mr. Brooke's colliers
once and again turned out, to the embarrassment of their
employer, who sought help from God. Enumerating
various promises given to him whilst the colliers were
on strike, Mr. Brooke writes, "all fulfilled. The men
have returned and begged on again. We have got rid
of a few. . I know where my help lies. 'In the time
of trouble, He shall hide me in his pavillion; in the
secret of His tabernacle shall He hide me. He shall set
me up upon a rock.' This is a wonderful deliverance,
if fully known in all its bearings."

The branch of industry in which Mr. Brooke had em-
barked was in its infancy, and its details were not to be
mastered without trouble. In some instances, valuable
knowledge had to be gained by a process of failure and
disaster involving no small harassment. "Trial upon
trial," writes Mr. Brooke, "Failure upon failure, pots
cracking, etc., etc., but verily there is a God, and we
shall rally and prosper." "There is no wisdom, nor
understanding, nor counsel against the Lord, and if He
pleases He can give me back all the customers. I see
His providence again and again, and wonder at His all-
controlling hand. Praise ye the Lord! He bringeth
them to the desired haven."

True to his principles, Mr. Brooke not only sought counsel of God, in relation to the management of his rapidly enlarging business, but gratefully gave God the glory of the success which ultimately crowned it. He writes in his journal,

"The Lord revealed to me a fresh scheme. Our mining agent and Mr. Green are delighted. On my return home, the Lord said sweetly to me, 'If thou draw out thy soul to the hungry, and satisfy the afflicted soul, then shall thy light rise in obscurity, and thy darkness be as the noon day, and the Lord shall guide thee continually.'"

Awhile after, when his son had made a successful trip to America, and opened foreign business connections, and taken extensive contracts, and the Fieldhouse wares were coming into high repute and wide demand, Mr. Brooke writes in his journal, "I see the good hand of God upon us for good. If He careth for us it is enough. When shall we realise this and go on our way rejoicing? If He says to events let that man succeed in his calling, opposition and difficulties are nothing. He gets forward. The blessing of the Lord it maketh rich, and He addeth no sorrow with it."

The Fieldhouse works were commenced and carried on by their founder in childlike dependence upon God. The counting-house was a closet where plans and projects, calculations, contracts, and trade arrangements, were spread before the Lord, and where the servant of God seeking counsel from above received, according to his own testimony, answers plain and unmistakable, as when above thirty years before, God said to him, "Thy sins which are many are all forgiven thee, go in peace and sin no more;" answers which rid him of all perplexity and fear about the course that he should take. Again and again, as he knelt before God in his counting-house, his path was lit up with heavenly light, so that he wrote in his journal, " I see how God can direct in the most minute affairs of life. . . . Now my way is plain, every doubt is removed, every scruple is banished. God will go before me and prosper me. It is astonishing, I am amazed. It is inexplicable, I am overpowered. I now see my way clear as if written with a sunbeam."

" Never such a day as this for full direction. I consulted the Lord, and an answer was given me. I see more clearly than ever, that every thing is under the immediate control and Providence of God. Abraham believed God, and I have only to act faith on the promises specially given to me, and I shall see them fulfilled in reference to temporal, spiritual, and eternal blessings,—and when I said I do believe, my heart was touched with burning love. The fire fell from heaven upon my soul."

Conversing about his affairs with the Rev. Martin Jubb, Mr. Brooke once said, " the best business that I have done in the world, has been done on my knees. God has given me my best business thoughts in prayer, and my most successful purchases on a large scale have been suggested to me on my knees."

" Them that honour me I will honour " is the announcement of a principle of the divine government remarkably exemplified in the case of Mr. Brooke. The Fieldhouse works, established in prayerful dependence upon God, now take their place amongst the recognised industries of Huddersfield. The lofty chimney, towering like a giant amid pigmies, a wonder in chimney architecture, attracts universal observation, and busy workmen and large store of material both raw and manufactured, with railway trucks and canal-boats, transporting their heavy freights to various destinations, far and near, testify to a large and thriving trade, exceeding the most sanguine expectations of its venturesome projector.

CHAPTER XVII

"A faithful witness of Thy grace,
  Well may I fill the allotted space,
    And answer all Thy great design ;
  Walk in the works by Thee prepared ;
  And find annex'd the vast reward,
    The crown of righteousness divine."

THE Fieldhouse fire-clay works being fairly established ; as
early as practicable, Mr. Brooke transferred the responsibilities of the business to his sons, that with the least
interference, he might pursue his higher and loved work.
The excessive labours of his earlier life had made permanent impression upon his vigorous constitution, and though
the will to work for God was strong as ever, the power was
materially lessened.

However patiently the body may seem, for awhile, to
endure the cruel exactions of the keen spirit that rules its
movements, it keeps accurate account of overtime, and
undue strain ; and strength given under pressure, in earlier
life, is commonly withdrawn from the latter end. Judicious self-restraint is, in the long run, the most generous
service. It is said that an admirer of the ardent Whitefield,
who preached almost incessantly, and as if gifted with
super-human strength, once asked John Newton how it
was that he, with his profession of love to Christ, and concern for the salvation of his fellow-men, preached less frequently than his energetic friend. John Newton wisely
replied that he intended, God willing, to preach as many

sermons as his brother Whitefield, but to take more time about it, and whilst Whitefield died at the age of fifty-six, a martyr to over-work, John Newton lived to extreme old age, preaching, at the age of seventy, six sermons a week ; and regularly preaching in his own church when he was upwards of four score.

Had Mr. Brooke acted upon John Newton's principle of spreading his labours over a wider period, instead of compressing the greatest possible amount of work into the least possible space of time, he might in all likelihood have attained unto the days of the years of his fathers, in the days of their pilgrimage, and done vigorous work at the age of three score years and ten ; but his impulsive nature, constrained by the love of Christ, spurned all thought of self-restraint in his Master's service, as if it were a temptation from beneath, and he worked under high pressure, until at length, nature unable to endure the strain, put in a resolute demand for gentler usage.

Mr. Brooke was now reluctantly compelled to reply in the negative, to more distant applications, and to invitations to conduct successive week-night services ; and, partly to reduce the number of remote and onerous engagements, and also from the desire to spend his remaining strength for the advantage of his neighbours, he ultimately entered into a standing engagement to reserve every alternate Sabbath for his own circuit.

"A prophet is not without honour, save in his own country and in his own house." Mr. Brooke was the exception which proves the rule. His determination to give additional labour to his own circuit was hailed with delight. His services were in general request. In the large town chapel, as well as in the smaller village chapels, the announcement of his name attracted overflowing congregations. It may be questioned whether Honley chapel ever contained a more densely packed mass of humanity than was found within its walls, when Mr. Brooke, for the last time, preached in connection with the Sunday school anniversary of his native place, or whether the Honley congregation ever listened to their old friend with greater interest or deeper feeling. The church, the army, the gentry of the neighbourhood, and the lowest of the population were all represented, and as the preacher illustrated the nature of conversion by allusion to his youthful history, and urged his hearers to decision, the good Spirit moved upon the people, hearts melted and tears flowed, and whether almost or altogether persuaded to become Christians, the preacher on bidding his hearers adieu, could say, " Notwithstanding, be ye sure of this, that the kingdom of God is come nigh unto you."

It was no small financial service which Mr. Brooke rendered to local interests, to circuit funds, and to the funds of the Connexion ; for, more frequently than he thought desirable, he was appointed to make collections, the unwonted largeness of which bore testimony to the preacher's popularity, and ensured his appointment for like service in the future, till sometimes he begged for the privilege of preaching without the usual finale, "now concerning the collection."

Nor were Mr. Brooke's later pulpit labours in his own circuit without spiritual result. God continued to honour His servant with signs following. Entering the pulpit on a Sabbath evening, a quarter or half an hour before time, he generally found a congregation awaiting his arrival, and after a short sermon, enlivened by occasional singing, he announced a prayer-meeting. Praying men rallied around him. Intercession was made, interrupted by brief exhortations and songs of praise, and the preacher seldom failed to lay hold of some, who, impressed by the discourse, were

R

induced to avow themselves seekers of salvation. Mr. Brooke retained to the last, his insatiate desire for immediate and visible fruit of his labour. It was a day of humiliation, when, preaching in his own circuit or elsewhere, he could advert to none as the seal of his ministry, and to such humiliation he was rarely subjected.

Mr. Brooke's services in his own circuit were deemed so important, that as some recognition of their value, and to guard against disappointment, successive superintendents were accustomed to appoint him according to his own arrangement. Shortly before the old plan ran out, the superintendent minister commonly received a list of the Sabbaths which Mr. Brooke had reserved for his own circuit, accompanied by a polite request for appointments on the dates specified. The communication always indicated a preference for country chapels. No place was too small or insignificant to be favoured with his services. As life advanced, it became not merely a difficulty, but an impossibility, to induce him to face the immense congregations which his appointment in the town chapels had attracted.

To his superintendent, who had requested him to preach in Huddersfield, on behalf of the trust funds of a country chapel, he replied,

Dear Sir,

I find the state of my nerves such, that I cannot consent to preach in Buxton Road chapel for Crosland Moor trust. This is my first answer.

Should you write again, I shall then answer and positively say, *I will not.* Kind regards to self.

I remain, respectfully,

EDWARD BROOKE.

In everything which bore upon the interests of the work of God in his own circuit, Mr. Brooke took the liveliest interest; and though he might sometimes fail to see as others saw, and oppose the views of others, or advocate his own, with an impetuosity of manner, and a seeming impatience to which calmer natures took objection, none ever questioned the purity of his motive, or the ardency of his attachment to God's cause and to the church of his early choice. His constant prayer for Jerusalem was, "Peace be within thy walls, and prosperity within thy palaces." He preferred Jerusalem above his chief joy.

Over Honley, where the Methodist Society had been blighted by "reform," and the congregation scattered, so that Methodism was reduced for a time, to the extreme of feebleness, he watched with the tenderness of a nursing mother. But for his generous and unfailing help, the faithful Honley chapel trustees had been crushed by an accumulating financial burden, involving results the most disastrous. Mr. Brooke, however, kept himself well informed of their position, and cheered their hearts by a standing order, to apply to him in every emergency. Large deficiencies he met out of his private purse; writing to Mr. McOwan, he says, "I have paid over and above other gifts, about £140 for Honley chapel, interest on money borrowed," and when the time came to free the chapel from its encumbrance of debt, so that to call it God's house should be no longer a misnomer, he largely assisted, and had the compensation of seeing Methodism in Honley revive and assume a more hopeful position than ever.

The village of Paddock, in the vicinity of Huddersfield, had a rapidly-increasing population, imperfectly supplied with means of grace. After consultation with the superintendent minister, Mr. Brooke proposed to concentrate his

efforts upon the evangelization of this locality, when not
engaged in more distant service. Again and again he
traversed the village, to discover a house which he might
rent or purchase as a place of worship, until more suitable
provision could be made. Discouraged by repeated disap-
pointments, he was earnestly imploring divine interposi-
tion, when, as God's answer to his prayer, there came an
impression, clear and strong, that a house was available at
the top of Paddock. Having recently concluded a vain
search, he was incredulous. The impression was repeated
with force which awakened his surprise. In the evening
when telling the small Society at Paddock, that unless he
could meet with a house, he should have to abandon his
purpose of spending his spare time amongst them, the
leader astonished him by saying, I have just heard that
there is a house to be let or sold at the top of Paddock.
Encouraged by this remarkable confirmation of the impression he had previously received, whilst on his knees, Mr.
Brooke hastened to the spot indicated, and found, in the
centre of the population, a house, which he quickly purchased, and which having transformed into a chapel, he
ultimately presented to the Wesleyan Methodist Connexion. The thanks of the Wesleyan Conference were
formally conveyed to Mr. Brooke for this acceptable gift.

From that time, Paddock became a recognised part of
the Huddersfield (Buxton Road) circuit. The Society
increased. The congregation soon outgrew the capacity of
the little sanctuary. Bold spirits projected a new erection,
and undaunted by the slenderness of their resources and
by manifold discouragements, originated a building fund,
to which all contributed, "the deep poverty" of many
abounding unto the riches of their liberality. Assisted by
wealthier neighbours, the Methodists of Paddock at length
achieved their object, and now rejoice in possession of a

new and commodious chapel, which it is hoped may prove the spiritual birth-place of many.

"There is that scattereth and yet increaseth." "Give and it shall be given unto you, good measure, pressed down and shaken together and running over shall men give into your bosom. For with the same measure that ye mete withal, it shall be measured to you again." In this principle of the divine administration Mr. Brooke had long firmly believed; and none is more sure. God lives in no man's debt. All that love gives to God comes back with increase, sometimes in kind, otherwise, in a still better form. Just after the purchase of the house at Paddock for God's worship, the Fieldhouse business received an impetus which Mr. Brooke regarded as God's recognition of his offering. He writes, "A great order has come in, which will clear me all I have given this last week or two, and also the purchase of the place at Paddock. Wonderful! There is a particular Providence over us. He will provide. The government is upon His shoulder, in reference to providence as well as grace and glory." Shortly after, he writes, "Business is rising, increasing, flourishing. I have just been on my knees to thank the Lord, and whilst kneeling the passage came to my mind, 'Thou hast wrought all our works in us,' or, for us. I more than ever see the controlling hand of God in all my affairs. While I work for Him, He works for me. Praise the Lord!"

Nor were temporal blessings the only or chief recompence which God bestowed upon His servant. In his own heart he realised increase of grace, and in working for God he saw fruit of his labour. He writes, "I am getting on in my soul. All is well. Salvation is mine. The Lord tells me that all He has is mine. I see wonders. The Lord is saving souls nearly every week, wherever I go." Upon his family also, there came a blessing, more prized than gold

and silver, and to which the following extract from a letter
addressed to one of his children alludes.

Your kind letter did me great good. Oh, how thankful
was I to hear you had received the favour of the Lord;
His forgiving mercy. What a wonder, what an astonishing
act of kindness—loving-kindness to you, after so many
years rejecting His offers of salvation. Oh, be thankful
and say with David, "What shall I render unto the Lord
for all His benefits?" Render! Your whole heart, your
undivided heart, your whole life, and then if so, happy
throughout life, happy in a dying hour, happy throughout
eternity. "Well done." Oh! my child, watch and pray ;
pray that you may watch. The enemy will try to shake
your confidence, but "resist the devil," "steadfast in the
faith," and cry "Lord help me," and He will empower you,
will support you, will deliver you. He will, I know He
will, from this time forth and for evermore. Amen and
Amen. You are now engaged in a war. Fight. You are
now engaged in a race. Run. But run carefully, speedily.
Run, "looking unto Jesus the author and finisher of our
faith." Oh! what mercy is before you, heights and lengths
and depths and breadths of Jesus' love. Look for more
grace, not only forgiving mercy, but sanctifying grace.
His blood cleanseth from all sin. Let your light shine.
Talk about Jesus. Love Him with all your heart and say,
"What would'st Thou have me to do?" But more when I
see you. In your prayers,

Remember

Your dear father.

Again, he writes to one of his daughters :—
"Let us not be weary in well doing." I now pray about
everything, every *little* thing : I did not formerly do so.

Never thought of it. I now see the necessity of praying about everything. It is reasonable, scriptural, well-pleasing to God, and honours the Saviour. He likes to hear from us. David said, " I will cry unto God Most High, who performeth all things for me." Let us be simple, faithful, honest, straight-forward, loving, kind, zealous, persevering, and hear a voice crying, " This is not your rest." Plead the blood, the atonement, the promises. Live in the temple, the glory, the heart of Jesus. I enclose you a letter from Mr. Reed. His motto is,

NONE BUT CHRIST.

To another daughter he writes :—

December 10th, 1861.

I am glad to say mother is better, so hope we shall go on favourably and improve. Write and say how you all are. All well, expect me home on Friday afternoon, without fail, at 4.55. Home, *home, home* for me. But there is another home in heaven above, and what avails anything and everything if at last we don't meet there. Oh! let us strive for that home. Pray earnestly for the Lord to give you real repentance, sorrow for sin, reformation from sin, and faith to believe that for Christ's sake He will save you, and give you an assurance that you are His child. " The Spirit itself beareth witness with our spirits that we are the children of God," He came to give us " the knowledge of salvation by the remission of sins." Never rest till you get it. He that believeth shall be saved, saved to-day. Jesus says, " I will give you rest."

CHAPTER XVIII.

BEREAVEMENT.

"Then fell upon the house a sudden gloom,
   A shadow on those features fair and thin,
And softly from that hush'd and darken'd room,
   Two angels issued where but one went in."

CLOUD and storm have their use in the economy of nature. Beautiful though the earth appears in calm, bright summer time, when bathed in golden light; unbroken sunshine and perpetual serenity would soon transform the fairest landscape into a wilderness; and in the moral world there are few natures beautified by grace, whose loveliness would not be marred by continuous prosperity, and none, to the perfecting of which the discipline of sorrow is not necessary. Suffering is an ordinance of God to which all God's children, at one time or other, must submit. "Whom the Lord loveth He chasteneth and scourgeth every son whom He receiveth."

At no period of his Christian life had Mr. Brooke been without the confirmation of his sonship, which divine chastening supplies. Once and again his health had failed under the severe strain of over-work, and whilst his ardent spirit was eager as ever for Christian usefulness, he had to submit to be "set aside as a broken vessel." The lives of loved ones had been endangered by disease. Babes who had lived long enough to awaken a father's love had been snatched from his embrace: and he had anxieties in relation to surviving members of his family which drove him, like David, in self-despair to

God's "everlasting covenant, ordered in all things and sure;" but at length came a sorrow, before which all previous sorrow seemed dwarfed into insignificance.

Mrs. Brooke's health gave way, and though for a time hope triumphed over fear, the case assumed a form which baffled alike the skill of the physician and the tender and assiduous care of daughters, whose filial love amounted to devotion; and over the happy household crept the shadow of death still darkening, until at length the death-stroke fell.

That sick chamber was the scene of holy triumph, which constituted a fit termination of a life of singular beauty and devotion. Having consecrated herself unto the Lord in youth, Mrs. Brooke had held fast the profession of her faith without wavering. Her ideal of the Christian life was of the loftiest order. She believed herself predestinated to be conformed to the image of God's Son. Her life was an aspiration after the mind that was in Christ, and an endeavour to walk as Christ also walked. Like her Lord and Master, she compassionated the wants of the necessitous and the miseries of the afflicted, and "went about doing good" to the bodies and souls of her fellow creatures. She walked within her house with a perfect heart, ruling her children and domestics with strictness, but in love. Her closet was the scene of mighty wrestlings with the God of Jacob, on behalf of the cause of God, and especially for the salvation of her family; and there, she received answers which gave radiance to her life, and made her a blessing and joy to others and to many. Mrs. Brooke's daily conduct was a beautiful exemplification of "whatsoever things are true, whatsoever things are honest, whatsoever things are just, whatsoever things are pure, whatsoever things are lovely, and whatsoever things are of good report." She was a "living epistle of Christ," whom none could read without conviction of the truth and loveliness of Christianity ; and when, at length, came unexpectedly the summons to depart, she girt up the loins of her mind and faced death with the calm dignity of faith. To her, death was but God's messenger to bid her home ; and the grave was the portal of the skies. Her family assembled around her bed, and as she gazed upon those objects of her intense solicitude and love, an inspiration came over the dying saint. She spake with superhuman eloquence and power, demanding what none of the weepers could withhold,—the promise to meet her in the world above ; and having solemnly pledged her children to follow in her footsteps, she felt that her work was done, and with expressions of trust and praise she joyously entered into rest.

The anticipation of this stroke, when imminent, awakened in the heart of Mr. Brooke feelings approaching to dismay, and the shock of its fall stunned him. A help-meet more thoroughly in sympathy with her husband and his evangelistic labours, and more entirely adapted to her difficult and responsible position than Mrs. Brooke, could not be. Burdens, which equally divided with her husband, had pressed heavily upon her heart, she bore, almost in full, that her husband might be unembarrassed in his work; and when God took her, and her love and sympathy and help were all found wanting, the loss was incalculable.

Addressing his old friend, Mr. Tindall, Mr. Brooke wrote,

Mother is gone. At ten minutes past one o'clock on Sunday morning. It is all that ever I can do, to hold up, but the Lord is my stay. But oh ! what an end ! What a victory ! What peace ! What sayings before she went! and sensible to the last. More, when calm and settled and quiet.

EDWARD BROOKE.

Fieldhouse, Monday Morning, Feb. 10th, 1862.

Prayer and occupation form the best antidote to immoderate sorrow. Instead of moodily brooding over his trouble, and as the certain result, sinking into the depths of despondency, Mr. Brooke betook himself to his knees, and in a short time, braced with new strength, he threw himself with renewed devotion into God's work.

"Laboremus," we must work, was the last watchword which a Roman emperor gave to his soldiers. "I must work the works of Him that sent me, while it is day; the night cometh when no man can work," said the great Captain of our salvation, as He approached the close of His earthly sojourn. "I must work," had long been Mr. Brooke's motto, and the brief record of his preaching engagements at this period, still preserved, shows how, when crushed by his great sorrow, he solaced himself by the continuous endeavour to do good, and was abundantly cheered by the manifestations of God's saving power. Again and again occur such entries as the following:

"Special seasons. Wonderful times. O what goodness!"

"Never more happy in preaching. Amazing liberty."

"Best day I have had for a long time. A mighty influence. A few in distress, and a few saved."

"Numbers in distress; a cry for mercy through the place. People blessed on all sides, and some saved."

"A woman roared out, 'Got saved,' and then shouted for joy."

"Hard soil: the people like heathens. An Irish mob broke the windows."

"A few saved : a fiddler and his wife among the rest."

"A mighty move : numbers in distress, and I hope some saved."

"I shall never forget this visit. One or two professed to get mercy. Nothing like soul-saving work."

"An old man aged seventy-one saved. He came fifty miles yesterday. His daughter prayed that he might get saved before he went back. Praise the Lord! Others I left weeping, praying, and struggling. Ten or twelve found peace, I was told. A good day."

Preaching at Green Hammerton on Sunday, July 9th, 1865, on the following Monday, Mr. Brooke writes, "I have seen nothing like it for the last ten years. It is supposed that from forty to fifty were seeking mercy. Masters and servants, husbands and wives, young and aged."

"Numbers in distress : some saved. Kept the prayer-meeting up till twelve o'clock at night."

"Never so tired in my life. One set at liberty."

"August 12th, 1866. At home. I am always uneasy when I don't preach. I must preach, Lord help me!"

"A good time : a few in distress. One man came out of prison, and I hope some got real good."

"Two glorious times. Full liberty, and a shout on all sides. A landlady saved."

In January or February, 1866, Mr. Brooke visited Derby, and afterwards writing to his friend, the Rev. Samuel Tindall, he says, "I hope my visit was made a blessing, but I never suffered more in my life than I have since then. I felt well on Sunday night. On Monday evening I could not preach from my favourite text, 'Sanctify them through thy truth,' etc. I am, and always was an excitable being, but the 'hallelujah men,' so called, shouted and went on so, that really I, with all my excitable feelings, could not do with it. I should not

like to meet those men again, and I dare not in Derby.
I like a good Amen, and sometimes a good hallelujah !
but they go beyond all bounds. I have never suffered
more than I have done from the excitement, and I, as
yet, cannot get over it. . . . . I do not like to give
offence to good pious Christians. Quiet but good."

In the same letter Mr. Brooke rejoices over good done
in several places : Slaithwaite, Honley, and Paddock. At
Stainland also, where there was "a wonderful revival, and
vast numbers saved." "At Halifax a mighty work, and
numbers saved." "At Netherton a glorious work is going
on. I was there last Sunday, and preached. Oh ! that I
could always preach as then : calm, steady, clear. A
sweet influence fell like the dew. I was amazed at the
heavenly, rich, flowing ideas, and language uttered purely
extemporaneously Never before. The people were silent
as death, and then burst into a heavenly amen and hallelujah ! Oh, that I could always preach so. I will try
and live for it."

Again addressing Mr. Tindall in March, 1867, he writes,
"Was at Littleboro' on Sunday and Monday. A number
in distress, and some professed to find mercy : a servant
girl where I stayed, a young boy in the shop, and numbers
more."

"A good work is going on in the Buxton Road circuit.
A few brought in at Deadmanstone. A wild, rough rifle-
man shot to the heart and felled to the ground, and others
cried out and were saved. But Linthwaite ! where we
have not had a good revival for thirty years, and which
has been the lowest place in our circuit ; last week, the
Lord came upon them like lightning and thunder. Last
Tuesday, I was told about twenty found peace. Thirty
on Wednesday. Forty on Thursday. How many since
I don't know, so you see the place is all on a move."

During the period referred to in the preceding extracts, Mr. Brooke preached somewhat frequently and with happy results, from a favourite text, and as the manuscript notes have been preserved, they are given, as a fair specimen of his pulpit preparations.

John xvii. 17.   Sanctify them through Thy truth.

Introduce by referring to John's vision.   He saw an innumerable company who had washed their robes. Patriarchs, prophets, apostles, martyrs.   Some of your fathers have joined that multitude.   They too have washed their robes.   Now go and ask them, Where they washed ? When they washed ? and if when thus washed, they did not long for others to be washed ?

Jesus the friend of sinners prayed for His disciples, and in heaven He still prays,   .

" Sanctify them through Thy truth."

Notice we then,

I. THE PRAYER OF THE REDEEMER, sanctify them through Thy truth.   Sanctify them.

1. *Not enlighten them.*   They were already enlightened. Christ the light of the world had given them to see themselves to be " wretched and miserable and poor and blind and naked," and had brought them out of the road to hell and into the road to heaven.

2. *Not justify them.*   They were already justified.   They had believed on the Saviour with the heart unto righteousness, and received the justifying grace of God, saved from guilt, they enjoyed peace with God and all the privileges of God's family.

3. *Not deliver them.*   He had delivered them out of one temptation after another.   The devil had laid many a snare for them, but they had experienced the fulfilment of Psalm xci. 16.   Still they were not sanctified.

4. *Not grant them wonderful success.* They had had seals to their ministry. Christ sent His disciples, two and two, before His face into every city, and they returned again with joy, saying, " Lord even the devils are subject unto us through Thy name." And has not many a preacher, leader, member been wonderfully successful in the salvation of souls, and yet not enjoyed the blessings of holiness ? It is possible for a man to be instrumental in the conversion of souls who is neither justified nor sanctified.

5. *Not glorify them.* They were not ready for the company of heaven, or for the kingdom prepared for them. Christ elsewhere prayed for their glorification, but not till He had prayed for their sanctification.

6. *Christ prayed for the sanctification of His disciples.*

(*a.*) *For the sanctification of their bodies.* The eye, ear, tongue, hands, etc. So that as they had yielded their members to be servants to uncleanness and to iniquity unto iniquity, even so, they might now yield their members servants to righteousness unto holiness.

The eye sanctified, so that it might beam with purity.

The ear sanctified, so that it might listen to the voice of the Son of God.

The tongue sanctified, so that it might speak forth the words of truth and soberness.

The hand sanctified, so that it might administer to the necessities of the saints.

The feet sanctified, so that they might " in swift obedience move." In short, the body with all its wondrous mechanism of bone and muscle, arteries and veins and nerves all sanctified.

(*b.*) For the sanctification of their souls.

That the *understanding* which is darkened might become full of light, and have written upon it, " HOLINESS UNTO THE LORD."

That the *imagination*, which is only evil continually, might become only good, and have written upon it, " HOLINESS UNTO THE LORD."

That the *memory* might be sanctified and become strong to retain divine and heavenly things, and have written upon it, " HOLINESS UNTO THE LORD."

That the *will* might be sanctified and sweetly yield to the will of God in providence and grace, and have written upon it, " HOLINESS UNTO THE LORD."

That the *conscience* might be sanctified, purged from dead works, and tender, and have written upon it, " HOLINESS UNTO THE LORD."

That the *affections* might be sanctified, loving God with all the heart, exemplifying the words of the Psalmist, " Whom have I in heaven but Thee ?" and have written upon them, " HOLINESS UNTO THE LORD."

That the *thoughts* might be sanctified, all brought into captivity to the obedience of Christ, and have written upon them, " HOLINESS UNTO THE LORD." In short, that every desire, motive, intention, design, etc., might be all sanctified.

(*c*.) *For the sanctification of their spirits.* Their entire nature. Their whole man. So that love, joy, peace, long-suffering, and every grace of the Spirit might have their perfect growth and sweetly harmonise, through life, in death, and in eternity.

The sanctification which Christ asked for His disciples.

(1.) Does not imply *freedom from error.* Infallibility belongs only to God. To err is the lot of humanity. We may err in a thousand minor points, and yet be sanctified. The head may be wrong when the heart is right.

(2.) Sanctification does not imply *the absence of temptation.* The Saviour, Himself, was the subject of strong temptation, and yet was without sin. St. Paul was dead indeed unto sin, and yet was severely tempted. St. Peter speaks of *saints* who now, for a season, if need be, are in heaviness through manifold temptation. The devil follows a sanctified soul right up to the city gates. I expect, said Mr. Wesley to a friend, that temptations will come about you,

> "'Thick as autumnal leaves that strew the vales."

(3.) Sanctification does not imply *freedom from heaviness or sorrow*, arising from *perplexities, trials, afflictions, tribulations*, etc. Jesus was exceeding sorrowful. Paul was sorrowful, but always rejoicing, and on his brethren's behalf, had great heaviness and continual sorrow in his heart.

(4.) Sanctification is not inconsistent with *further growth and increase in grace.* "Jesus increased in wisdom and stature and in favour with God and man." Dr. Clarke says, "No man can grow in grace as he ought until the roots of sin are destroyed." Garden. Weeds, etc. We may grow all through life, up to death, and through eternity in knowledge, love, and happiness.

II. Sanctify them. WHEN ?

1. *In Purgatory ?* There is no such place. "He that is filthy let him be filthy still." That one Scripture is enough to overthrow the doctrine of purgatory.

2. At *death ?*

3. At *some future time ?* Next year *?* next month ? next week ? to-morrow ?

4. Why not *now ?* If one day is with the Lord as a thousand years and a thousand years as one day, why not now ? If the wisdom and power and mercy and will of the Lord are the same now that they ever were, or ever will be, why not now ? If the Lord would ten thousand

s

times rather cleanse you than leave you uncleansed, why not now? "Lord increase our faith." Behold now is the accepted time : behold now is the day of salvation." " I will, be thou clean." The will of God is your sanctifition.

III. Sanctify them. How or by what means? "Through Thy truth," *i.e.*, through faith in Thy truth. How?

1. *Through their good desires?* No. Some of you have desired long enough. "The way to hell is paved with good intentions," and the way to heaven too.

2. *Through their prayers?* No. You may make long prayers and pray till you sweat as it were great drops of blood, and never get it unless you believe.

3. *Through their fasting?* No. You may fast twice a week like the Pharisees. Three days like the disciples. Forty days like Moses and Elijah ; nay till you cannot walk, and till you have scarcely any flesh upon your bones, and still never get it till you believe.

4. *Through their almsgiving?* No. You may give shilling after shilling, pound after pound. You may sell house after house, field after field, farm after farm, and give all away, and give your body to be burned, and never get it unless you believe.

5. *Through their vows and resolutions?* Vows! You have made scores, hundreds, some of you thousands, and broken them every one, and you may vow again that you will do this and do the other, if the Lord will only sanctify you, but you will never get it unless you believe.

But sanctify them *through Thy truth;* through *faith in Thy truth.* Through faith in its declarations and promises.

Believe it is a blessing *purchased.* To redeem us from all iniquity Christ gave Himself.

Believe it is a blessing *promised.* " Then will I sprinkle clean water ,upon you, and ye shall be clean," etc. " He shall redeem Israel from all his inquities."

Believe in the 'ability and willingness and readiness of God to bestow it. Believe with your heart just now. Cast yourself upon His mercy in Christ Jesus. Take Christ as a full Saviour. Receive Him not only as your wisdom and righteousness, but as your sanctification and redemption. Believe man. Believe woman. Only believe. Try, venture, dare. " If thou canst believe, all things are possible to him that believeth." Dost thou now believe ? " Lord increase our faith."

IV. Sanctify them.- WHAT FOR ?

1. *To enable them to perform their duties better.* Duties relating to themselves. The church. The world. Prayer. Searching the Scriptures. Reproving sin. Visiting the sick. Exhortation. Preaching. Class leading.

2. *To enable them to run faster in the way to heaven.* No man can run as he ought with weights about him. A stone weight of pride. Two stones of malice. Three stones of politics. Five of unbelief. Ten of anger. Fifteen of impatience. How can a man with such weights leap over a wall, or run through a troop ? Or how can a woman run with four ounces of curls upon her head, and three of extra ribbons, and two of artificial flowers, and one of self-consequence ?

3. *That they may be witnesses to the world and church of God's full power to save.* And such witnesses have been. See Enoch, Elijah, Isaiah, the Apostles in the upper room. The disciples. " Now are ye clean," and· there are witnesses now.

4. *To make them more useful in the conversion of souls.* See Isaiah i. God purely purged away His people's dross,

and then her converts were redeemed with righteousness. Read Ezekiel xxxvi. Israel must be cleansed, and then the wastes were to be filled with flocks of men. See the Apostles. Three thousand were converted. But when ? After they were cleansed. Then they set Jerusalem on fire. When Stephen got the sanctifying power, what numbers were converted. Barnabas was "a good man, full of the Holy Ghost and of faith, and much people was added unto the Lord." Paul, when sanctified, could say, " Now thanks be unto God, which always causeth us to triumph in Christ, and maketh manifest the savour of His knowledge by us in every place." " Create in me a clean heart," prayed David, . . . "then will I teach transgressors Thy ways, and sinners shall be converted unto Thee."

5. *To prepare them for a dying hour.* See John. Paul. I am ready to be offered. Sanctified persons are ready, made meet to be partakers of the inheritance of the saints in light. Ready. The work is done. The devil bruised. The world overcome. Sin destroyed. Salvation won. Ready. Hallelujah !

6. *To make them ready for an immediate and triumphant entrance into heaven.* See Stephen. The thief upon the cross.

(1.) An immediate entrance.

(2.) An abundant entrance.

(3.) A triumphant entrance.

(4.) A final entrance.

7. *That they may stand perfect* and complete in Christ at the bar of God, and be presented by the Redeemer to the Father without spot or wrinkle or any such thing, etc.

Some talk about sanctification when they want justifying, their backslidings healed, etc., etc.

Hymns 15, 16, 17.

The foregoing notes, though fairly illustrating Mr. Brooke's mode of preparing for the pulpit, convey a very imperfect idea of his pulpit ministrations. A mere glance will suffice to show how greatly the effect of the discourse depended upon the preacher's state of soul and body, upon the inspiration of the time, upon the various circumstances favourable or adverse to freedom of thought and utterance, in which the preacher might happen to be placed, and, above all upon the divine influence which accompanied the spoken word.

When explaining the position "that no man can grow in grace as he ought, until the roots of sin are destroyed," the Squire's favourite illustration before rustic congregations was derived from the cottager's onion bed, an illustration merely indicated in the notes, but which he often worked out with singular felicity, captivating the attention of his audience and carrying conviction to their hearts. More than one of Mr. Brooke's hearers, when informed that the foregoing notes were available for publication, have asked "Do they contain any allusion to the onion bed?" The use which the squire made of this illustration left a deep and permanent impression upon one youthful hearer, as the following communication from the Rev. Henry W. Holland attests.

"When a boy, I often heard Mr. Brooke preach, and always with great profit to my soul. His freedom and homeliness in the pulpit suited my boyish fancy, and his earnest spiritual appeals always went home to my heart. I well remember, his preaching from 'Sanctify them through Thy truth, and, in fact, I never heard him preach without hearing a great deal about entire sanctification, whether it belonged to his text or not. But on the particular occasion to which I refer, the squire was in one of his happiest moods, and seemed to be under a very heavenly influence. In the course of his sermon, he referred to some objections which might be urged against entire sanctification, and amongst the rest, that it would hinder people from growing in grace. In answer to this, he appealed to the gardening experience of the poor in something like the following terms. You have a little garden, and, perhaps, a nice onion bed in it. The bed has cost you much thought and care, and you are delighted to find that the young onions are beginning to grow. But after awhile, the weeds begin to spring up, they grow faster than the onions, and will smother them if they are not taken out, so you weed the onion bed until it is quite clean. And when the weeds are gone, do the onions cease to grow? (The people here, at once saw the point of the illustration, and some cried, Hallelujah! and others, glory be to God!) You know the onions will grow faster when the weeds are gone than they ever grew before, especially when the sun shines upon them, and the refreshing showers fall. So it is with the human heart. The converted man's heart is the garden of the Lord. But some seeds of sin are left in it, and they grow up into weeds and hinder the growth of the plants which are of the Lord's right hand planting. Weeds are no ornament to a garden, and the weeds of sin disfigure the garden of the soul, and they are hurtful to it. Thank God entire sanctification comes to take away the weeds of sin; and, when they are all gone, does that hinder the plants of the Lord from growing? No. Glory be to God! the garden of the Lord flourishes more than ever when the weeds are gone."

One of Mr. Brooke's sons having resolved to emigrate, his father addressed him a letter, from which the following paragraph is extracted.

"You do not know what I feel towards you : an affection which I believe will never be broken. I have thought about you, I have prayed for you a thousand times, and a thousand more. I have given you the best advice a father can, namely, to secure the favour of God, through faith in Christ's death. You are now entering into life without a father's protection. Oh! be steady. Keep from smoking and drinking, and be careful how you contract acquaintances with young men. Find out if you can a pious lad, a steady, thinking, diligent youth. Read your Bible every day and never neglect prayer. Oh! remember a mother's heart, how she yearned over you, loved you, cared for you, watched over you. Her greatest and highest wish was *your salvation.* Write to me every month. Tell me your whole mind, what you are doing, or intend doing. If you are in straits or difficulties, tell me so, and you shall have a father's heart and a father's hand. If it had been the will of the Lord for you to stay in England, I should have preferred it in relation to both time and eternity, but I think you are right in going. You will see life and learn lessons you never would have done at home. But above all, never rest without a clear sense of sins forgiven. Oh! be open with me. Tell me all your wants and cares, and if you don't feel settled and comfortable. The will of the Lord be done. The blessing of the Lord be upon you in time and in eternity, and as a family unbroken, may we meet on that eternal shore in heaven, where storms will for ever cease.

Your loving Father."

On Thursday, June 27th, 1867, Mr. Brooke was united in marriage to Mrs. Bellshaw, for many years an intimate and valued friend of the family. This lady's intelligent and earnest piety, her gentle disposition, her intimate acquaintance with Mr. Brooke's character and habits, and her reverential appreciation of his Christian worth and usefulness, made her a most suitable companion. The union was of brief duration. It was, however, productive of mutual happiness, and the knowledge that she lovingly ministered to the comfort of one so greatly honoured of God, and who now joyously awaits his final promotion "at the end of the days," is no small solace to the widow in her widowhood.

During the summer of 1867, Mr. Brooke paid occasional visits to surrounding circuits, and in some rare instances, to places more remote. He still preached twice upon the Sabbath, but these efforts became increasingly exhaustive, and, for the most part, he was compelled resolutely to decline week-night engagements. An air of languor in painful contrast with the buoyancy of former years, sometimes impressed his friends with the fear that secret mischief was undermining the foundations of his strength; but the mention of some interesting topic relating to the prosperity of the work of God, in his own circuit or elsewhere; or an allusion to his past labours, or to some incident of his career, seemed to rekindle the failing fire; his eye sparkled as of old, and he conversed with the sprightliness of his best days. An hour's chat with the squire at this season of his comparative feebleness was bracing, and few left his company without increase of strength. In spite of occasional forebodings, all clung to the hope that this honoured servant of God might be spared for years longer, to serve the church with maturity of wisdom and love, if with less physical vigour, but He in whose hand are our "times" ordained otherwise.

CHAPTER XIX.

GOING HOME.

"To the saints while here below,
With new years new mercies come ;
But the happiest year they know
Is the last, which leads them home."

THE symptoms of failing health,—the loss of strength and occasional syncope which Mr. Brooke now suffered, he was slow to recognise as notice to quit his "earthly house of this tabernacle." Length of days seemed to be the heritage of his family, and making too small allowance for the strain which he had put upon his constitution by the excessive labours of his earlier life, he anticipated a few more years of Christian toil, lightened by happy companionship. Struggling against increasing infirmity, he still preached, though gradually narrowing the circle of his labours, till at length he seldom ventured beyond the limits of his own circuit.

His diary of this date contains little more than a bare record of his preaching engagements, with the occasional recognition of special help and the enumeration of Scripture promises applied to his heart in seasons of devotion. It shows that every now and then he was unequal to the fulfilment of his public duties, and that his pulpit was taken by a substitute. This he felt to be no small trial of his patience, as appears from the recurring entry "At home, oh ! dear." To the last he loved his work. He had a passion for preaching, and was never more in his element than when pointing sinners to "the Lamb of God which taketh away the sin of the world." When silenced

by affliction, preaching was the almost constant subject
of his thought. Even with failing memory, and when
sustained thought was difficult, he was ever revolving
some passage of Scripture in his mind, throwing it into
sermonic form,, and picturing the execution he might do
with the. sharp blade of truth, had he but strength to
wield it as aforetime. Conversation upon the subject of
preaching was to him like the sound of the trumpet or
the rattling of musketry to the old war-horse; or like the
notes of the horn or the baying of hounds to the aged
hunter. The ruling passion of his life seemed never
stronger, than in old age and feebleness. God only knows
the severity of the trial which his servant bore when,
unexpectedly, the infirmities of age disabled him, when
hearing failed, and memory was shaken, and his limbs
lost their activity; and his evangelistic work, the work
that he loved so ardently was of necessity suspended,
and when, week after week, he pensively filled up the
vacant spaces in his day-book with the entries, " At
home poorly." " Bad cold; very deaf." " Poorly at
home; my head!" God only knows how his great heart,
so full of love to God and the souls of his fellow men,
yearned to be at its loved work once more, and yet
there was no murmuring at God's dealings with him,
but complete Christian submission. Conversing with his
minister about his failing strength he said, in cheerful
accents, " I have had my day, and now let the children
have theirs. It is all right." Loving life though he did,
reciprocating the affection of his family, delighting in
God's beautiful earth on which he never seemed weary
of gazing, and rejoicing in Christian service, he was
ready to depart, and he joyfully anticipated an abundant
entrance into the everlasting kingdom of his Lord and
Saviour Jesus Christ.

Sunday, July 17th, he spent at Ilkley, in company

with Mrs. Brooke. He was too unwell to attend public worship, but though withheld from the house of God he enjoyed sweet converse with God in his retirement. By a singular coincidence, whilst Mrs. Brooke was listening in the sanctuary to a sermon on the duty of covenanting with God, her sick husband was engaged in renewing his covenant at home, and entered the following record in his diary,

"This day I covenant with the Lord to be His for ever, and to serve Him better.

At Ilkley, Witness my hand,
EDWD. BROOKE."

And then follows, "I was just thinking what a blessing it is to know that I please the Lord and have His smile; and immediately came the passage, 'Son thou art ever with me, and all that I have is thine.'"

October 22nd, 1870. After enumerating consolatory passages of Scripture, brought to his remembrance whilst engaged in his devotions, he writes underneath, "Certain as I live. I prayed the day before. No answer came. It is come this morning, unsought."

The last entry in his diary is dated November 29th. "In returning and rest shall ye be saved: in quietness and in confidence shall be your strength."—"Thou shalt see greater things than these."—"Thou preventest him with the blessings of goodness."—"I will do better unto you than at your beginnings."—My soul is even as a weaned child." And then, possibly to express his fuller apprehension of the infinite mercy of his covenant God, and a firmer trust than he had heretofore exercised, he writes with a trembling hand that is soon to forget its cunning, "Never before."

Mr. Brooke's visit to Ilkley appeared to be of some service. For a time, his strength slightly rallied. Once

and again, he preached to his neighbours in the little
preaching-room adjoining his house, and was purposing,
with the help of Mr. William Donkersley, to attempt
another service at Honley; but the Honley pulpit, in
which he had so often preached Jesus and persuaded
men, he was to enter no more. His testimony in that
place, over which his heart yearned, and for which he
prayed to the last, was fulfilled.

The Sabbath previous to his fatal attack, he went to
his class at nine o'clock in the morning. He seemed to
be in a particularly calm and happy frame, and the members were much struck with the beauty and earnestness
of his remarks. Relating his experience in few words,
he said that he felt the infirmities of age, which reminded
him of his latter end; that he was packing up and preparing to go home, and that he felt that the blood of
Jesus Christ, the Son of God, cleansed him from all sin.
In the evening, he conducted a service in his little sanctuary, and preached from Acts xi. 21, "And the hand of
the Lord was with them, and a great number believed
and turned unto the Lord." He dwelt much upon Christ's
intercession, and afterwards remarked that he had had "a
very sweet time." It was his last discourse. On the
morning of the following Sabbath, January 22nd, 1871, he
was taken ill, and rapidly grew worse. He was unable to
converse, but when asked if Christ was precious, he
emphatically answered "yes;" and on several occasions,
when passages of Scripture were repeated for his comfort,
he said "Praise the Lord!" One of his daughters repeated to him the lines,

> "Who suffer with our Master here,
> We shall before His face appear,
> And by His side sit down."

when, with special emphasis, he again said, "Praise the
Lord!" The Friday before his death, about seven o'clock

in the morning, he appeared to be in a particularly happy frame, and whispered "the Lord is here."

His afflicted family still clung to the hope of his recovery, doing all that love could devise or labour, to detain him a while longer, but all in vain. During the night of Saturday a change for the worse took place. Nature was exhausted. The sufferer rapidly grew weaker. All could see that he was now taking the last solemn steps of life's journey,—walking "through the valley of the shadow of death." A Christian neighbour, for many years a faithful and valued servant in the family, offered prayer by her old master's bed. He appeared to understand and enjoy the exercise. As the day advanced, his breathing became difficult, and intermittent. His departure was at hand. All gathered around the bed and solemnly awaited the event, when, the dying saint, turning his eyes towards a corner of the room, they flashed once more with light, and gazed intently, as though fascinated by some bright vision. A beautiful smile passed over his wan features, which seemed lit up with heavenly radiance. The chariots had arrived. The angels were in waiting and beckoned him away, for the Master, who saith, "Where I am there shall also my servant be," had called for him. His glad spirit hasted to obey; and then was realized a scene he pictured some thirty years before, in the pulpit of the old French church in Spitalfields, when anticipating his decease; he described his soul's escape from the prison of mortality, and flight upwards to the new Jerusalem, and the angels on the city battlements wistfully watching his approach, and shouting in loud acclaim, as Edward Brooke passed through the gates into the city, another trophy of redeeming grace, and a bright star in the Redeemer's crown.

The bereavement which transformed that pleasant home at Fieldhouse into a house of mourning, and awakened in some hearts a sense of desolateness never felt before, spread sorrow throughout a wide circle. Many an old, decrepit man, and many a poor lone widow, whose slender means Mr. Brooke had supplemented by his unfailing bounty, felt that his removal had deprived them of their best earthly friend; and yet almost forgot the blow which had fallen on themselves, in sympathy with those whose hearts were still more severely stricken. There were few members of the church with which Mr. Brooke had been so long and closely identified, on whose hearts the sad tidings of their venerable friend's decease fell not with the shock and the sorrow of a personal bereavement. The weeping crowds who followed his remains to their last resting-place, and reluctantly retired from the ground to which his precious dust had given renewed consecration, and the mighty throng of mourners who, weeks after the funeral, assembled in Buxton Road chapel, and listened with manifestations of intense interest and deep emotion to his funeral discourse, bore testimony to Mr. Brooke's goodness, and to the high estimation in which he was held by all classes, more eloquent and impressive than the most laboured eulogy that tongue could utter or pen indite. Resolved that the memory of this good man, this earnest lover of mankind, shall be transmitted to succeeding generations, the people amongst whom he lived and laboured, have raised a subscription for the erection of monumental schools, to stand in close proximity to the Honley chapel, and on a spot of ground which Mr. Brooke had been long wishful to secure for religious uses; and these schools bearing his name, conducted in harmony with his principles, and through successive years imparting to the youth of Honley the priceless blessing of a sound Christian education, shall be an enduring verification of the words of scripture, "The memory of the just is blessed," and the commendation of a right noble life to the consideration of Posterity.

CHAPTER XX.

"To hide true worth from public view,
Is burying diamonds in their mine;
All is not gold that shines, 'tis true,
But all that *is* gold—*ought to shine.*"

THE venerable James Loutit, for three years the honoured
superintendent minister of the Huddersfield Buxton Road
circuit, who by his wise administration and energetic
labours laid Methodism in that circuit under a lasting
obligation, enjoyed beyond most men, Mr. Brooke's confidence and love. Of all Mr. Brooke's personal friends, no
man is more competent to supply a discriminating and just
estimate of his character and life; and a contribution
which the Rev. James Loutit, now of Halifax, has supplied,
with others forwarded by the Revs. John E. Coulson, John
Gostick, Thornley Smith, and John Wood, B.A., will fitly
close the present memorial of departed worth.

From the Rev. James Loutit:

1. To judge correctly of the late Edward Brooke's
Christianity—of its life, and of its fruits—it is needful to
bear in mind his natural disposition, and the mode in
which he was led to the Saviour.

2. Naturally he was manly, generous, and compassionate, withal jovial and comic; possessing considerable penetration into character and readiness of apprehension, with a power of seizing the leading points of a
subject—especially in their practical bearing. About the

artificial rules of logic he knew little and cared less, but he possessed no small share of natural logic, and soon saw through the fallacy of an argument.

3. He was no common-place person, passing through life without leaving a footprint. For good or for evil, Edward Brooke was certain to leave his mark on his generation. It forms one of the green spots of the writer's journey through a long and checkered public life, to have known and enjoyed his friendship and confidence for well nigh the last seven years of his life. His like will never be re-produced. For the present, the die is broken up, to re-appear hereafter in a superior type; or, as Dr. Franklin, of America, expresses it in his monumental inscription, "the covering of an old book—stript of its lettering and gild-ing lies here food for worms; yet the work itself shall not be lost, for it will appear once more in a new and more beautiful edition, corrected and amended by *the Author*.

4. Mr. Brooke's disposition imparted identity to his con-version. That event was a conflict between the carnal and the spiritual—between "the ruler of the darkness of this world—spiritual wickedness in high places," and the Spirit of God and of Christ. It was a giving up all for all, and issued in the victory of grace. The mere idea of Squire Brooke, of Honley—the jovial—the sportsman—turning Methodist! The worldling concluded that he was "cracked," or, as Festus of old sneeringly said to Paul, "Thou art beside thyself."

Satan had hurried him on in worldliness, and malignantly calculated on nothing short of his destruction, when *he* would be the first to mock his victim! Even his strong heart, his indomitable will, had quailed in the conflict; but Jesus the stronger had cast out the strong one and spoiled his goods—for ever! He was a brand plucked from the

burning—a wild olive grafted into Christ the good olive—
thenceforth to bear the fruits of grace.

5. There was a pause, a lull, a taste of the great rest.
A temporary reaction set in. The young disciple was in
heaviness.   Consulting the Primitive Methodist whose
words had been the instrument in the hands of God of
leading him to the Saviour—by name Thomas Holladay—
what he should do, the answer was decisive—" He that
doubteth is damned : " a passage which is certainly suscep-
tible of another interpretation, viz., to do an action with a
doubtful conscience, is condemnation.   But the words in
the higher sense of indecision were well spoken, and were
decisive.   And the person to whom they were addressed
needed them ; and, spoken with thrilling emphasis, they
were a voice from the Holy Ghost, and the young squire
from that day forth looked upward and onward.

Conversing with him one day on the subject of his
becoming a Christian, the writer inquired, " Well, Mr. B.,
when you found yourself at the strait gate—that gate
through which all who are saved must pass—what did you
do with that fine horse and the trained dogs, etc. ? " Fixing
his eyes, and with a look which seemed verily to recall the
whole, he said, " Sir, the gate *was* strait.   I pressed into
it myself, and left horse, dog, and the world outside."
The camel had gone through the eye of the needle !   The
revolution in the outer man was only the sign of the
greater within : the world looked on and wondered, and
the half and half religious—a people who sojourn in
churches and chapels—significantly inquired, " Cannot we
be Christians without altogether renouncing the world ?
Surely religion does not require us to make fools of ourselves,"—and so on.   Well, there is a Book which says,
" If any man among you seemeth to be wise in this world,
let him become a fool that he may be wise."   Squire

T

Brooke knew—knew in the depth of his being—it must be with *him*, Christ or Satan, that between those antagonist Masters there was no medium, and no compromise.

6. *His preaching.* Having found Christ, he was a living witness of the *truth* of Christianity, and what is far more, of *its salvation.* Without *this* qualification, all intellectual gladiatorship—doctrinal knowledge (by the learned termed dogmatics), degrees, whether in arts or divinity, are mere tinsel : *with it,* the peasant—witness Samuel Hick, of Micklethwaite, Charles Richardson, the Lincolnshire thrasher (both well known to the writer), and many more, were mighty through God to the ingathering of Christ's sheep.

Well, the squire had this experience, saying with no faltering voice, " Christ is mine, and I am His." This tendered his heart, yet imparted the courage of the lion for his Master. In *His* service he could afford to be the butt of the self-righteous. Then he thought, and thought truly, that in addition to, and beyond the ordinary call to do spiritual good, as there was opportunity, there must be the call of the Holy Ghost to preach, with which there is the corresponding promise of the *gift.* So said one of the old Honley Methodists on his death-bed —" You have to preach the Gospel and be the means of bringing hundreds of souls to God." The word was spoken from faith, to faith. It entered the seat of his sorrows and his joys. The voice from the inner sanctuary, Who will go, and whom shall we send ? he answered, " Lord, here am I, send me." And from that day, to the close of his life he was faithful.

7. His preaching was impressive and awakening, Not a few thought and said, " Squire Brooke preaches extempore." If by this is meant that he neglected preparation, it was as untruthful as slanderous. With the Bible he was familiar ;

and he was, especially in his early ministry, a careful reader of the Methodist and other standard works in theology, *e.g.*, Matthew Henry's Commentary on the Old and New Testament, 6 vols. 4to, was conned over, and its margin crammed full of memoranda. This book will no doubt be carefully preserved by his children and grand-children. To name no more, his Common-place Book (formed on John Locke's system) and his manuscript preparatious for the pulpit attest his industry. He studied, prayed, and laboured for *present fruit*, and he was signally successful. To this point his texts—plan of sermon—prayers—state of his own heart, all converged. And the Holy Ghost was with him. O, how many has he met in paradise, and how many are on the way thither, to whom he was the minister of salvation, and as an angel of God! It was a rare thing for him to return from his Sabbath or week-day labours in circuits without having been a fisher of men. In this he triumphed with a triumph transcending earthly joy! The *people* distinguished between his sermons and those of the *mere* professional. By the instincts of a new nature, or a yearning for its attainment, they welcomed the man who led them at once to the Saviour.

8. Of the extent and length of his labours others will speak. This I know, that from the commencement to the close of his arduous services he travelled at his own cost. The writer of these lines ventured to say, " Mr. Brooke, I can well understand your giving your *services gratuitously*— that you do for Christ: but would it not be better to charge your bare expenses?" With an earnest and fixed eye, he quickly said, "Say no more on that subject, I have my reasons."

And not only did he cost nothing, but he assisted the numerous circuits which he visited, to an extent which will never be known until the day shall declare it.

9. "But was he not very eccentric?" If by eccentricity be meant, either 1—"deviation from the centre," the answer is No. His centre was during the four quarters of the year, CHRIST and HIS KINGDOM. Or, 2—If by this hackneyed phrase be meant, "departing from the usual course," it is admitted that he had his own way of working; but who gave the other servants the right to depreciate a zealous servant of Christ because, forsooth, he followed not *them* in their frigid decorum, and because his fervour was not toned down to their propriety? Perhaps—and this is spoken in good temper—their seals are few and far between. His were multitudes. No, no! Edward Brooke was consistent with himself. He had a passion for souls. The poor heard him gladly. Many came from curiosity to see and hear—a rare thing—a rich man who had become a Christian. Others to listen to one who had renounced the glories of the turf and turned preacher; or some, perhaps, to relish the piquant remarks—now of his own, and it may be upon other occasions, borrowed from Matthew Henry—who remained to pray, and were caught in the gospel net.

And not the poor only, but some rich who ever were willing to acknowledge him as their spiritual father. And while on the topic of preaching let me not omit to add that he did not restrict his labours to the pulpit. He was in season and out of season. He availed himself of every opening, and often *made openings* to recommend his Master. On his journey through a certain village, and meeting a man, he inquired if he could inform him the way to "Paradise Lane." The man stared, and answered that he had lived in that village forty years, and had never heard of such a lane.

B. "And is there no place near called Paradise?"

Man. "No; never heard of such a place!"

B. "What, not of Paradise! I am going there."

Man (after a pause). "Ah, master, I understand you now."

And a serious conversation ensued. Would that all Christians—aye, and Christian ministers—were assiduous and ingenious in winning the lost for whom Christ died. Souls are perishing, and the regularity of moderatism seems to do very little in the great work of snatching them from impending ruin.

In his own circuit, where he had preached for so long, his services were to the last acceptable and successful. The writer found, on entering it at the Conference of 1864, that he had been in the habit of giving one Lord's day in three, or somewhere in that proportion. At his request, he consented to give every alternate Sabbath, or two monthly, as he felt he must restrict his labours, and give additional services to his own circuit.

11. At the urgent request of the circuit stewards and others, the writer was appointed to Huddersfield. He can never forget the hearty reception which he received from the departed, accompanied with his assured conviction that "he *knew* God had sent him thither." And he has lived to see this verified more ways than one. From that Conference the Buxton Road Circuit has advanced, spiritually and materially. And it would not be well to conceal the fact that, although he had his attachments, yet, when he saw—as he had long seen—the circuit crippled by party, he sighed for a better state of things, and was willing to uphold the heart and hands of one who desired to rise above it, and prosecute, as far as God might give him a door, the *one interest* of Christian extension. Mr. Brooke had not attended the Quarterly meeting for years, but he did so then, and was found ready to cheer his brethren and assist in the good works then commenced.

Chiefly through him the ground for the new chapel at Netherton was obtained. Often has his gig been at the Buxton Road chapel gates, prompt to the moment, to take journeys, and they were not a few, in the service of the circuit.

And *in* the circuit as well as out of it Edward Brooke was liberal. Very true, he had *his own way of action, e.g.,* the Linthwaite Methodist church, which cost £3,000, was generously erected at the sole expense of one gentleman, upon condition that a minister should reside there, and that a house should be erected for his residence, the donor himself being the first subscriber of £100. He and the writer waited upon Mr. Brooke to solicit a subscription. His answer was, " I will think of it." Shortly thereafter, preaching in the Linthwaite old chapel, he announced his subscription to the new house as "4,000 thrippenies."

12. The writer cannot close without adding a word on Mr. Brooke's sympathy with the afflicted. When waves and billows passed over him, he sought retirement at a distance, in the house of an old friend, where he was grateful to receive the following unexpected and characteristic letter :

Mr. Loutit.
Dear Friend,

I am glad you are at a retired spot, and not alone. No, no. Where My servant is, there am I also.

The services of the 9th . . . " Lo I am with you always, etc.," but still, I think it will be too much for your tried nerves.

We will publish for Friday, the 28th, all well. " The circuit needs my presence." It does, and we shall be glad to see you. Of course you know . . . We hope on all sides it is for the best. Let us keep the prize in view.

" What thou knowest not now, thou shalt know hereafter."
Oh, that we could always say, "Thy will be done." Fanny
and Lizzie and self send our best respects.

In your prayers remember,

December 3rd, 1866. EDWARD BROOKE.

13. *Edward Brooke—a neighbour.* It was gratifying to
accompany him in his drives to the surrounding neighbourhood, and to mark his influence for good, and the honest
respect shown him. He would stop at this and the other
door in his way, and kindly inquire for all under the roof—
recommend Christ the present Saviour of stricken sinners
—encourage Zion travellers—help by quietly dropping a
coin into the hand of the needy. After all, it was not his
riches, or his position, which gained the love of the people.
It was their confidence in his genuineness as a man and a
Christian. In him they saw Christianity humanized.

14. *The burning and shining light tapering.* Many precious seasons has the writer experienced in preaching in
the cottage which he had fitted up for religious service, and
as a school, near his own residence. At most of those
services he was present, and generally concluded with a
brief, sententious, deep-worded, and deep-hearted prayer.
And it is pleasing to think that for some weeks before
his death, he had preached every Sabbath evening in
the little school-room. The last time he did so was
January the 15th. His text was Acts xi. 21, remarking
as he came away that he had had "a sweet time." The
text is a epitome of his life's service.

I shall no more see Edward Brooke, the elder, upon
earth; but in my seventy-first year I have come to the
margin, and shall shortly, through grace, rejoin him in
the paradise of rest,—to be for ever with the Lord.

J. LOUTIT.

Halifax, December 8th, 1871.

The Rev. John E. Coulson, referring to Mr. Brooke as a preacher, writes :—

All his utterances in the pulpit were earnest, godly, and breathing intense love for souls and desire to glorify God. Self-exaltation was not seen in anything he said. Many of his sentences were home-thrusts at the hearts and consciences of his hearers, very impressive and awakening. He never failed to keep up intense interest in the audience; and he was useful where other and more gifted preachers would have failed. It pleased God very frequently to make his ministry the means of saving sinners. He had cause to rejoice hundreds of times over souls born again into a new life, and placed at the feet of Jesus by his instrumentality.

Soon after he went to reside at Sheepridge, Mrs. Coulson was visiting at his house (she was then Miss Booth, of Penistone) : late one night Mr. Brooke came home from preaching somewhere. Soon after he got into the house, he laid down on the sofa somewhat exhausted, and began to groan audibly as if in deep distress. Miss Booth said, " Mr. Brooke, what is the matter ? " He replied, " Oh, I have had a bad time; no souls have been saved !" and it was some time before he could join in conversation. This condition of mind he carried about with him almost continually. Before a religious service, he was full of anxiety as to whether souls would be saved or not; and he prayed much and wept before God for the salvation of the people he was going to preach to; and when the service was ended, all he could or would talk about for some time was the salvation of souls, either praising God for the triumphs of grace he had seen, or mourning over the unproductiveness of his own services. Mr. Brooke's spirit was always right with respect to preaching, and if other more gifted preachers could only go into the pulpit and live in the spirit which he had, one might expect the speedy conversion of the world.

As a Christian man, his personal piety and character were of a very high order. He counted all things lost for Christ's sake. He made many sacrifices in relation to worldly position, friends, and fortune, in order to maintain his faith's integrity. He was a man of much closet-prayer, loved and read and re-read his Bible. He walked with God, and made everything subservient to his religious duties. "Lord, what wilt Thou have me to do?" was his daily cry, and when he was clear that God directed him in the path of duty, his was a frame of mind that would have carried him, like a hero of the cross, through fire and water to do the will of his heavenly Master.

In the early part of his Christian life he held views on many subjects which might be pronounced Puritanical. Ministers ought to dress plainly like the Quakers, he thought; and indeed for many years his clothes were cut much in the style of the Friends. Ladies ought not to sin by wearing curls or veils, so he thought and said. In after years, however, he somewhat changed in respect to these points. In the furniture of his house he was particular to avoid ornamentation, believing that Christian simplicity was endangered by the gratification of taste, and that money might be better expended in acts of charity to the poor, of whom he was ever mindful. To the Lord's poor especially he was attentive and kind.

Mr. Brooke was very zealous for God. Phineas-like he was a man to stand in the gap and cry, "Who is on the Lord's side?" Zeal was, perhaps, the most prominent feature of his religious character.

From the Rev. Thornley Smith.
My recollections of Mr. E. Brooke go back to the days of

my youth, when he visited the city of York, and conducted several services, most of which I had the happiness to attend. This was some time after his conversion, and I well remember the effect produced on a crowded congregation in New Street chapel, when he recited, in his own very telling way, the facts connected with his renunciation of the world and its sinful pleasures. A deep impression was made, and in the prayer-meeting which followed there were numbers of penitents, many of whom entered that night into the liberty of the sons of God. I believe the revival which then took place was very extensive, and its results very permanent and blessed. A few years later I was residing in the Driffield circuit, when he paid a visit to that town, and then, too, many were awakened and found the pearl of great price. I was at that time myself a seeker, and though I did not then realise what I sought, I never lost the impression made upon my mind of the vast importance of eternal things as Mr. Brooke tried to set them forth. Later still I was a student at Hoxton, when I heard that Mr. Brooke was coming to London, and was to preach in Spitalfields chapel. Several of the students went to hear him, and his fame attracted a very large congregation. I heard it said that the reporters intended to take down his sermon, and that hearing of this he said, "They won't be able;" and he was right, for he spoke very rapidly, and the discourse, though good, was of such a character, that it certainly would have appeared strange in print. In the midst of it he gave out a verse of a hymn, and the organ struck up a tune which was sung most lustily. The organist was about to repeat the two last lines, when Mr. Brooke shouted, "Stop, that's enough just now," and then went on. There were many penitents that night, and some of us remained to a late hour pleading with them and directing them to Christ.

In the year 1865 I was stationed in the Buxton Road circuit, Huddersfield, when I became a frequent visitor at Mr. Brooke's house, and was always received with the greatest kindness and affection. I delighted to hear him talk, and he generally did so very freely, sometimes respecting the interests of the circuit, and often about preaching and the preparation of sermons. He used to tell me of the texts he had thought of, and the way in which he intended to treat them, and then would ask my opinion on the subjects referred to. I was riding with him one day when he said, " What do you think ? I got a new sermon some weeks ago, and I preached it, and it did execution, so I thought I would preach it again, but it wouldn't go a bit, and I put it on the shelf. But I looked at it again, and I thought the devil wants to cheat me out of that sermon because it did execution when I preached it the first time; but he shan't, I'll preach it again, and I preached it the other day, and it went grandly, and did execution again."

He took considerable pains in the preparation of many of his sermons, and though very impulsive and dependent on the emotions of the time, he often preached well, and of him, as of his Master, it might be said, " the common people heard him gladly." And not the common people only, for the best and most intelligent of our hearers were always glad of the opportunity of listening to him, for they felt and knew that he spoke out of the abundance of his heart.

In the little room near his dwelling in which we held service, I have spent many a precious hour and received many a rich blessing. And all the more so when he was present, as I knew that he prayed for me, and that he had great power with God. He often adverted to his remarkable conversion, and when riding through the neighbourhood, as we sometimes did in the afternoon of the day, he would say, "These are the fields in which I used to hunt with my dogs and my gun before I knew anything of religion. What a blessing I gave them all up!"

Mr. Brooke was a genuine character in every respect. I could say much respecting him were it needful; but the above will suffice. I esteemed him highly as a man of God, and I doubt not that by his preaching, his piety, and his large liberality, he served his generation well, and has obtained a bright reward.

From the Rev. John Wood, B.A.
Dear Sir,

I had an hour to spare the other day, and I employed it in setting down the thoughts that occurred to my mind respecting our common friend, the late Mr. Brooke. You will not be surprised when I tell you that the first I noticed was *his eccentricity*, because it was the most prominent of his character, and the first which would arrest the attention of a stranger. It displayed itself in a certain austerity of manner, and roughness, though not coarseness, of expression; and ran through the whole of his demeanour, being not less conspicuous in the pulpit than in private life. He himself was quite conscious of it, and was never unwilling to avow it; but his close friends knew quite well that it only covered, without concealing, a genial and tender nature which was ever manifesting itself;—witness his generous care for the poor, his liberal support of Methodism in his own circuit, as well as in its Connexional institutions, and his constant preaching of the Gospel for more than forty years in all parts of England without fee or reward. Those who knew him best loved him most, because they had no difficulty in getting over his peculiarities, which they had learned to regard as having no mischief in them.

The next thing I set down was *the thorough religious-ness of his character.* With him piety was not a thing kept on hand, to be called for and used when wanted : it was interwoven with all his habits, it mingled in his ordinary talk, and appeared in every phase of his life. What preacher, who shared his friendship, does not call to mind the eagerness with which he inquired into the work of God in the circuit, beginning with Buxton Road at the top of the plan, and going right down to the bottom, calling at every place on his way ? Who does not remember his readiness to discuss texts, and sermons, and "sketches;" the "good times" he had had in preaching, and the "new thoughts" that had come to him in his studies ? He knew his Bible well, and delighted himself in the Lord.

When I came to his *preaching,* I felt that I could not give a very confident judgment, on account of not having heard him often. I apprehend it would not bear to be criticized according to the common standard : it was all of a piece with his general character, and was like nobody else's. A rapid utterance, racy remarks, original anecdotes, descriptions from his "sporting life," homely illustrations, and very frequent rests in the discourse to "sing a verse," constituted a powerful attraction to multitudes. I dare say there would be sober-minded Christians that could not do with all this ; but "the common people heard him gladly," and it always struck me as a most remarkable thing, and one which said much in his praise, that in a forty years' course of preaching in Huddersfield and the neighbourhood, where everybody knew all about him, he was as popular at the end as at the beginning. I rather think that he preached more sermons than any other layman that Methodism ever produced ; and his converts are everywhere.

His memory is a pleasant one to me ; and I cannot but think that a man who untiringly expended his strength, and time, and talents, and money for the salvation of others, denying himself largely of the domestic comforts and social advantages which Providence, with no sparing hand, had put in his way, deserves to be had in everlasting remembrance.

In respect of the facts and incidents of his remarkable career, 1 can furnish you with nothing beyond what is already known to the generality of his friends. You will of course have access to his private records, and his family will be able to supplement them with other information.

I wish you much happiness in your labour of love ; and the memoir which you will produce will doubtless be of much service in furthering the interests of Christ's kingdom.

From the Rev. John Gostick.

I have very strong and cherished recollections of "Squire Brooke," though they are confined to a brief and not recent period—the years from 1836 to 1842. The influence of his character and labours on me at that time was such as to lead me often to speak of him, in after years, as my spiritual father.

I attended various never-to-be-forgotten services which he conducted in the Sleaford, Grantham, Leicester, Higham-Ferrers, Wellingborough, Bedford, and other circuits, when God greatly owned him in the quickening of believers, and in the conversion of many careless, unawakened people. These were of all sorts and conditions, and nearly of all ranks and degrees. Not a few of the conversions were of a striking and remarkable character, at once overcoming the doubts of some good men, and reducing to silence, at least for a season, even the boldest and most profane.

Amid a chorus of grateful joy from those who had renewed their strength, and from those who had found the Lord, Mr. Brooke had to meet with opposition, and it came not *only* from the two widely different classes just referred to. In one instance, a county newspaper, in the interest of superscilious churchmanship as well as worldliness and sin, pursued him from week to week with scurrility and falsehood, both in its leading articles and in the anonymous attacks of correspondents.

Mr. Brooke acted in a spirit and under motives which made such opposition ineffectual, and it rarely ever even drew from him a remark. He had one idea—one work : ·he sought the salvation of souls and the glory of God in an eminently simple and direct way, and thousands know he was an apostle to them. His spirituality of mind, his perpetual devotion, his fervent, universal love, can never be forgotten. They often seemed to bathe his countenance in heavenly radiance. And many and constant were his secret benefactions to the poor, revealed after he had left the place, although his journeys were always free of cost to the place that he visited. He nowhere shone more brightly than in the houses where he was entertained, leaving an example deserving imitation down to the minutest point, and discipling almost as many in the home as in the sanctuary. It is worthy of notice, too, that Mr. Brooke ever remained the *gentleman* after he had given himself to labours and sacrifices so unlikely to be accepted by his social class. This was illustrated in the care he took that all arrangements for his services were made with the sanction of the superintendents of the circuits. I could say much more, but will only add that I love and revere Mr. Brooke's memory more than I can express, and that, in my judgment, the fruit of his labours has been more lasting than that of any similar labours I have known.